International praise for Rica

- INTERNATIONAL RÓMULO GALLEGOS NOVE...
- NATIONAL CRITICS PRIZE, 2011
- THE BEST NOVEL IN SPANISH OF THE YEAR 2010, CHOSEN BY 55 CRITICS AND JOURNALISTS OF *El País*

"Piglia demonstrates perfect mastery of his art. Nothing is there just for the sake of it." —*El País*

"Ricardo Piglia is an extremely important literary figure. He has inherited Borges' quizzical intelligence, enthusiasm for the tireless exploration of literature and attraction to hidden depths. Piglia's fictions trace inventive parabolas over the past nightmarish events of his country." —*The Independent*

"Ricardo Piglia, the rebel classic." —J.A. MASOLIVER RODENAS, *La Vanguardia*

"One of the sharpest minds on the latino-hispanic-american scene today— not just in Argentina."—*El Cultural*

"Argentine writer Piglia is the most perceptive contemporary reader of that nation's literature and perhaps its best practitioner..."—...A DO...A CWILICH, *Publishers Weekly*, on *Formas Breves*

"Latin American noir at its best—and further evidence of Piglia's remarkable versatility and skill."—*Kirkus Reviews* on *Money to Burn*

"One of Latin America's most highly regarded novelists. Piglia brings into play a swirl of tales mixing dark truths with hallucinatory adventures." —GWEN KIRKPATRICK, author of *The Dissonant Legacy of Modernismo*, on *The Absent City*

"Piglia is Argentina's most important novelist, a compelling writer and committed intellectual who relentlessly deals with the complicated relationships between politics and fiction. And Sergio Waisman is an exceptionally gifted translator with a wonderful ear and eye for the reverberations of Spanish in English."—FRANCINE MASIELLO, author of *Between Civilization and Barbarism: Women, Nation, and Literary Culture in Modern Argentina*, on *The Absent City*

TARGET IN THE NIGHT

—

Ricardo Piglia

TRANSLATED FROM THE SPANISH
WITH AN INTRODUCTION BY
SERGIO WAISMAN

DEEP VELLUM PUBLISHING

DALLAS, TEXAS

Deep Vellum Publishing
2919 Commerce St. #159, Dallas, Texas 75226
deepvellum.org · @deepvellum

Deep Vellum Publishing is a 501C3
nonprofit literary arts organization founded in 2013.

ISBN: 978-1-941920-16-9 (paperback) · 978-1-941920-17-6 (ebook)
LIBRARY OF CONGRESS CONTROL NUMBER: 2015946455

———

Work published within the framework of SUR Translation Support Program of the Ministry of Foreign Affairs, International Trade and Worship of the Argentinian Republic.

Obra subsidiada en el marco Programa SUR del
Ministerio de Relaciones Exteriores y Culto de la República Argentina.

———

Cover design & typesetting by Anna Zylicz · annazylicz.com

Text set in Bembo, a typeface modeled on typefaces cut by Francesco Griffo
for Aldo Manuzio's printing of *De Aetna* in 1495 in Venice.

Distributed by Consortium Book Sales & Distribution.
Printed in the United States of America on acid-free paper.

Experience is a dim lamp that
only lights the one who bears it.
LOUIS-FERDINAND CÉLINE

INTRODUCTION

WHAT'S IN A TITLE? FROM "BLANCO NOCTURNO" TO "TARGET IN THE NIGHT"

Ricardo Piglia was born in Adrogué, in the Province of Buenos Aires, Argentina, in 1941. One of Latin America's most important living writers, Ricardo Piglia is known for his sophisticated combination of formal experimentation and political and cultural engagement. The author of fourteen books of fiction and non-fiction, Piglia's work has been translated, among others, into French, German, Italian, Dutch, Polish, Chinese, Arabic, Hungarian, and Portuguese, as well as English. *Target in the Night* was originally published in Spanish in 2010 as *Blanco nocturno*, and in 2011 it won the Rómulo Gallegos Award and the National Critics Prize, two of the most prestigious awards given to a single work of Spanish-language literature in the world. In 2015, Ricardo Piglia was awarded the Formentor Prize, which recognizes a lifetime contribution to literature, previously awarded to Borges, Beckett, Bellow, and Gombrowicz, and most recently Fuentes, Goytisolo, Marías, and Vila-Matas.

Target in the Night is a kind of literary thriller set in the pampas of Argentina. Tony Durán, a Puerto Rican mulatto from New Jersey, arrives in a small town in the province of Buenos Aires with a suitcase full of American dollars. All indications are that Durán comes in pursuit of two beautiful women, the Belladona sisters, whom he met in Atlantic City, and with whom he formed a hasty trio. But the Belladona sisters may not have been the real, or at least not the only, reason for Durán going to Argentina. A few weeks after Durán's arrival in the small Argentine town, a murder ensues. Inspector Croce, the local, somewhat-rambling genius detective, investigates the crime. A writer from *El Mundo*, a newspaper in Buenos Aires, is sent to the remote area to cover the story; the journalist is Emilio Renzi, the author's well-known alter-ego figure, who appears in most of Piglia's fictions.

As *Target in the Night* unfolds, the investigations by Croce—and by Renzi—uncover a series of hidden associations that lead to further inquiry. The story involves a powerful local family, a corrupt public prosecutor, and the relationships that Inspector Croce and the investigative journalist Renzi have and develop with the town residents. The initial enigma drives the narrative, and the different storylines in the novel all hinge around the initial crime. But there is also a larger mystery that lies as if hidden beneath the town and the text. The mystery at the heart of *Target in the Night* is an actual mystery and a pretext for the telling of a complex family story—which turns out, in many ways, to be the story of Argentina.

Experimenting with form, innovating with narrative, recounting gripping tales that revolve around a central plot, *Target in the Night* starts as a detective novel, and soon turns into much more than that. Piglia takes the genre of the detective story and transforms it into what can be called, using Piglia's own term, "paranoid fiction." Everyone in the novel is a suspect of a kind, everyone feels persecuted. In Piglia's paranoid fiction, individuals are accused of—and some commit—crimes, but the category of a "criminal" no longer applies only to isolated individuals. Groups with power over other groups maneuver to conserve or gain more power through hidden as well as overt moves. No one understands what is happening, the clues and testimonies are contradictory, and suspicion is always in the air, because the versions of the story change with every point of view. As we follow Croce and Renzi through *Target in the Night*, the potential—and the intrigue—of the story expand with the many voices interwoven throughout the narrative. Important in Piglia's book is the exploration of what is left unsaid, of what is hidden but cannot be forgotten. The initial crime is a point of departure for a series of unpredictable events and a fascinating inquiry into the machinations of society and storytelling in a small town in Argentina. Machinations that have everything to do with contemporary fiction—and with contemporary reality.

★★★

Ricardo Piglia's *Target in the Night* is deeply rooted in its nation's literary tradition, and in a certain Río de la Plata kind of Spanish (*castellano rioplatense*). The context of a small town in the pampas, the language used by the narrator and spoken by the characters in the novel, and the foundational importance of the Argentine countryside in the history of Argentine literature make translating *Target in the Night* a big challenge. At times, *Target in the Night* echoes some of the Argentine greats that came before Piglia: Macedonio Fernández, Jorge Luis Borges, Roberto Arlt, Manuel Puig, Rodolfo Walsh. At others, the novel resonates with Modernists like Joyce and Faulkner, Fitzgerald and Hemingway, Brecht and Kafka, as well as the narrative worlds of Thomas Pynchon, Don DeLillo, and William Burroughs, or the hardboiled mysteries of Raymond Chandler and Dashiell Hammett. These are some of Piglia's influences in *Target in the Night*, crossed and reworked in a thoroughly original style in the remote Argentine landscape where the mystery takes place.

How do you translate *Blanco nocturno*—a novel so rooted in Argentine tradition, a novel where the Argentine landscape and ways of speaking are so important—into English? How does one go from *Blanco nocturno* to *Target in the Night*? One of the most difficult things to translate about *Blanco nocturno*, in fact, is the title itself. In Spanish, *Blanco nocturno* has several meanings, and there is no obvious way to reproduce those multiple meanings in English—*Target in the Night* comes at the end of a complex process that always seems to create as many or more questions as answers.

"*Blanco nocturno*," translated literally, would be "Nocturnal White," which does not make much sense in English. White Nocturne was a possibility, and it was never far from Target in the Night. But "*blanco*" in Spanish is not just "white." The most important meaning of "*blanco*" in the context of the novel is probably "target." "*Tiro al blanco*" is target shooting; "*dar en el blanco*" is to hit the target. While *blanco* does mean white, it also means blank, as in a blank space. Tony Durán, the mulatto Puerto Rican from New Jersey, the strange foreigner who travels to a small town in the Province of Buenos Aires, is a dark man at the center of a dark mystery. He is also a target from the moment he sets foot in the Argentine town. Or perhaps Durán has gone to the town with a secret target in mind. These possibilities emerge from the title and from a number of scenes in the novel that work by juxtaposing opposites: black and white, day and night, past and future, presence and absence, tradition and innovation.

I considered a number of titles as I worked on the translation, before arriving at *Target in the Night*. The centrality of the target, as well as the feel of the story, outdid the lyricism of White Nocturne. Nocturnal Target, or Night Target, were not far off. White Night would have overly simplified things, although it would have kept the *blanco-nocturno* binomial. Night Blanks, or Blank Night sounded mysterious, but too ambiguous. Night Vision, although intriguing, would have changed the meaning too much. Likewise, I considered A Shot in the Dark, but found it to be off the mark. Conrad Aiken has a lovely poem entitled "White Nocturne," and while there are some very beautiful passages in Piglia's novel, and while there is definitely something poetic about *Blanco nocturno,* the novel has a jazzy, driving feel to it, a noirish hook much closer to *Target in the Night*.

In many ways, *Blanco nocturno* is the brilliantly untranslatable title of this brilliant novel. There may be better options, but now that the translation is complete and the novel has begun this version of its afterlife, *Target in the Night* is starting to feel very much like the right title in English. With any luck, some readers will be reminded of Fitzgerald's masterful *Tender Is the Night*. Readers, of course, are the ones who will decide what they think of *Target in the Night*, including the title.

★★★

Target in the Night—née *Blanco nocturno*—is the third book of Piglia's that I have translated into English, and there is, I hope, more to come. From the moment I first read Piglia in Spanish, I felt an almost unexplainable need to say the same (to speak the same voice) that I was reading—but to say it (to speak it) so it could be heard (so it could be read) in English. It is a great honor to be one of Piglia's translators. It is also a great challenge, full of responsibility as well as potential. How does a literary tradition like Argentina's, one influenced by so many travelers and outsiders, a tradition with so many translations and rewritings as part of its own national formation—how does such a tradition travel abroad, beyond its own borders? How do you translate a writer like Ricardo Piglia, who is so immersed in the language and the tradition in which he writes? How to translate *Blanco nocturno* from the Argentine countryside into English in the U.S. and arrive at *Target in the Night*? A lot of hard work and conjecture; in the end, the translation becomes a kind of answer.

The first book I translated by Ricardo Piglia was *Nombre falso*, published in English (by Latin American Literary Review Press) as *Assumed Name*. From the beginning, I liked the play with names, attribution, authorship, and property found in that book, and in translation. When I translated Ricardo Piglia's *La ciudad ausente* (published, by Duke University Press, as *The Absent City*) I felt, at times, as if my work as a translator was a direct and natural projection of the machine at the center of the novel, with its ceaseless output of stories that are reworkings and recombinations of other stories, in turn reproduced and circulated throughout a city somehow composed of the stories themselves. A mechanism of narrating as if projected from the original itself, though clearly of another sort.

With *Blanco nocturno*, I felt transported to the small town in the Argentine pampas, even as I was trying, paradoxically, almost impossibly, to transport the novel to another place, in another tongue: *Target in the Night*. I was submerged in the mystery and the investigation and the various characters and relationships, and then released in the second half of the novel by the lyricism of the narrative and the expanding imagination of Luca (one of the Belladona brothers) working in his factory with the stuff that dreams are made of. As with the other projects, I communicated with Piglia as I worked on the translation, and as always he was extremely generous in his responses. At one point, I had a question about Inspector Croce's dog, which roams around town and sometimes goes out to Luca's factory, as if chasing an invisible trail. Piglia answered my query by e-mail—"*[Cuzco] es un perro vagundo de tamaño chico, mutt estaría bien*" [(Cuzco) is a small street dog, mutt would be fine]—and added: "*Sigo imaginariamente tu traducción*" [I am following your translation imaginarily]. As *Blanco nocturno* was becoming *Target in the Night*, changing languages and being reimagined in the North, so to speak, I imagined Piglia following my translation far away in the South, in the dark distance, fading yet always present, leading even as I wrote my version, letting go so others might find the story and take the intrigue where it needed to go.

Because the scene of translation almost always remains invisible, the processes that take place in that scene often remain unknown. Somewhere between creative writing and scholarly research, between invention and investigation, the scene of translation emerges as a third space, mysterious and unexplored, in between languages and texts, suspected—and suspect. Something happens in the scene of translation; there is a potential found there and few places else that deserves to be unveiled. A movement between reading and writing as much as it is a movement between languages and cultures, translation offers insights into all manner of questions about authorship and originality, voice and identity, communication and understanding, cultural borders and linguistic movement. Translating a text is an odd experience: you produce an entire text that is yours, *you* write it, you put it down on paper, you undertake your stylistic and syntactic decisions—but when you are done, you sign *someone else's name* to it instead of your own. Or equally startling, you sign your name *in addition to* someone else's; thus the text gains a double, or a phantom authorship. By signing your words over to someone else, by putting another's name to your language, you willingly sacrifice yourself. Handing over your identity card, if you will, it is as if you were making yourself invisible. Many say that such self-erasure is the necessary duty of the translator, whose task it is—allegedly—to serve the original at all costs.

But translation is also always at least partially selfish, because translation is a mode of reading that is by definition one of appropriation. Translation may be an attempt at careful reproduction, translation may involve a hermeneutic motion the end goal of which may be to restitute signification so that the target might successfully recreate the meaning of the source in an analogous text, but we know that translation always distorts and transforms, as it seeks to say the same in another language. Literary translation requires humility, and also daring, and passion. Somewhere between performance and copying, between building bridges and destroying originals; somewhere between theft and plagiarism, on the one hand, and altruism and empathy, on the other.

Is it possible to speak the same voice in another tongue? A nearly impossible task, in which one ends up remaining nearly invisible. For some, the less one sees of the translator in the text, the better. And yet the translation we read is written by the translator—rewritten by the translator, I should say. When we read a translation, we know that we are reading a text that is actually two texts: the version we have in our hands, and the version that came before, both there somehow, encoded in the same book. Seeking to speak the same voice in another tongue.

In the end, the original we so covet (*Blanco nocturno*, in this case) is perceived—heard, felt, intuited—in the translation itself, reflected and distorted, refracted, literally reworded, in an attempt to say the same (to speak the same voice) in the target language (*Target in the Night*, now). What is found in the scene of translation? Fleeting glances of the other in the same, sliding mirrors and shifting floors, moving targets in darkened spaces. Almost enough to make us think of alchemy, forbidden formulas, melodies forgotten yet not entirely lost, a deceptive shape hovering in the fog—like the distant horizon fading in the Argentine countryside at dawn.

On the relationship between translation and the novel, Piglia has said: "*Habría que reflexionar sobre qué quiere decir leer mal; qué tipo de efecto puede producir una lectura que se desvía de lo que en principio pueden ser los sentidos dados del texto…La traducción es el espacio de los grandes intercambios y de las circulaciones secretas.*" [We should think about what it means to mis-read. What kind of effect is produced by a reading that deviates from what may have been, at first, the assumed meanings of the text…Translation is the space of great exchanges and secret circulations.]

A space of great exchanges and secret circulations. An organic machine that reads in one language and writes in another. What's in a name? What meanings and implications are hidden in the town where Croce and Renzi pursue their investigations? A paranoid fiction, full of potential. What is *Target in the Night*? I leave it to the reader.

Sergio Waisman
Kensington, MD, July 2015

PART I

I

Tony Durán was an adventurer and a professional gambler who saw his opportunity to win the big casino when he met the Belladona sisters. It was a ménage à trois that scandalized the town and stayed on everyone's mind for months. He'd show up with one of the two sisters at the restaurant of the Plaza Hotel, but no one could ever tell with which because the twins were so alike that even their handwriting was indistinguishable. Tony was almost never seen with both at the same time; that was something he kept private. What really shocked everyone was the thought of the twins sleeping together. Not so much that they would share the same man, but that they would share each other.

Soon the rumors turned into stories and elaborate tales, and before long no one could talk about anything else. People went on about it throughout the day—in their homes, or at the Social Club, or at Madariaga's Store and Tavern. Everyone had a detail to add, commenting as easily as if they were talking about the weather.

In that town, like in all the towns in the Province of Buenos Aires, more news was batted around in a single day than in any large city in a week. The difference between regional and national news was so vast that the residents could retain the illusion that

3

they lived an interesting life. Durán had come to enrich that mythology, and his figure reached legendary heights long before the time of his death.

You could take Tony's comings and goings through the town and draw a map from them. An outsider's ramblings along the elevated sidewalks, his walks to the outskirts of the abandoned factory and the deserted fields. He deciphered the order and hierarchies of the place in short order. The dwellings and houses stand clearly divided according to the social level of the inhabitants. The territory seems to have been drawn by a snobbish cartographer. The wealthy live at the top of the hill, and in a circle of about eight blocks is the so-called historical center of town,[1] which includes the square, the town hall, the church, and the main street with the stores and the two-story houses. Finally, sloping down on the other side of the railroad tracks, are the poorer neighborhoods where over half of the darker-skinned population lives and dies.

Tony's popularity and the envy he aroused among the men could have led to anything. But in the end his downfall was simply a matter of chance, which is what had brought him here in the first place. It was incredible to see such an elegant mulatto in that town full of Basques and Piedmontese gauchos, a man who spoke Spanish with a Caribbean accent but looked as if he came from the

---

1   The town is toward the south of the province of Buenos Aires, 340 kilometers from the capital. A military stronghold and the location of troop settlements during the time of the Indian Wars, the small town was really founded in 1905 when the railroad station was built, the plots of the downtown area were demarcated, and the lands of the municipality were distributed. In the 1940s the eruption of a volcano covered the plains and the houses with a mantle of ash. The men and women defended themselves from the gray dust by covering their faces with beekeeping and fumigation masks.

province of Corrientes or from Paraguay, a mysterious foreigner lost in a lost town in the middle of the pampas.

"He was always happy," Madariaga said, looking in the mirror at a man pacing nervously along the store's stacked bottles, a riding whip in his hand. "And you, Inspector, will you have a gin?"

"Grappa, maybe. But never on duty," Inspector Croce replied.

Tall, of indefinite age, with a red face and gray moustache and hair, Croce chewed pensively on an Avanti cigar as he paced back and forth, hitting the legs of the chairs with his riding whip. As if he were shooing away his own thoughts, crawling along the floor.

"How could no one have seen Durán that day?" Croce asked, and everyone in the country store looked at him silently, guiltily.

Then he said that he knew that everyone knew but that no one was talking, and that they were thinking up a bunch of lies and going round and round the obvious to try to find a fifth leg to the cat.

"I wonder where that expression comes from?" Croce said, stopping to think, intrigued. He got lost in the zigzag of his thoughts, flashing like lightning bugs at night. He smiled, and began pacing again. "Just like Tony," he said, remembering. "An American who didn't look like an American, but he was an American."

Tony Durán was born in San Juan, Puerto Rico. His parents moved to Trenton when he was five years old, and he was raised in New Jersey as a typical American. The only thing he remembered from the island was that his grandfather was a gamecock breeder who used to take him to the fights on Sundays. He also remembered that the men would cover their pants with newspapers to protect their clothes from the spraying blood of the fighting cocks.

When he arrived and found a secret cockfighting ring in the town of Pila, and saw the country laborers wearing sandals and the little pygmy roosters strutting around in the sand, he laughed, saying that that's not how it was done. But in the end he got excited about the suicidal fierceness of a Bataraz rooster that used its spurs like a lightweight boxer uses his hands to come out swinging. Quickly, deadly, ruthless, going straight for his rival's death, his destruction, his end. When he saw the rooster, Durán started betting and got worked up about the cockfight, as if he were already one of us (*one of us*, as Tony himself would have said, in English).

"He wasn't one of us, though, he was different, but that's not why they killed him. They killed him because he looked like what we imagined that he had to be," the Inspector said, as enigmatic as always, and as always a bit crazy. "He was nice," he added, looking outside at the countryside. "I liked him," the Inspector said, stopping in his tracks, near the window, leaning back against the wall, lost in his thoughts.

At the bar of the Plaza Hotel, in the afternoons, Durán would recount fragments from his childhood in Trenton, about his family's gas station off of Route One. How his father got up before daybreak because someone had turned off the highway and was honking his horn, how you could hear laughter and jazz from the radio, how Tony looked out the window, half asleep, to see the expensive cars speeding by with happy blond women in ermine jackets in the back seats. A bright vision in the middle of the night confused—in his memory—with fragments from a black and white film. The images were secret and personal and didn't belong to anyone. He didn't even remember if the memories were his. Sometimes Croce felt the same about his own life.

"I'm from here," the Inspector said all of a sudden, as if he had just woken up. "And I know all the cats around here, and I've never seen one with five legs, but I can imagine this young man's life perfectly. He seemed to come from somewhere else," Croce said calmly, "but there is nowhere else." He looked at his young assistant, Saldías, who followed him everywhere and always agreed with him. "There is nowhere else, we're all in the same boat."

Durán was elegant and ambitious and so good at dancing the *plena* in the Dominican clubs of Spanish Harlem that he became the emcee of the Pelusa, a dancehall on East 122nd Street in Manhattan. This was in the mid 1960s, and he had just turned twenty. He climbed quickly because he was quick, because he was fun, because he was always willing and because he was loyal. Before long he was working the hotels in Long Island and the casinos in Atlantic City.

Everyone in town remembered how amazed they were when they heard the stories that he told at the bar in the Plaza Hotel, drinking gin-and-tonics and eating peanuts, chatting in a low voice as if he were sharing secrets. No one was sure if those stories were true, but no one cared about a detail like that. They listened, grateful that he was confiding in provincial folk like them, people who still lived where they were born, where their parents and their grandparents were born, and who only knew about the lifestyle of guys like Durán because they saw them on the Telly Savalas detective show on Saturday nights. He didn't understand why they wanted to hear the story of his life. His story was the same as anyone else's, he said. "There aren't that many differences, when you get down to it," Durán used to say. "The only thing that changes is who your enemy is."

After a time in the casinos, Durán broadened his horizon, particularly with women. He developed a sixth sense that allowed him to determine a woman's wealth, to differentiate rich women from female adventurers who were looking for a catch of their own. Small details would grab his attention, a certain caution when betting, a deliberately distracted look, a carelessness in their dress and a use of language that he immediately associated with abundance. The more money, the more laconic the woman, that was his conclusion. He had the class and skill to seduce them. He'd tease and string them along, but at the same time he treated them with a colonial chivalry he had learned from his Spanish grandparents. Until one night in early December 1971, in Atlantic City, when he met the Argentine twins.

The Belladona sisters were the daughters and granddaughters of the town founders, immigrants who had made their fortune from the lands they owned in the area of Carhué, at the end of the Indian Wars. Their grandfather, Colonel Bruno Belladona, came with the railroad and bought lands now administered by a North American firm. Their father, the engineer Cayetano Belladona, lived in the large family house, retired, suffering from a strange illness that kept him from going out but not from controlling the town and county politics. He was a wretched man who cared only for his two daughters (Ada and Sofía). He had a serious conflict with his two sons (Lucio and Luca), and had erased them from his life as if they'd never existed. The difference of the sexes is the key to every tragedy, Old Man Belladona thought when he was drunk. Men and women are different species, like cats and vultures. Whose idea was it to make them cohabitate? The males want to kill you and kill each other, while the women want to go to bed with you, climb into the nearest cot with you at siesta time, or go to bed together, Old Man Belladona would ramble on, somewhat deliriously.

He'd been married twice. He had the twin girls with his second wife, Matilde Ibarguren, a posh lady from Venado Tuerto who was a certifiable nut. The two boys he'd had with an Irishwoman with red hair and green eyes who couldn't stand life in the countryside and had run away, first to Rosario, and then back to Dublin. The strange thing was that the boys had inherited their stepmother's unhinged character, while the girls were just like the Irishwoman: red-haired and joyful, lighting up the air wherever they went. Crossed destinies, Croce called it, the children inherit their parents' crossed tragedies. Saldías the Scribe carefully jotted down all the observations that the Inspector made, trying to learn the ins and outs of his new position. Recently transferred to the town by order of the Public Prosecutor's Office, which was trying to control the overly rebellious Inspector, Saldías admired Croce as if he were the greatest investigator[2] in Argentine history. Assistant Inspector Saldías took everything that Croce said entirely seriously; and the Inspector would, in jest, sometimes call him Watson.

In any case, their stories—Ada and Sofía's on the one hand, Lucio and Luca's on the other—remained separate for years, as if

2   Investigator was the name used, at the time, for a plainclothes policeman.

they belonged to different tribes. They only came together when Tony Durán was found dead. There had been a monetary transaction; apparently Old Man Belladona had been involved with some transfer of funds. The old man went to Quequén every month to oversee the shipments of grain that he exported, for which he received a compensation in dollars paid to him by the State under pretext of keeping internal prices stable. He taught his daughters his own moral code and let them do whatever they wanted, raising them as if they were boys.

Ever since they were little the Belladona sisters were rebellious. They were audacious, they competed with each other all the time, with tenacity and delight, not to differentiate themselves, but to sharpen their symmetry and to learn to what extent they were really identical. They'd go out on horseback and explore the night like viscachas, in winter, in the frost-covered countryside. They'd go along the ravine and into the swampy ground crawling with black crabs. They'd bathe naked in the rough lake that gave its name to the town and hunt ducks with the double-barreled rifle their father bought them when they turned thirteen. They were very developed for their age, as they say, so no one was surprised when—almost overnight—they stopped going hunting and horseback riding and playing fútbol with the country laborers, to become young society ladies who sent out to have their identical clothes made in an English shop in the capital. With time they went to study agronomy at the university in La Plata, following the wish of their father, who wanted them in charge of the fields soon. People said that they were always together, that they passed their exams easily because they knew the countryside better than their teachers, that they shared their boyfriends, and that they wrote their mother letters to recommend books and to ask her for money.

Around that time the father suffered the accident that left him half paralyzed, so the sisters abandoned their studies and came back to town. There were several versions of what had happened to the old man. That his horse had thrown him when he was surprised by a swarm of locusts from the north, and that he spent the whole night lying in the middle of the field, his face covered with the insects and their razor-sharp legs. That he suffered some kind of stroke when he was screwing a Paraguayan at Bizca's brothel and that the girl had saved his life, almost without realizing it, because she went on giving him mouth-to-mouth resuscitation. Or also, that one afternoon he discovered, or so people said, that someone very close to him had been poisoning him. He didn't want to believe it might be one of his sons. Apparently, someone had been adding a few drops of the liquid used to kill ticks in the whiskey he drank at the end of every day, at dusk, on his flower-filled balcony. By the time they realized what it was, the poison had done part of its job, and from that point on the old man couldn't walk anymore. In any case, before long the family was not seen around town anymore. The father because he stayed in his house and never went out; and the sisters because, after taking care of their father for a few months, they grew bored of being locked in and decided to go abroad.

Unlike all their friends who were going to Europe, the sisters went to the United States. They spent time in California, then crossed the continent by train on a trip that took several weeks with long stops in various cities along the way, until they reached the East Coast around the beginning of the northern winter. They spent the trip staying in large hotels, gambling wherever they could along the way, living the life and playing the part of South American heiresses in search of adventure in the land of upstarts and the nouveau riche.

This was the news about the Belladona sisters that reached town. The information arrived with the evening train that left the mail in large canvas bags on the station platform. It was Sosa, the post office agent, who reconstructed the itinerary of the young women from the postmarks on the envelopes addressed to their father. Complemented by the detailed stories of the travelers and businessmen who came to the bar of the Plaza Hotel to recount what was rumored about the twins among their fellow students in La Plata—to whom they would boast on the telephone, apparently, about their North American conquests and discoveries.

Then, toward the end of 1971, the sisters reached the New York area. In a casino in Atlantic City they met the pleasant young man of uncertain origin who spoke a Spanish that seemed to come straight out of a television series. At first, not realizing there were two of them, Tony Durán went out with both sisters, thinking there was just one. This was a system the sisters had always practiced. It was like having a double do the disagreeable (and the agreeable) tasks for you, which is how they took turns with everything in life. In fact, people in town used to say, each sister only went through half of school, half of their catechism, and even half of their sexual initiation. They were always drawing straws to see which of them was going to do whatever they had to do.

Is that you, or your sister? Was the question everyone asked when one of the two showed up at a dance, or at the dining room of the Social Club. Doña Matilde, their mother, would often have to clarify which was Sofía and which was Ada. Or the other way around. Because their mother was the only one who could tell them apart—by their breathing, she said.

The twins' passion for gambling was the first thing that attracted Durán to them. The sisters were used to betting against each other, and he became part of the game. From that point on he dedicated himself to seducing them—or they dedicated themselves to seducing him. They were always together (dancing, dining, listening to live music) until one of the two would insist on staying a bit longer to have another drink at the bar in the hotel, while the other would excuse herself and go back to the room. He would stay with Sofía; with the twin who said she was Sofía. Everything worked out for a few days.

Then, one night, when he was in bed with Sofía, Ada came in and started undressing in front of them. That was the start of the stormy week they spent in the motels of Long Island's South Shore, in the freezing winter, sleeping together, the three of them, enjoying the bars in the resorts that were nearly empty in the off-season. The three-way game was hard and brutal and the cynicism was the hardest thing to bear. Perdition and evil make life fun, but conflicts evenutally arise. The two sisters would plot behind Tony's back and make him say too much; he, in turn, would plot with the women, trying to turn one against the other. Sofía was the weakest, or the most sensitive, and the first to give up. One night she left the hotel and flew back to Buenos Aires.

Durán continued traveling with Ada. They went back to the same hotels and to the same resorts, until one night they decided that they, too, would go to Argentina. Durán sent her ahead and came a few days later.

"But did he come for them? I don't think so. And he didn't come for the family money, either," Inspector Croce said, stopping to light his cigar. He leaned against the counter while Madariaga cleaned glasses behind the counter. "He came because he was never at peace, because he couldn't keep still, because he was looking for a place where he wouldn't be treated like a second-class citizen. That's why he came, and now he's dead. In my time things were different." The Inspector looked around the tavern, but no one said anything. "We didn't need a half-Latino, half-mulatto, fake gringo coming here to complicate life for a poor country Inspector like me."

Croce was born and raised in the area. He became a policeman during Perón's first government, and had been in charge of the district ever since—except for a brief period after General Valle's revolution in 1956. The Inspector went gray overnight, that year, when he found out the military had executed the workers who had risen up asking for Perón's return. The week before the uprising Croce had been rallying the local police stations, but when he learned the rebellion had failed he wandered through the countryside speaking to himself for days, without sleeping. By the time they found him it was already as if he were someone else. His hair white, his head agitated, he locked himself in his house and didn't come out for months. He lost his post that time, but he was reinstated during Frondizi's presidency in 1958 and has kept it ever since, despite all the political changes. He was supported by Old Man Belladona who, as they say, always defended him, although they weren't particularly close.

"They want to catch me slipping up somehow," Croce said, smiling. "They have me under surveillance. But it won't work, I won't let them."

He was legendary, much loved by all, a kind of general consultant in town. Everyone thought Inspector Croce had a bit of a screw loose, especially when people saw him riding through the countryside in his one-horse cart. Always the lone ranger, he'd detain cattle rustlers and horse thieves, or round up bums and rich kids from the large ranches when they came back drunk from the bars near the port. His style sometimes provoked scandals and grumbling, but he got such great results that everyone ended up thinking that his was the way every country Inspector should behave. He had such extraordinary intuition, he was like a psychic.

"He's a bit off," everyone said. A bit off, maybe, but not like Madman Carousel, who circled around town all dressed in white, talking to himself in an incomprehensible tongue. No, a bit off but in another way, like someone who can hear a song in his head but can't quite play it on the piano. An unpredictable man who ranted at times, had no set rules, but was always right and always remained impartial.

Croce got it right so often because he seemed to see things that others didn't. He caught a man who had raped a woman, once, because he saw the perpetrator coming out of the same movie theater—twice. It turned out that the man had raped a woman in the theater where *God Bless You* was playing, but the clue that had led Croce to the arrest hadn't meant anything to anyone else. Another time he discovered that someone was a rustler because he saw the man taking the early-morning train to Bolívar. If he's going to Bolívar at that time of day, it's because he's going there to sell stolen loot, Croce said. Said and done.

Sometimes they'd call him from one of the surrounding towns to solve an impossible case, as if he were a criminal faith healer. He'd ride over in his one-horse cart, listen to the different stories and testimonies, and come back with the case solved. "The priest did it," he said once in the case of a set of farm fires in Del Valle. A Franciscan pyromaniac. They went to the parish and found a trunk full of fuses and a can of kerosene in the atrium.

His whole life was dedicated to his job. After a strange love affair with a married woman, Croce remained unattached, although everyone thought he had an intermittent relationship with Rosa, Estévez's widow, the woman in charge of the town's archives. He lived by himself on the edge of town, on the other side of the tracks, where the police station operated.

Croce's cases were famous throughout the province. His assistant, Saldías the Scribe, a student of criminology, had fallen under the Inspector's spell, too.

"Fact is no one really understands why Tony came to this town," Croce said, and looked at Saldías.

The assistant took out a little black notebook and reviewed his notes.

"Durán arrived in January, on the fifth of January," Saldías said. "Exactly three months and four days ago."

2

On that day, in the still glare of summer, a stranger was seen getting off the northbound express. Very tall, with dark skin, dressed like a dandy, with two large suitcases that he left on the train platform—and a fine leather brown bag that he refused to let go of when the porters approached—he smiled, blinded by the sun, and gave a ceremonial bow, as if that was the way people greeted each other around here. The ranchers and laborers talking in the shade of the casuarina trees responded with a surprised murmur, as Tony—in his sweet voice, in his musical language—looked at the stationmaster and asked where he could find a good hotel.

"Would you be so kind as to tell me, sir, where there might be a good hotel near here?"

"The Plaza is right over there," the stationmaster said, pointing to the white building on the other side of the street.

He registered at the hotel as Anthony Durán, showing his U.S. passport and using his traveler's checks to pay a month in advance. He said he had come for business, that he wanted to make some investments, that he was interested in Argentine horses. Everyone in town tried to figure out what type of business he might have with horses. They thought that maybe Durán was going to invest in the stud farms in the area. He said something vague about a polo player in Miami who wanted to buy ponies from the Heguy Ranch, and something about a trainer in Mississippi who was looking to race Argentine stallions. According to Durán, a show jumper named Moore had been here before him, leaving convinced of the quality of the horses bred in the pampas. That was the reason he gave when he first arrived. A few days later he started visiting the local corrals and checking out the colts and fillies grazing in the pastures.

At first it looked as if he had come to buy horses. Everyone became interested in him—the cattle auctioneers, the consignees, the breeders, the ranchers—thinking there was some kind of profit to be made. The gossip buzzed from one end of town to the other like a swarm of locusts.

"It took us a while," Madariaga said, "to catch on to his connection to the Belladona sisters."

Durán settled in at the hotel in a room on the third floor facing the plaza and asked to have a radio installed (a radio, not a television). He asked if there was anywhere in the area where he could get rum and frijoles, but he quickly got used to the local food in the hotel restaurant and to the Llave gin that he had sent up to his room every afternoon at five.

He spoke an archaic Spanish, full of unexpected idiomatic expressions (*copacetic, what's the deal, in the thick of it*) and bewildering words in English or in ancient Spanish (*obstinacy, victor, frippery*). It wasn't always possible to understand the words he used, or how he put sentences together, but his language was warm and soothing. Also, he'd buy drinks for anyone who listened to his stories. That was his moment of greatest esteem, and that's how he started to circulate, to become known, to visit the most varied of places, and to become friends with the young men in town, regardless of their level on the social scale.

He was full of stories and anecdotes about that strange outside world that people in the area had only seen in the movies or on TV. He had lived in New York, a city without any of the ridiculous hierarchies of a small town in the province of Buenos Aires—or at least where they weren't as visible. He always looked happy. Everyone who spoke to him or ran into him on the street felt important because of how he listened to them. How he agreed with them. One week after being in town, he had established a warm and sympathetic aura about him, and he became popular and well known even among people who hadn't met him.[3]

He had a certain ability to win over the men, and this seemed to draw the women to his side as well. They talked about him in the ladies room in the coffee shop, and in the halls of the Social Club, and in endless telephone conversations on summer afternoons. The women were the ones, of course, who started saying that Tony

---

3   Tony's older brother had died in Vietnam. The sun reflected off of his glasses as he was crossing a stream in the forest near the Mecong Delta, making him visible to a Vietcong sniper who killed him with a single shot—fired from such a distance that it went unheard. *He died in battle, but his death was so unexpected and so peaceful that we thought he had died of a heart attack*, said the condolence letter signed by Colonel Roger White, the ranting author in charge of writing these letters on behalf of the Military Assistance Command in Vietnam. The troops referred to Colonel White as *the fucking poet*. After the shot, the squad fell back into the rice fields, fearing an ambush. Tony's brother was carried away by the current. They found him a week later, devoured by dogs and scavenger birds. Colonel White didn't say anything about these circumstances in his condolence letter. As grace for his brother's death, Tony wasn't called up into the army. They didn't want two dead brothers in the same family, even in a Puerto Rican family. His brother's remains came back in a sealed, lead coffin. His mother was never certain that the body—buried in the military cemetery in Jersey City—was really her son's.

had actually come to town after the Belladona sisters.

Until finally, one afternoon, he walked into the bar of the Plaza Hotel with one of the two sisters—with Ada, they say. They sat at a table in a far corner and spent the afternoon talking and laughing softly. It caused an explosion, a show of joy and malice. That very night was the start of the hushed comments and the stories full of innuendos.

They were said to have checked in at the Inn on the road that leads to the town of Rauch. And that the sisters used to receive him in a small house of theirs, in the vicinity of the closed factory that stood like an abandoned monument some ten kilometers from town.

It was all rumors, provincial chatter, stories that only served to further elevate his prestige—and that of the sisters.

The Belladona sisters had always been ahead of their time, they were the precursors of everything interesting that happened in town: the first to wear miniskirts, the first not to wear bras, the first to smoke marijuana and take the pill. It was as if the sisters had decided that Durán was the right man to help them complete their education. An initiation story, then, like in those novels in which young social climbers conquer frigid duchesses. The sisters weren't frigid, or duchesses, but Durán was a young social climber, a Caribbean Julien Sorel—as Nelson Bravo, the writer of the society pages for the local paper, eruditely put it.

At this point the men changed from looking at him with distant sympathy to treating him with blind admiration and calculated envy.

"He used to come here, peaceful as could be, and have a drink with one of the sisters. Because at first (people say) they didn't let him into the Social Club. Those snobs are the worst, they like to keep everything hidden. Simple folks, instead, are more liberal," Madariaga said, using the word in its old sense. "If they do something, they do it out in the light of day. Didn't Don Cosme and his sister Margarita live together for over a year as a couple? And didn't the two Jáuregui brothers share a woman they got in a brothel in Lobos? And didn't that old guy Andrade get involved with a fifteen-year-old girl who was a pupil in a Carmelite convent?"

"Surely," one of the patrons said.

"Of course if Durán had been a blond gringo everything would've been different," Madariaga said.

"Surely," the patron repeated.

"Surely, surely...Shirley got put in the clink," Bravo said, sitting at a table near the window toward the back of the tavern. Stirring a spoonful of bicarbonate in a glass of soda water. For his heartburn.

Durán liked living in a hotel. He'd stay up all night, wandering the empty hallways while everyone slept. And sometimes he'd talk with the night concierge, who went around trying the doors at all hours, or took brief naps on the leather chairs in the large reception hall downstairs. Talking is a figure of speech, though, because the night porter was a Japanese man who smiled and said yes to everything, as if he didn't understand Spanish. He was small and pale, slicked down, very servile, always wearing a bow tie and jacket. He came from the countryside, where his family ran a flower nursery. His name was Yoshio Dazai,[4] but everyone

---

4   The son of an officer of the Imperial Army who died hours before the

in the hotel called him the Japo. Apparently, somehow, Yoshio was Durán's main source of information. Yoshio was the one who told Durán the history of the town and the real story of Belladona's abandoned factory. Many wondered how the Japanese porter had ended up living like a cat by night, shining a light on the hotel's key cabinet with a small lantern, while his family grew flowers in a farm out in the country. Yoshio was friendly and delicate, very formal and very mannered. Quiet, with gentle, almond-shaped eyes, everyone thought the Japanese night porter powdered his face and that he went as far as applying a touch of rouge, a soft palette really, on his cheeks. He was very proud of his straight, jet-black hair, which he himself called *raven's wing*. Yoshio became so fond of Durán that he followed him everywhere, as if he were his personal servant.

Sometimes, at daybreak, the two would come out of the hotel together and walk down the middle of the street, across town to the train station. They'd sit on a bench on the empty platform and watch the dawn express speed by. The train never stopped, it raced south toward Patagonia like a flash. Leaning against the lighted windows, the faces of the passengers behind the glass were like corpses at the morgue.

It was Yoshio who, one early February day at noon, handed Durán the envelope from the Belladona sisters inviting him to visit the family house. They had drawn a map for him on a sheet of notebook paper, circling the location of their mansion on the

---

signing of the Armistice, Dazai was born in Buenos Aires in 1946. Raised by his mother and his aunts, as a child he understood only feminine Japanese (*onnarashii*).

hill in red. Apparently he was invited to meet their father.

The large family house was up the slope in the old part of town, at the top of the hills looking over the low mountains, the lake, and the gray, endless countryside. Dressed in a white linen jacket and matching shoes, Durán walked up the steep road to the house in the middle of the afternoon.

But they had Durán come in through the back service door.

It was the maid's mistake, she saw that Tony was a mulatto and thought that he was a ranch hand in disguise.

He walked through the kitchen, through the ironing room and the servants' rooms, and into the parlor facing the gardens where Old Man Belladona was waiting for him, thin and frail like an old, embalmed monkey, his eyelids heavy, his legs knock-kneed. Durán very politely bowed and approached the Old Man, following the respectful customs used in the Spanish Caribbean. But that doesn't work in the province of Buenos Aires, because only the servants treat gentlemen in that way here. The servants (Croce said) are the only ones who still use the aristocratic manners of the Spanish Colonies, they've been abandoned everywhere else. And it was those gentlemen who taught their servants the manners that they themselves had abandoned, as if depositing in those dark-skinned men the customs they no longer needed.

So Durán behaved, without realizing it, like a foreman, or a tenant, or a farmhand slowly and solemnly approaching his master.

Tony didn't understand the relationships and hierarchies of the town. He didn't understand that there were areas—the tiled paths in the center of the plaza, the shady sidewalk along the boulevard, the front pews of the church—where only the members of the old families could go. That there were places—the Social Club, the theater boxes, the restaurant at the Jockey Club—where you weren't allowed to enter even if you had money.

People asked themselves, though, if Old Man Belladona wasn't right to mistrust. To mistrust, and to show the arrogant foreigner from the beginning the rules of his class, of his house. The Old Man had probably wondered, as everyone wondered, how a mulatto who said he came from New York could show up in a place where the last black people had disappeared—or had dispersed until they blended completely into the landscape—fifty years earlier, without ever clearly explaining why he had come here, insinuating rather that he had come on some kind of secret mission. They said something to each other that afternoon, it came out later, the Old Man and Tony. It seems he had come with a message, or with an order, everything under wraps.

The Old Man lived in a spacious parlor that looked like a racquetball court. They had knocked down several walls to make room for him, so Old Man Belladona could move from one end to the other, between his tables and desks, speaking to himself and spying out the window at the dead movement on the road beyond the gardens.

"They're going to call you Sambo around here," Old Man Belladona told him, smiling caustically. "There were a lot of blacks in the Río de la Plata area during colonial times, they even formed a battalion of mulattos and Negros, very determined, but they were all killed in the War of Independence. There were a few black gauchos, too, out on the frontier, but in the end they all went to live with the Indians. A few years back there were still a few blacks in the hills, but they've died off. They're all gone now. I've heard there are a lot of ways of differentiating skin color in the Caribbean, but here the mulattos are all sambos.[5] Do you understand, young man?"

Old Man Belladona was seventy years old, but he seemed so ancient that it made sense for him to refer to everyone in town as young. He had survived every catastrophe, he ruled over the dead, everything he touched disintegrated, he drove the men in the family away and stayed with his daughters—while his sons were exiled ten kilometers to the south, in the factory they built on the road to Rauch. Right away the Old Man told Tony Durán about the inheritance. He had divided up his possessions and ceded his property before dying, but that had been a mistake. Ever since it had been nothing but wars.

"I don't have anything left," Old Man Belladona said. "They started fighting, and they've nearly killed me."

His daughters, he said, weren't involved in the conflict, but his sons had gone about it as if they were fighting over a kingdom. (*"I'm never coming back,"* Luca had sworn. *"I'll never set foot in this house again."*)

"Something changed at that point, after that visit, and that conversation," Madariaga said from behind the bar, to no one in particular, and without clarifying what the change had been.

It was around that time that people started to say that Durán was a *carrier*.[6] That he had brought money, which wasn't his, to

---

5   Sambos, mestizos of mixed Indian and black blood, were considered the lowest rung on the social ladder of the River Plate region.

6   "Tax evasion is due, primarily, to the activities of so-called *carriers*, known

buy crops under the table. People started saying that this was his business with Old Man Belladona. That the sisters were only a pretext.

Quite possibly, it wasn't that rare, except that people who carried money under the table tended to be invisible. Men who looked like bankers and traveled with a fortune in dollars to avoid the Tax Office. There were a lot of stories about tax evasion and the trafficking of foreign currency. Where it was hidden, how it was carried, who had to be greased. But that's not the point, it doesn't matter where they hide the money, because they can't be discovered if no one says anything. And who's going to say anything if everyone's in on it: the farmers, the ranchers, the auctioneers, the brokers who trade in grains, everyone at the silos who keeps prices down.

Madariaga looked at the Inspector in the mirror again. Croce paced nervously from one end of the tavern to the other, his riding crop in his hand, until he finally sat at one of the tables. Saldías, his assistant, ordered a bottle of wine and something to eat. Croce continued his monologue, as he always did when he was trying to solve a crime.

"Tony Durán came with money," Croce said. "That's why they killed him. They got him excited about the country races and the horse from Luján."

"They didn't need to get him excited, he was already excited before he got here," Madariaga said, laughing.

---

as such because they carry cash in briefcases. They offer better prices to suppliers, to the owners of the winter pastures, and to agricultural producers in general. They trade under the table and make out receipts to inexistent firms" (*La Prensa*, February 10, 1972).

Some people say that a country race was set up especially for him and that he became obsessed about it. But it would be more accurate to say that the horse race, which they had been preparing for months, was moved up so Tony could be there. And that some saw in this the hand of fate.

Tony quickly realized that there were several kinds of very good horses in the province, basically falling into three categories: the polo ponies, very extraordinary, bred mostly in the area of Venado Tuerto; the purebred locals, from the stud farms near the coast; and the short-distance racers, which are very fast, with great pickup, flashing bursts, nervous, used to running in pairs. There are no other horses—or races—like these anywhere else in the world.

Durán began to learn the history of the races in the area.[7] Right away he realized there was more money at play here than at the Kentucky Derby. The farmers and the ranchers bet big, the laborers gamble their entire salary. The country races are set up with much anticipation, and people round up their money for the occasion. Some horses accumulate a kind of prestige, everyone knows that they have won so many races in such and such places. Then a challenge is made.

The town's horse was a dapple gray that belonged to Payo Ledesma, a very good horse, retired, like a boxer who hangs up his gloves without ever having lost. A rancher from Luján with an undefeated sorrel had been trying to challenge him for some time. It seems at first Ledesma didn't want to accept, but that he

---

7   The best-known short-distance racer in the history of Argentina was *Pangaré azul*, property of Colonel Benito Machado. This horse won every race in which it ever participated. It died hanged in its stall due to some trainer's carelessness.

finally rose to the challenge, as they say, and accepted the call. Which is when someone looked over and got Tony involved. The other horse, the one from Luján, was named *Tácito*, and he had quite a history. *Tácito* was a purebred that had been injured and now couldn't run more than three hundred meters at a time. He had started out in the racetrack in La Plata and had won in the Polla de Potrillos, but then one rainy Saturday afternoon, in the fifth race at San Isidro, he'd had an accident. On one of the turns he broke his left leg and was left damaged. He was the son of one of *Embrujo's* sons. They wanted to put him out to pasture and just breed him, but the horse's jockey—and trainer—stepped in and took care of him. Until, slowly, the horse was able to run again, damaged and all. Apparently they convinced the rancher in Luján to buy him and he had won every country race in which he had raced since. That was the story everyone told about him. The horse was truly impressive, a sorrel with white feet, surly and mean. He had ears only for his jockey, who spoke to him as if he were a person.

The horse was brought to town in an open pickup. When they let him out in the field the folks who had gathered watched from a respectful distance. A horse of great height, with a blanket on its back and one leg bandaged, spirited, surly, darting its wide eyes from fright or anger, like a true purebred.

"Yah," Madariaga said. "Ledesma's dapple gray against the undefeated sorrel from Luján. Something happened there."

3

It was a cool Sunday afternoon. Men from the farms and estancias from throughout the district lined up against the fence that separated the track from the surrounding houses. A couple of boards were placed over a pair of sawhorses to set up a stand to sell empanadas, gin, and a coastal wine so strong it went to your head just by looking at it. The fire for the grill was already lit, there were racks of ribs nailed on a cross, and entrails stretched out on a tarp laid out on the grass. Everyone was gearing up as if for a big fiesta; there was a nervous, electrified murmuring through the crowd, typical of a long-awaited race. There were no women in sight, only males of all ages, boys and old men, young men and grown men, wearing their Sunday best. Laborers with embroidered shirts and vests; ranchers with suede jackets and scarves around their necks; young men from town with jeans and sweaters tied at their waists. Large numbers of people milling about. The betting started right away, the men holding bills in their hands, folded between their fingers, or behind the headbands of their hats.

A lot of men from out of town came to watch the race, too, and they were all gathered toward the end of the track, at the finish line, near the bluff. You could tell they weren't from the area by how they moved, cautiously, with the uncertain step of someone not on home turf. The loudspeakers from the town's advertisement company—*Ads, auctions, and sales. The voice of the people*—played music first, then asked for a round of applause for the judge of that afternoon's race: Inspector Croce.

The Inspector arrived wearing a suit and a tie and a thin-brimmed hat. He was with Saldías the Scribe, who followed him around like a shadow. Some scattered applause sounded.

"Long live the Inspector's horse!" a drunk yelled.

"Don't get smart with me, Cholo, or I'll throw you in jail for contempt," the Inspector said. The drunk threw his hat in the air and shouted:

"Long live the police!"

Everyone laughed and the atmosphere eased up again. Croce and the Scribe very formally measured the distance of the track by counting the requisite number of steps. They also placed a linesman on either side, each holding a red towel to wave when everything was set.

During a break in the music, a car was heard driving up at full speed from behind the hill. Everyone saw Durán driving Old Man Belladona's convertible coupe with both sisters beside him in the narrow front seat. Redheaded and beautiful, they looked as if they hadn't gotten enough sleep. While Durán parked the car and helped the young ladies out, the Inspector stopped, turned around to look at them, and said something softly to Saldías. The Scribe shook his head. It was strange to see the sisters together except in extraordinary situations. And it was extraordinary to see them there at all because they were the only women at the race (except for the country women selling empanadas).

Durán and the twins found a place near the starting line. The young women each sat on a small canvas folding chair. Tony stood behind them and greeted people he knew, and joined in making fun of the out-of-towners who had crowded together at the other end of the track. His thick, black hair, slicked back, shone with some kind of cream or oil that kept it in place. The sisters were all smiles, dressed alike, with flowery sundresses and white ribbons in their hair. Needless to say, had they not been the descendants of the town owner, they wouldn't have been able to move about with so much ease among all the men there. They, the men, looked at the Belladona sisters out of the corner of their eyes with a combination of respect and longing. Durán was the one who'd return the looks, smiling, and the men from the countryside would turn around and walk away. The two sisters also immediately started betting, taking money out of a diminutive leather purse that each carried around her shoulder. Sofía bet a lot of money on the town's dapple gray, while Ada put together a stack of five-hundred and one-thousand bills and played it all on the sorrel from Luján. It was always like that, one against the other, like two cats in a bag fighting to get out.

"Fine, that's fine," Sofía said, and raised the stakes. "The loser pays for dinner at the Náutico."

Durán laughed, joking with them. People saw him lean forward, between the two, and reach toward one of the sisters, and warmly tuck a rebellious strand behind an ear.

Then everything froze for an endless instant. The Inspector motionless in the middle of the field; the out-of-towners quiet as if asleep; the laborers studying the sand on the track with exaggerated attention; the ranchers looking displeased or surprised, surrounded by their foremen and farm hands; the loudspeakers silent; the man in charge of the grill with a knife in his hand suspended over the flames of the barbeque; Calesita the Madman circling slower and slower until he too stood still, barely rocking in place as if to imitate the swaying of the canopies over the carousel in the breeze. (*Carousel*: a word Tony taught Calesita one time when he stopped to speak with the town's madman in the main square.) It was a remarkable moment. The sisters and Durán appeared to be the only ones who continued on, speaking softly, laughing, he still caressing one of them, the other pulling on the sleeve of his jacket to get him to bend toward her and hear what she had to whisper in his ear. But if everything had stopped it was because, on the other side of the row of trees, the rancher from Luján—Cooke the Englishman—had shown up, tall and heavy as an oak. Next to him, swaying his hips as he walked with a studied smugness, his riding crop tucked under his arm, was the small jockey. Half yellowish-green from drinking so much *mate*, he looked at the men from the country with disdain because he had raced in the hippodromes in La Plata and San Isidro, and because he was a professional turf racer. The story had reached the town of how the jockey had lost his license when he jostled a rival coming out of a curve at full speed. The move apparently forced the other horse to roll, badly killing the jockey, crushed underneath the animal. People said that he spent time in jail at first, but was later released when he claimed that his horse was spooked by the whistle of a train pulling into the station in La Plata, directly behind the racetrack. People said that he was cruel and quarrelsome, that he was full of tricks and wiles, that he was responsible for two other deaths, that he was haughty, tiny, and mean as pepper. They called him el Chino because he was born in the District of Maldonado, in the Oriental Republic of Uruguay—but he was so cocky and arrogant, he didn't seem like someone from Uruguay.

One-Eyed Ledesma's dapple gray was ridden by Little Monkey Aguirre, a trainee of at most fifteen years who looked as if he'd been born on a horse. Black beret, scarf around his neck, espadrilles, baggy trousers, thick riding crop, Little Monkey. In front of him, the other jockey, diminutive, dressed in a colorful vest and jodhpurs, a glove on his left hand, his scornful eyes two wicked holes in a yellow plaster mask. They looked at each other without saying anything: el Chino with his crop under his arm and the black glove on his hand, like a claw, and Little Monkey kicking stones out of the way, as if he wanted to clear the ground, stubborn, fussy. His way of focusing before a race.

When everything was ready, they set about mounting their horses. Little Monkey took off his sandals and got on barefoot, putting his large toe through the rope of the saddle, Indian style. El Chino used short stirrups, up high, English style, half-standing on his horse, both reins in his gloved left hand, while he patted the horse's head with his right and whispered in the horse's ear in a distant, guttural tongue. Then they weighed them, one at a time, on a maize-weighing scale that lay flat on the ground. They had to add weight to Little Monkey; el Chino had about two kilos on him.

They decided the horses would take off with a running start and then race a distance of three blocks, barely three hundred

·meters, from the shadow of the casuarina trees to the embankment of the downhill slope, near the lake. One of the linesmen laid out a yellow sisal string at the starting line, which shone in the sun as if it were made of gold. The Inspector stepped to the line and waved his hat to indicate that everything was set. The music stopped, silence settled over everything again, the only sound the soft murmur of a handful of people placing the last few bets.

The racehorses took off in a trot from underneath the tree covering. There was one false start and two different attempts to get the horses lined up again. Finally, they came running up from the back in a light gallop, perfectly even, picking up speed, expertly mounted, nose to nose, and the Inspector clapped his hands loudly and shouted that it was a fair start. The dapple gray seemed to jump forward and right away took a head's length lead over el Chino, who was riding draped over his horse's ears, without touching him, his whip still under his arm. Little Monkey came up whipping his animal wildly. Both ran as fast as a light.

The loud cheers and insults formed a chorus that surrounded the track. Little Monkey led for the first two hundred meters, at which point el Chino started hitting his sorrel and quickly closed in on him. They raced to the end, neck and neck. When they crossed the finish line Ledesma's dapple gray had a nose on the sorrel from Luján.

El Chino jumped off of his horse, furious, and immediately shouted that it had been a false start.

"The start was fair," the Inspector said, unfazed. "Little Monkey won, at the finish line."

A ruckus started up. Amid the confusion, el Chino started

arguing with Payo Ledesma, owner of the winning horse. First he insulted him, then he tried to hit him. Ledesma, who was thin and tall, put his hand on el Chino's head and kept him at an arm's length, while the small, enraged jockey kicked and swung his arms in vain. Finally, the Inspector intervened. He yelled until el Chino calmed down, dusted himself off, and turned toward Croce.

"I get it. The horse is yours, right?" el Chino asked. "No one in this town beats the Inspector's horse, is that it?"

"Inspector's horse my ass," Croce said. "You jockeys. When you win everything's fine and dandy, but when you lose the first thing you do is claim that the race was fixed."

Feelings ran high, everyone was arguing. The bets hadn't been paid yet. The sisters stood up on their small canvas seats to see what was going on. They balanced themselves by each holding on to one of Durán's shoulders. Tony stood between them, smiling. The rancher from Luján seemed very calm, holding his horse by its bridle.

"Relax, Chino," he said to his jockey, and turned to Ledesma. "The start wasn't clear. My horse was cut off and you," he said, looking at Croce, who had lit a small cigar and was smoking furiously, "you saw it and still gave the sign for a fair start."

"In that case, why didn't you speak up earlier and say that it was a false start?" Ledesma asked.

"Because I'm a gentleman. If you claim that you won, that's your business, I'll pay the bets. But my horse is still undefeated."

"I disagree," the jockey said. "A horse has his honor, he never accepts an unfair defeat."

"That little doll-man is crazy," Ada said, with astonishment and admiration. "Really stubborn."

As if he could hear them all the way from the other end of the field, el Chino looked at the twins up and down with audacity, first at one and then the other. He turned to face them, insolent and vain. Ada raised her hand and formed the letter *c* with her thumb and index finger, smiling, to indicate the small difference by which he had lost.

"That little guy is all cocked and ready to crow," Ada said.

"I've never been with a jockey," Sofía said.

The jockey looked at both of them, bowed almost impercep-tibly, and swayed away, as if one of his legs was shorter than the other. His whip under his arm, his little body harmonious and stiff, he walked to the pump by the side of the house and wetted his hair down. While he was pumping the water, he looked at Little Monkey, sitting under a tree nearby.

"You beat me to it," he said.

"You talk too much," Little Monkey said, and they faced each other again. But it didn't go any further than that because el Chino walked away. He went to the sorrel and spoke to him, petting him, as if he were trying to calm the horse down, when he was the one who was upset.

"I'll say it's okay, then," the rancher from Luján said. "But I didn't lose. Pay the bets, go on." He looked at Ledesma. "We'll go again whenever you want, just find me a neutral field. There are races in Cañuelas next month, if you want."

"I thank you," Ledesma said.

But Ledesma didn't accept the rematch and they never raced again. They say the sisters tried to convince Old Man Belladona to buy the horse from Luján, including the jockey, because they wanted the race to be restaged, and that the Old Man refused—but those are only stories and conjectures.

March arrived and the sisters stopped going swimming at the pool in the Náutico. After this, Durán would wait for them at the bar of the hotel, or he'd say goodbye to them at the edge of town and walk to the lake, making a stop at Madariaga's Tavern to have a gin. He was seen at the bar of the hotel almost every night, he kept up a tone of immediate confidence, of natural sympathy, but slowly he started growing more isolated. That's when the versions of his motives for coming to town started changing, people would say that they'd seen him, or that he'd been seen, that he'd said something to them, or that someone had said something—and they'd lower their voices. He looked erratic, distracted, and he seemed comfortable only in the company of Yoshio, while the latter appeared to become his personal assistant, his cicerone and his guide. The Japanese night porter was leading him in an unexpected direction that no one entirely liked. They swam naked together in the lake during siesta time. Several times Yoshio was seen waiting for Durán on the edge of the water with a towel, and then drying Tony vigorously before serving him his afternoon snack on a tablecloth stretched out under the willows.

Sometimes they'd go out at dawn and fish at the lake, rent a boat and watch the sunrise as they cast their lines. Tony was born on an island in the Caribbean, and the interconnected lakes in the south of the province, with their peaceful banks and their islets with grazing cows, made him laugh. Still, he liked the empty landscape of the plains, beyond the gentle current of the water lapping on the reeds, as they saw it from the boat. Expanding fields, sunburnt grass, and occasionally a water spring between the groves and the roads.

By then the story had changed. No longer a Don Juan, no longer a fortune seeker who had come after two South American heiresses, he was now a new kind of traveler, an adventurer who trafficked in dirty money, a neutral smuggler who snuck dollars through customs using his North American passport and his elegant looks. He had a split personality, two faces, two backgrounds. It was impossible to reconcile the versions because the other, secret life attributed to him was always new and surprising. A seductive foreigner, an extrovert who revealed everything, but also a mysterious man with a dark side who fell for the Belladona sisters and got lost in the whirlwind that followed.

The whole town participated in fine-tuning and improving the stories. The motives and the point of view changed, but not the character. The events themselves hadn't actually changed, only how they were being perceived. There were no new facts, only different interpretations.

"But that's not why they killed him," Madariaga said, and looked at the Inspector again in the mirror. Nervous, his riding crop in his hand, Croce was still pacing from one end of the tavern to the other.

The last light from the late March afternoon seeped in, sliced by the window grilles. Outside, the stretched-out fields dissolved like water in the dusk.

They spoke from late afternoon until midnight, sitting on the wicker chairs on the porch facing the back gardens. Every so often Sofía would get up and go into the house to refresh the ice or get another bottle of white wine, still talking from the kitchen, or as she went in or out the glass door, or when she leaned on the railing of the porch, before sitting down again, showing off her suntanned thighs, her bare feet in sandals with her red-painted toes—her long legs, fine ankles, perfect knees—which Emilio Renzi looked at in a daze as he followed the girl's serious and ironic voice, coming and going in the evening—like a tune—only occasionally interrupting her with a comment, or to write a few words or a line in his black notebook, like someone who wakes up in the middle of the night and turns on a light to record on any available piece of paper a detail from a dream they have just had with the hope of remembering it in its entirety the next day.

Sofía had realized long ago that her family's story seemed to belong to everyone, as if it were a mystery that the whole town knew and told over and over again, without ever managing to completely decipher. She had never worried about the different versions and alterations, because the various stories formed part of the myth that she and her sister, the Antigones (or was it the Iphigenias?) of the legend didn't need to clarify—"to lower themselves to clarify," as she said. But now, after the crime, amid all the confusion, it might be necessary to attempt to reconstruct—"or understand"—what had happened. Family stories are all alike, she said, the characters always repeat—there is always a reckless uncle; a woman in love who ends up a spinster; there is always someone who is mad, a recovering alcoholic, a cousin who likes to wear women's clothing at parties; someone who fails, someone who succeeds; a suicide—but in this case what complicated everything was that their family story was superimposed with the story of the town.

"My grandfather founded the town," she said disdainfully. "There was nothing here when he arrived, just the empty land. The English built the train station and put him in charge."

Her grandfather was born in Italy and studied engineering and was a railroad technician, and when he arrived in Argentina they brought him out to the deserted plains and put him at the head of a branch line, a stop—a railroad crossing, really—in the middle of the pampas.

"And now sometimes I think," she said later, "that if my grandfather hadn't left Turin, Tony wouldn't have died. Or even if we hadn't met him in Atlantic City, or if he had stayed with his grandparents in Río Piedras, then they wouldn't have killed him. What do you call that?"

"It's called life," Renzi said.

"Pshaw[8]!" she said. "Don't be so corny. What's wrong with you? They picked him out on purpose and killed him, on the exact day, at the exact hour. They didn't have that many opportunities. Don't you understand? You don't get that many chances to kill a man like that."

---

8   Sofía liked to use the onomatopoeias she always saw reading comics throughout her childhood.

4

The cleaning lady found Durán dead on the floor of his hotel room, stabbed in the chest. She heard the phone ringing inside and went in when no one picked up, thinking the room was empty. It was two in the afternoon.

Croce was drinking vermouth in the bar of the hotel with Saldías then, so he didn't have to go anywhere to start the investigation.

"No one leaves the premises," Croce said. "We'll take their statements before they can go."

The occasional guests, the travelers, and the long-term lodgers stood around in groups of three or four, or sat on the leather chairs in the reception hall, whispering to each other. Saldías set up at a desk in the office of the hotel manager and called them in one at a time. He made a list, wrote everyone's personal and contact information, asked them exactly where in the hotel they had been at two o'clock, and told them that they remained at the disposal of the police and could be called back as witnesses anytime. Finally, he separated the ones who had been close to the scene of the event, or who had direct information about the murder, and asked them to wait in the dining room. The rest could go on about their normal activities, pending further notice.

"Four people were close to Durán's room at the time of the crime. They all say they saw someone suspicious. They should be questioned."

"We'll start with them."

Saldías realized that the Inspector was hesitant to go up and see the body. Croce didn't like the expression of the dead, that strange look of surprise and horror. He had seen plenty of them, too many, in all sorts of positions and from the oddest causes of death, but always with the same look of shock in their eye. His hope was always to be able to solve a crime without having to examine the corpse. Too many corpses, dead bodies everywhere, he said.

"We have to go upstairs," Saldías said, and used an argument that Croce himself had used in similar circumstances. "It's better to look at everything before talking to the witnesses."

"True," Croce said.

Tony had been staying in the best room in the hotel. It faced out to the street corner and was isolated at the end of the hallway. Durán, dressed in black trousers and a white shirt, was lying on the floor in a pool of blood. He seemed as if he were about to smile. His eyes were open in a look that was at once frozen and terrifying.

Croce and Saldías stood before the body with that strange sort of complicity that forms between two men who look at a dead man together.

"Don't touch him," Croce said. "Poor devil."

The Inspector turned his back on the body and carefully started to examine the floor and the furniture. Everything in the room was in order, *at first sight*. Croce walked to the window facing the square to see what you could see from the street, and also to see what you could see from the room if you looked out. The killer had probably stopped at least for a moment to look out the window and see if anyone could see what was happening inside the room. Or maybe there had been an accomplice downstairs who gave him a sign.

"He was killed when he opened the door.

"He was pushed back in," Croce said, "and was killed right away. First he recognized the person who came in. Then he was surprised." Croce walked back to the body. "The knife wound is very deep, very precise, it's the kind of blow used to kill a calf. A perfect strike, the killer used a local knife technique. Brought down from above, with force, the edge of the blade facing in, between the ribs. A clean blow," he said, as if he were narrating a movie he had seen that afternoon. "There was no noise, just a moan. I'm sure the killer held him up so he wouldn't fall too hard. There's not that much blood. You hold the body up, like a sack of bones, and by the time you set your victim down, he's already dead. Short and chubby, the killer," Croce concluded. He could tell from the wound that an ordinary blade had been used, it would be like many of the kitchen knives used in the country to slice beef. A carving knife, there were thousands of them in the province.

"I'm sure they threw the weapon into the lake," the Inspector said, with a lost look in his eye. "A lot of knives at the bottom of the lake. When I was little I used to dive down there, and I'd always find one—"

"Knives?"

"Knives and bodies. It's a cemetery down there. Suicides, drunks,

Indians, women. Corpses and more corpses at the bottom of the lake. I saw an old man once, his hair long and white, it had kept growing. It looked like tulle in the clear water." He paused. "The body doesn't rot in the water, the clothes do, that's why dead bodies float naked among the weeds. I've seen pale corpses on their feet with their eyes open, like big, white fish in an aquarium."

Had he seen it, or dreamt it? He would suddenly have visions like that, Croce would, and Saldías would realize that the Inspector was already somewhere else, just for a moment, speaking with someone who wasn't there, chewing furiously on his extinguished cigar stub.

"Not that far away, out there, in the nightmare of the future. They come out of the water," he said enigmatically, and smiled, as if he had just woken up.

They looked at each other. Saldías held him in high esteem and understood that Croce would sometimes get suddenly lost in his thoughts. He'd be gone for a moment and always come right back, as if he had psychic narcolepsy. Durán's body, becoming whiter and more rigid, was like a plaster statue.

"Cover the deceased," Croce said.

Saldías covered Tony Durán with a sheet.

"They could have thrown him out in a field, left him for the vultures. But they wanted me to see him. They left him on purpose. Why?" Croce looked around the room again, as if seeing it for the first time.

There was no other sign of violence except for a poorly closed drawer, from which a tie was slightly sticking out. Perhaps it was closed quickly and, when he turned around, the killer didn't see the tie. The Inspector pushed the drawer shut with his hip, sat on the bed, and let his gaze drift through the skylight on the ceiling.

Saldías took inventory of what they found. Five thousand dollars in a wallet; several thousand Argentine pesos stacked on the dresser, next to a watch and a keychain; a pack of Kent cigarettes; a Ronson lighter; a package of Pink Veil prophylactics; a U.S. passport issued to Anthony Durán, born February 5, 1940, in San Juan. There was a cutout from a New York newspaper with the results from the major leagues; a letter written in Spanish by a woman;[9] a photograph of the nationalist leader Albizu Campos speaking at a function, the Puerto Rican flag waiving behind him. A photograph of a soldier with round glasses, in a Marine uniform. A book of poetry by Palés Matos, a salsa long-play by Ismael Rivera, dedicated to *My friend Tony D.* There were a lot of shirts, many pairs of shoes, several jackets, no journal or datebook. Saldías listed off the items to the Inspector.

"What a corpse leaves behind is nothing," Croce said.

Such is the mystery of these crimes, the surprise of a man who dies unprepared. What did he leave unfinished? Who was the last person he saw? The investigation always starts with the victim, he

---

9   "Tony, you know I'm not looking for love anymore, not of any kind. I've passed my twenty-five summers, oh Lord, and I will not live with love again, nor with tenderness. I have looked for it, for love, yes, but the times that I've found it, it has gone poorly. You know that a girl at first believes everything she hears, men [*illegible*] a girl like me who is so naïve and has so much understanding. A man shows up with 'I love you,' he promises villas and castles, he hollers two or three times, and then, to hell with me. When I left Lalo, I was the biggest flirt, one tease after another and then I'd light it up, I was the worst. When an American came around I'd go crazy, *Honey, Honey*, he'd have me and the next day, it was like he didn't even know me [*the next page is missing*]."

is the first trace, the dark light.

There was nothing special in the bathroom: a jar of Actemin, a jar of Valium, a box of Tylenol. In the dirty-clothes wicker hamper they found a novel by Ben Benson, *The Ninth Hour*, a map from the Automobile Club with the roads of the Province of Buenos Aires, a woman's bra, and a small, nylon bag with American coins.

They went back to the room. They had to prepare a written report before the body was photographed and taken to the morgue for the autopsy. A fairly thankless task that the Inspector delegated to his Assistant.

Croce paced back and forth from one end of the room to the other, making observations in starts, constantly moving, muttering, as if he were thinking out loud in a kind of continuous murmur. "The air is strange," he said. *Tinted, a kind of rainbow against the sunlight, a blue light. What was it?*

"See that?" he asked, his eyes fixed on the light in the room.

He pointed at the traces of a nearly invisible dust that seemed to be floating in the air. Saldías was under the impression that Croce saw things at an unusual speed, as if he were half a second (half a thousandth of a second) ahead of others. They followed the trail of the light blue dusting—a fine mist swayed by the sun, which Croce saw as if it were footprints on the ground—to the far end of the room where there was a hanging on the wall, a black cloth square with yellow arabesques, a kind of Batik or tapestry from the pampas. It looked shabby, not like an actual decoration, it was clearly covering something. The corners of the tapestry flapped slightly in the wind that blew through the open window.

Croce removed the hanging with a letter opener that hung off of his keychain, and found that it was hiding a double-hung internal window. Opening it easily, they saw that it led into a kind of pit. There was a rope. A sheave.

"The service pulley."

Saldías looked at him, not understanding.

"They used to serve food up to the room, if the guest ordered it. You'd call and they'd send it up through here."

They leaned over the opening. Between the ropes they could hear the murmur of voices and the sound of the wind.

"Where does it lead?"

"To the kitchen, and the basement."

They moved the rope on the sheave and raised the box from the small pulley up to the edge.

"Too small," Saldías said. "No one would fit."

"I don't know," Croce said. "Let's see." He leaned over again. Through the cobwebs, he could see a faint light below, and at the bottom a floor with checkered tiles.

"Let's go," Croce said. "Come on."

They went down the elevator to the ground level and down a further flight of stairs to a blue hallway that led into the basement. They found the old, out-of-service kitchens and the boiler room. To the side there was a door that opened into a large closet with blue-tiled walls and an old, empty refrigerator. At a turn at the end of the hallway, behind a grille, was the telephone switchboard. On the other side, a half-opened, iron door connected to a storage room filled with items from lost-and-found and old items of furniture. The storeroom was wide and tall, with a black-and-white tiled floor. A window at the back wall, closed with a double-paned shutter, was the base of the service pulley with the cables connecting up to the higher floors.

The storage room contained the remainders from the hotel's past life, randomly piled up. Trunks, wicker baskets, suitcases, tacks with messages, rolled-up canvases, empty frames, clocks, a 1962 calendar from the Belladona factory, a blackboard, a birdcage, fencing masks, a bicycle without its front wheel, lamps, lanterns, ballot boxes, a headless statue of the Virgin, a crucifix (whose eyes seemed to follow you around), sleeping cots, a wool carding machine.

There was nothing especially noticeable—except, in a corner, for a fifty-dollar bill on the floor.

Strange. A brand-new bill. Croce put it in a clear envelope with the other evidence and looked at the issue date. A fifty-dollar bill. Series 1970.

"Whose is it?"

"Could be anyone's," Croce said. He looked at one side of the bill and then the other, as if he were trying to identify who had dropped it. Accidentally? They paid for something and it fell out. Maybe. He saw General Grant's face on the bill: *the butcher*, the drunk, a hero, a criminal, the inventor of the strategy of razing the earth, he'd go in with the army from the North and burn down cities and the fields, he'd only go into battle when he outnumbered his opponents five-to-one, he'd have all prisoners executed—Ulysses S. Grant, the butcher. Look where he ended up, on a dropped bill on the floor of a lousy hotel in the middle of nowhere. Croce stood there, thinking, the clear envelope in his hand. He showed it to Saldías as if it were a map. "See? Now

I understand, my son. I mean, I think I know what happened. They came to steal from him, they went down the service pulley, they split up the money. Or they were putting it away? In their rush they dropped a fifty-dollar bill."

"They came down?"

"Or they went up," Croce said.

Croce leaned into the opening of the service pulley and looked up again.

"Maybe they just sent the money down and someone was waiting for it here."

They went out the blue hallway. The telephone switchboard was off to one side, in a kind of cell, behind a glass screen and a grille.

They questioned the hotel's operator, a Miss Coca. Thin and slight, freckly, Coca Castro knew everything about everyone, she was the best-informed person in town, she was always invited to people's houses because everyone wanted to hear about what she knew. She made people beg. But in the end she always went and brought all the news and updates with her—and this is why she never married. She knew so much that no man dared. A woman who knows things scares men off, Croce said. She went out with import-export agents and men traveling through, and was a very good friend to the young women in town.

Croce and Saldías asked her if she had seen anything, if she had seen anyone go in or out. No, she hadn't seen anyone that day. Then they asked her about Durán.

"Thirty-three is one of the three rooms in the hotel with a telephone," the operator clarified. "Mr. Durán asked especially for this."

"Who did he speak with."

"There were a few calls. Several in English. Always from Trenton, New Jersey, in the United States. But I don't listen to the guests' conversations."

"And today, when he didn't pick up. Who was calling? Around two in the afternoon. Who was it?"

"A local call. From the factory."

"Was it Luca Belladona?"

"I don't know, they didn't say. It was a man. He asked for Durán, but he didn't know the room number. When no one answered, he asked me to try again. He waited on the line, but no one picked up."

"Had he ever called before?"

"Durán had called there a couple of times."

"A couple?"

"I have the records. You can take a look."

The operator was nervous, in a murder case everyone believes the police are going to make their life complicated. Durán was a darling, he had asked her out twice. Croce immediately thought that Durán wanted information from her, that was why he would have asked her out, she could have told him things. She had refused out of respect for the Belladona family.

"Did he ask you anything specific?"

The woman seemed to roll up and retreat, like a spirit in an Aladdin's lamp, until you could only see a red mouth.

"He wanted to know who Luca spoke with. That's what he asked me. But I didn't know anything."

"Did he ever call the Belladona sisters at home?"

"A few times," Coca said. "He spoke with Ada about everything."

"Let's call them, I want them to come identify the body."

The operator dialed the number of the Belladona house. She had a satisfied expression on her face, as if she were the protagonist of an exceptional situation.

"Hello, yes, this is the Plaza Hotel," she said. "I have a message for the Belladona Misses."

The sisters arrived late in the afternoon and quietly entered the hotel. The occasion was such that they had decided to break the taboo, or superstition, which had kept them for years from being seen together in town. The sisters were like replicas, the symmetry between them was so similar it was almost sinister. Croce had a familiarity with them that came not only from seeing them around town occasionally.

"Who told you?"

"Cueto, the public prosecutor. He rang us up," Ada said.

They went up to identify the body. Covered with the white sheet, it looked like an item of furniture. Saldías pulled the sheet back. Durán's face had an ironic sneer now and was already very pale and stiff. Neither sister said anything. There was nothing to say, all they were supposed to do was identify the body, and it was him. Everyone knew it was him. Sofía shut his eyes for him and walked to the window. Ada looked as if she had been crying, or maybe it was the dust from the street burning her eyes; she looked at the objects in the room distractedly, the open drawers. She was tapping her foot nervously in a motion that didn't mean anything, like a spring bouncing outdoors. The Inspector looked at the movement and, without intending to, thought about Regina Belladona, Luca's mother, who used to make that same motion with her foot. As if the body—as if a part of the body—was the site where all desperation gathered. *The crack in a crystal glass.* Croce would suddenly receive strange sentences like these, as if someone were dictating to him. Even the feeling that someone or something was dictating to him was—for him—evidence of their significance. He grew distracted. When he snapped back to, he heard Ada speaking, she seemed to be answering some question from his assistant, the Scribe. Something referring to the telephone call to the factory. She didn't know if Durán had spoken with her brother. Neither one of them knew anything. Croce didn't believe them, but he did not insist because he preferred to have his intuitions revealed when it was no longer necessary to confirm them. All he wanted to know from them was a few details about Tony's visit to their house.

"He came to speak with your father."

"He came to our house because my father wanted to meet him."

"Something was said about the will."

"This shitty town," Ada said, with a delicate smile. "Everyone knows we can split the inheritance whenever we want because my mother is incapacitated."

"Legally," Sofía said.

"Toward the end people saw him with Yoshio frequently, you know the rumors."

"We don't worry about what people do when they're not with us."

"And we're not interested in rumors."

"Or gossip."

As if it were a flash, Croce recalled a summer siesta: both sisters playing with newborn kittens. They must have been five or six years old, the girls. They had lined up the kittens, crawling along the tiles, warmed by the afternoon sun; each girl would pet a kitten and pass it to the other, holding them by their tails. A fast game, which went even faster, despite the kittens' plaintive meowing. Of course he had ruled out the sisters from the start. They would've killed him themselves, they wouldn't have delegated such a personal issue. Crimes committed by women are always personal, Croce thought, they don't trust anyone else to do it for them. Saldías continued asking questions and taking notes. A telephone call from the factory. To confirm he was there. At the same time. Too great a coincidence.

"You know my brother, Inspector. It's impossible, he wouldn't have called," Sofía said.

Ada said that she didn't have any news from her brother, that she hadn't seen Luca in a while. They weren't close. No one saw him anymore, she added, he lived shut away in the factory with his inventions and his dreams.

"What's going to happen?" Sofía asked.

"Nothing," Croce said. "We'll have him sent to the morgue."

It was strange to be speaking in that room, with the dead man lying on the floor, with Saldías taking notes, and the tired Inspector looking kindly at them.

"Can we leave?" Sofía asked.

"Or are we suspects?" Ada asked.

"Everyone's a suspect," Croce said. "You better leave out the back.

And please don't tell anyone what you saw here, or what we talked about."

"Of course," Ada said.

The Inspector offered to walk them out, but they refused. They were leaving on their own, he could call them anytime if he needed them.

Croce sat down on the bed. He seemed overwhelmed, or distracted. He wanted to see the notes Saldías had taken. He studied them calmly.

"Okay," he said after a while. "Let's see what these scoundrels have to say."

A rancher from Sauce Viejo declared that he had heard the sound of chains from the other side of the door, outside Durán's room. Then he had heard clearly someone say, in a nervous, hushed voice:

"I'll buy it for you. You can pay me later, somehow."

He remembered the words perfectly because he thought it sounded like a threat, or a joke. He couldn't identify who had spoken, but the voice was shrill, as if they were speaking in falsetto, or like a woman's voice.

"Falsetto, or like a woman's voice?"

"Like a woman's voice."

One of the travelers, a certain Méndez, said that he had seen Yoshio walk down the hallway and squat to look through the keyhole of Durán's door.

"Strange," Croce said. "He squatted?"

"Against the door."

"To listen, or to look?"

"He seemed to be spying."

An import-export agent said that he saw Yoshio go into the bathroom in the same hallway to wash his hands. That he was dressed in black, with a yellow scarf around his neck, and that the sleeve of his right arm was folded up to his elbow.

"And what were you doing?"

"Relieving myself," the import-export agent said. "I was facing away from him, but I could see him through the mirror."

Another of the guests, an auctioneer from Pergamino who always stayed at the hotel, said that around two o'clock he had seen Yoshio leave the bathroom on the third floor and go downstairs, agitated, without waiting for the elevator. One of the maids from the cleaning staff said that at that same time she had seen Yoshio leave the room and head down the hallway. Prono, the tall, fat, hotel security man who had been a professional boxer and had retired to the town seeking peace and quiet, accused Dazai right away.

"It was the Japo," he said, with the nasal voice of an actor from an Argentine cowboy movie. "A fight among faggots."

The others seemed to agree with him. They all hurried to give their testimony. The Inspector thought that so much unanimity was strange. Some witnesses had even created problems for themselves with their testimony. They could be investigated, their statements had to be corroborated. The rancher from Sauce Viejo, a man with a flushed face, for one, had a lover in town, the widow of Old-Man Corona. His wife, the rancher's, was in the hospital in Tapalqué. The maid who said she saw Yoshio leave Durán's room in a hurry couldn't explain what she was doing in the hallway on that floor when she should already have clocked off by that time.

Yoshio had locked himself in his room—terrified, according to what everyone said, distraught by the death of his friend—and would not answer the door.

"Let him be for now, until I need him," Croce said. "He won't go anywhere."

Sofía seemed furious, she looked at Renzi with a strange smile. She said that Tony was crazy for Ada, maybe not in love, probably just horny for her, but that there were other reasons why he'd come to town. The stories that people told about the trio, about the games they had played or imagined, they had nothing to do with the crime, they were phantoms, fantasies that she could tell Emilio about some other time, if the opportunity arose, because she had nothing to hide, she wasn't going to let a gaggle of old, resentful women tell her how she should live— "or with whom," she added—she and her sister should go to bed with. Nor would they allow the prudish bastards of a small town, the fat, pious slobs who go straight from church to the Cross-Eyed Woman's brothel—or vice versa—lecture them about proper behavior.

Country people lived in two separate realities, with two sets of morals, in two parallel worlds. On the one hand they dressed in English clothes and drove around the pampas in their pickup trucks waving at the laborers as if they were feudal lords, and on the other they got mixed up in all the dirty dealings and shady arrangements with the cattle auctioneers and exporters from the Capital. That's why when Tony arrived people knew that there had to be another play involved, in addition to the sentimental story. Why would an American come all the way here if not to bring money for some kind of business?

"And they were right," Sofía said, lighting a cigarette and smoking

in silence for a while, the cigarette's ember glowing in the afternoon dusk. "Tony had an errand to carry out, that's why he came looking for us. Once he found us, he went with us to the casinos in Atlantic City, stayed in the luxury hotels, or in flea-ridden motels by the side of the road, we had fun living the life, while they finished arranging the affair with which they had entrusted him."

"An errand?" Renzi asked. "What affair? Did he already know about that when he found you and your sister in the U.S.?"

"Yes, yes," she said. "In December."

"In December, that's not possible. What do you mean in December? But your brother——"

"Maybe it was January, it doesn't matter. It doesn't matter, who cares? He was a gentleman, he never spoke out of turn, and he never lied to us. He only refused to go into certain details," Sofía said, and resumed her litany, as if she were a child singing in a church choir. Renzi had a flash with that image, the little redheaded girl in church, singing in the choir, dressed in white…"And on top of everything, Tony was a mulatto. The fact that my sister and I were turned on by him scared the farmers around here to no end. You know they actually started calling him Zambo, like my father had anticipated."

Tony's death could not be understood without talking about the dark side of the family, especially Luca's story, the other mother's son, my half-brother, Sofía was saying. Renzi tried to get her to slow down. "Hold on, hold on," Renzi said, but Sofía became irritated and continued, or went back to restart the story somewhere else.

"When the factory collapsed, my brother didn't want to sell. I shouldn't say that he 'didn't want to,' it was more like he wasn't able to. He couldn't imagine the possibility of giving up, of giving in. Understand?

Imagine a mathematician who discovers that two plus two is five, and to keep everyone from thinking that he's crazy, he has to adapt the entire mathematical system to his formula. A system wherein two plus two, needless to say, is not five, or three—and he's able to do it." She served herself another glass of wine and added ice, and stayed still for a moment; then she turned to face Renzi, who looked like a cat, sitting on the couch. *"You look like a cat,"* she said, *"plopped down on that couch like that. And I'll tell you something else,"* she continued. *"That's not what it was like, he's not that abstract, imagine a swimming champion who drowns. Or better yet, picture a great marathon runner who's in first place, only five hundred meters from the finish line, when something goes wrong, he gets a cramp that paralyzes him, but he keeps going, because he never thinks about giving up, no way whatsoever, until finally, when he crosses the line, it's already nighttime and there's no one else left in the stadium."*

"What? What stadium?" Renzi asks. *"What cat? No more comparisons, please. Tell it straight, will you?"*

"Don't rush me, hold on. We have time, don't we?" she said, and stood motionless for a moment, looking at the light coming in through the back window, from the other side of the patio, between the trees. *"He realized,"* she said after a pause, as if hearing a tune in the air again, *"that everyone in town had plotted to get him out of the way. Two plus two is five, he thought, but no one knows it. And he was right."*

"He was right about what?"

"Yeah," she said. *"The inheritance from his mother. Understand?"* she said, and looked at him. *"Everything we have is inherited, that's the curse."*

She's delirious, Renzi thought, she's the one who's drunk. What was she talking about?

"We've spent our lives fighting over the inheritance, first my grandfather, then my father, now the two of us, the sisters. I always remember the wakes, the relatives arguing at the town's funeral parlor while they cried over the deceased. It happened with my grandfather and with my brother Lucio, and it's going to happen with my father, and with the two of us, too. The only one who kept his distance and didn't accept any part of the bequest and made himself what he is, by himself, is my brother Luca. Because there is nothing to inherit except death and the land, and the land must not change hands, the land is the only thing of any value, as my father always says, and when my brother refused to accept what was his, that's when all the conflicts started which led to Tony's death."

5

Yoshio was in the small quarter where he lived, in a kind of oversized closet near the elevator shaft, facing the hotel's inner courtyard. Pale, his eyes tearful, slight and thin like a porcelain doll, he was holding a small, lady's embroidered handkerchief in his hand. When Croce and Saldías entered, he remained calm, as if the sorrow of Durán's death was greater than his own misfortune. On one of the walls in his room there was a picture of Tony on the beach by the lake, half-dressed. Yoshio had it framed and had added a line in Japanese. It said, he told Croce, *We are as our friends see us*. On another wall there was a picture of the Emperor Hirohito on horseback reviewing the imperial troops.

The idea that someone might dislike him, that he might be criticized or looked down upon, was unbearable for Yoshio. That was the defining quality of his work. The only thing servants have, if they want to survive, is the acceptance of others. Yoshio was overwhelmed, he was going to have to leave town, he could not comprehend the consequences of what had happened. What does it mean to be accused of a crime? How can one bear to know that everyone thinks that you're a criminal? The witnesses had condemned Yoshio. Many of them were his friends, but they were acting in good faith: they had seen him, they said, at the scene of the episode, at the time of the crime. There was no way for him to account for himself, accounting for himself would be the same as acknowledging his guilt. He knew the secrets of all the guests in the hotel. He was the night porter. But his discretion didn't do him any good, because nothing can save a servant from suspicion when he falls into disgrace. A servant must be invisible, his visibility is his worst sentence.

Yoshio spoke Spanish slowly, using many popular expressions, for his was the world of radio. He showed them his portable Spica as if it were a gem, the small radio fit in his hand and had a patterned leather cover and a headphone that he could put in his ear so he could listen without bothering anyone. He was a Nikkei: an Argentine of Japanese origins. He was very proud, he didn't want people to think that his fellow countrymen were only florists or dry cleaners or billiard-room barkeeps. Japanese industrial technology was gaining ground, producing small, perfect machines (Yashica cameras, Hitachi recorders, and Yamaha Mini-iMotos filled the cover of the magazine that the Embassy had sent him and which he showed to his guests). He always listened to X8 Radio Sarandí, the Uruguayan station that played Carlos Gardel tangos around the clock. Like all Japanese, Yoshio loved the tango; guests would sometimes hear him singing "Amores de estudiante, A student's love," as he walked down the empty hallways of the hotel, imitating Gardel—but pronouncing the r's as if they were l's in the verse *flores de un día son.*

They found two small balls of opium toward the back of the closet.

"I'm not innocent," he said. "Because no one is innocent. I have my transgressions, but they are not the ones that others attribute to me."

"No one is accusing you…yet," Croce said, addressing him informally. Yoshio realized that the Inspector distrusted him, like everyone else. "There's no need to get defensive ahead of time. Tell me, what did you do today?"

He had woken up at two in the afternoon, like always, he had had breakfast in his room, like always, he had done his exercises, like always, he had prayed.

"Like always," Croce said. "Did anyone see you? Can anyone vouch for you?"

No one had seen him, everyone knew he was off from his nighttime duties in the afternoon, but no one could vouch for him. Croce asked him when he had last seen Durán.

"Not seen him today," Yoshio answered, imitating gaucho-speak. "I haven't seen him the whole blessed day," he corrected himself. "I'm the night porter, I'm a porter and I live by night and I know the secrets of everyone's life in the hotel, and everyone who knows that I know fears me. Everyone in the hotel knows that at the time Tony was killed I am always asleep."

"And what do they fear, the ones who fear you?" Croce asked.

"Children pay for the sins of their parents. Mine is having slanted eyes and yellow skin," Yoshio replied. "And that's why you're going to find me guilty, for being the most foreign of all the foreigners in this town of foreigners."

Croce slapped him in the face with the back of his right hand, unexpectedly, hard. Yoshio's nose started bleeding, and he closed his eyes without making a sound, affronted.

"Don't get contrary with me, and don't you lie to me," Croce said. "Write down that the suspect hit himself against the corner of the open window."

Saldías, shocked and nervous, jotted down a few lines in his notebook. Yoshio dried his blood on his small, embroidered handkerchief. He was on the verge of crying.

"It wasn't me, Inspector. It wasn't me, it wouldn't ever be me," Yoshio was standing stiff, livid. "I... I loved him."

"It wouldn't be the first time that someone is killed for that reason," Croce said.

"No, Inspector. He was very good to me, he was a friend, he honored me with his trust. He was a gentleman—"

"So why was he killed?"

Croce moved about the room restlessly. His hand hurt. He had done what he had to do, he wasn't there to feel sorry for anyone, he was there to interrogate a criminal. Sometimes he got carried away with an excess of anger that he couldn't control, the servant-like humility of the Japanese man exasperated him. But the slap across the face had forced him to react, and now Yoshio was starting to give his real version of events.

He said that Durán was unhappy, that just yesterday he had insinuated that he intended to leave soon, but he had certain affairs to resolve first. He was waiting for something, Yoshio didn't know what. That is all the Japanese man declared, in his own way he explained everything he knew, without actually saying anything.

"You're going to need a lawyer, my man," the Inspector said to him, and became pensive. "Let me see your hand." Yoshio looked at him, surprised. "Like this," Croce said, turning Yoshio's palms face up. "Squeeze my arm. Harder. That's as hard as you can squeeze?" Yoshio looked at him, confused. The Inspector released his hands; Yoshio kept them like that, in the air, like two dead flowers. "We'll take him to the station," Croce said. "There'll be trouble, for sure, when we take him out of the hotel."

And there was. The neighbors crowded around the hotel entrance, as soon as they saw Yoshio they started insulting him, calling him a "murderer," and trying to strike him.

An old man named Unzué threw a rock that hit Yoshio on the forehead. Calesita the Madman started spinning in place and screaming obscenities. Souto's sister rushed up, pushed against Saldías's arms (who was trying to cover Yoshio), bent her gray face forward, and spit on the criminal's face.

"Murderer!" the woman yelled, hatefully but with an impassive look, as if she were reciting a line, or sleeping.

Prosecutor Cueto showed up in the middle of the mess. He told everyone to settle down, assuring them that he was there to make sure justice was carried out. He was a man of about forty years, thin and tall, although from a distance he looked deformed. There was a moment of calm, and the Prosecutor went into the hotel to speak with Inspector Croce.

"What does the police have to say?" he said as he walked in. When Yoshio saw the Prosecutor come in, he turned away and stood facing the wall.

Cueto had a stealthy way of moving, at once violent and sly, and he insulted everyone as a matter of principle. He produced a stiff smile and brought his left fingers together as if he were about to ask something.

"And what does the pansy Jap have to say for himself?"

"Nothing's settled yet. Yoshio's been detained, we're going to take him to the station as the leading suspect. Which doesn't mean that he's guilty," Croce explained.

Cueto looked at him with a false expression of surprise, and smiled again.

"Give her a good beating first, that'll get her talking. A simple procedural suggestion, Inspector. You know."

"Our opinion has already been formed," the Inspector said.

"Mine too, Croce. And I don't understand that plural of yours, 'our.'"

"We'll be writing up the report and we'll present the charges tomorrow. You can proceed with your work after that."

"Can you tell me," Cueto said, addressing Saldías, "why you didn't investigate that mulatto as soon as he arrived? Who was he? Why did he come here? Now we have this whole scandal to deal with."

"We don't investigate people without cause," Croce said.

"It's true, he didn't do anything illegal," Saldías added timidly.

"That's exactly what you're supposed to find out. A guy shows up out of nowhere, he settles here, and the two of you don't know anything? Now that's strange."

He's pressuring me, Croce thought, because he knows something and he wants to see if I know what he knows, too. And he wants to shut the case quickly by declaring it a sex crime.

"Whatever happens will be your responsibility, Croce, do you understand?" Cueto said, and went outside to harangue the crowd of people on the sidewalk.

He never called him Inspector, as if he didn't recognize the title. In fact, Cueto had been waiting for months for a chance to retire him, but he hadn't found the way yet. Maybe now things would change. From the street they could hear shouts and angry voices.

"We're heading out," Croce said. "You think I'm afraid of those idiots?"

The three of them walked out and stood outside the hotel entrance.

"Murderer! Degenerate Japo! Justice! We want justice!" the people around the door shouted.

"Get out of the way. I don't want any trouble," Croce said, moving forward. "Anyone comes close, you get a night in jail."

The crowd moved back as they moved forward. Yoshio refused to cover his face. Proud and diminutive, very pale, he walked through a sort of corridor that was formed from the front of the hotel to the car as the people shouted and yelled insults at him.

"Folks, we're close to solving the case, I'd ask for your patience," the Prosecutor said, having immediately taken over the scene.

"We'll take care of it, boss," one man said.

"Murderer! Faggot!" they shouted again, and started pushing in.

"That's enough," Croce said, taking out his weapon. "I'm taking him to the station and he'll stay there until he has his trial."

"You're all corrupt!" a drunk yelled.

A myopic, nervous man approached. He was the editor of *El Pregón*, the local newspaper.

"You have the guilty party, Inspector."

"Don't write what you don't know," Croce said.

"Are you going to tell me what I know?"

"I'm going to throw you in jail for violating the confidentiality of the investigation."

"Violating what? I don't follow, Inspector," the myopic said. "It's the usual tension between power and the press." He shrugged, turning toward the crowd to make sure everyone heard him.

"The usual tension of stupid-ass journalists," the Inspector said.

The editor of *El Pregón* smiled, as if the insult were a personal triumph. The press would not allow itself to be intimidated.

Inspector Flies Off the Handle—would be the headline, for sure. What did "off the handle" mean? Croce wondered for a moment, while Saldías took advantage of the confusion to get Yoshio into the back of the car.

"Let's go, Inspector," he said.

What they called the police station was a rural outpost with one guard posted inside. It was basically a hovel with a room set aside to lock up the bums who endangered the crops by lighting fires near the fields to heat up their *mate*, or who slaughtered animals from the ranches in the area to make themselves a little barbeque.

Croce lived in another room in the same small building. That night—after leaving Yoshio locked up in the cell with the guard at the door—he went out to the vine-covered patio to drink *mate* with Saldías. The light from the oil lamp illuminated the dirt patio and the near side of the station.

In the Inspector's mind, the hypothesis that a Japanese night porter, quiet and friendly as an old lady, would kill a fortune-hunting Puerto Rican did not add up.

"Unless it was a crime of passion."

"But in that case he would've stayed in the room, hugging the body."

Croce and Saldías agreed that if Yoshio had let himself be driven by anger or jealousy, he wouldn't have behaved as he did. He would have stumbled out of the room with the knife in his hand, or they would have found him sitting on the floor, staring at the dead man's face in shock. Croce had seen a lot of cases like that. This didn't seem to be a case of violent emotion.

"Too much stealth," the Inspector said. "And too visible."

"The only thing missing was someone taking a picture of him while he was doing the killing," Saldías agreed.

"As if he were sleeping, or *acting*."

An idea seemed to push against the external tissue of Croce's brain. Like a bird trying to get into a cage from outside. His thoughts would escape sometimes, flutter away, so he would say them out loud.

"As if he were sleepwalking, or a zombie," he said.

As if by instinct Croce understood that Yoshio had been caught in a trap that he didn't quite comprehend. A mass of facts had fallen upon him from which he would never be able to free himself. The weapon hadn't been located, but several eyewitnesses had seen him enter and leave Durán's room. It was an open-and-shut case.

The Inspector's mind had become a flock of mad thoughts flying too fast for him to catch. Like the wings of a pigeon, the uncertainties about the guilt of the Japanese night porter flapped fleetingly inside the cage, but not the conviction about his innocence.

"For example, the fifty-dollar bill. Why was it down there?"

"He dropped it," Saldías said, following his train.

"I don't think so. They left it on purpose."

Saldías looked at him, he didn't understand. But he trusted Croce's power of deduction, so he sat still, waiting.

There was over five thousand dollars in the room which hadn't been taken. It wasn't a robbery. *So we'd think that it wasn't a robbery.* Croce started pacing *in his mind*, out in the field, to clear up his ideas. The Japanese had been the barbarians in World War II, but after that they'd been model servants, servile and laconic. There was a prejudice in their favor: Japanese never commit crimes. This was an exception, a detour. That's what it was about.

"Barely 0.1% of crimes in Argentina are committed by Japanese," Croce said, target shooting in the dark, and fell asleep. He dreamt that he was riding a horse bareback again, like when he was little. He saw a hare in the lake. Or was it a duck? Up in the air, he saw a figure, like a frieze. And against the horizon he saw a duck that turned into a rabbit. The image appeared very clearly in the dream. He woke up and kept talking, as if resuming the paused conversation. "How many Japanese do you think live in our province?"

"In the province I don't know, but in Argentina[10]," Saldías improvised. "Out of a population of 23 million inhabitants, there must be some 32,000 Japanese."

"Let's say there are 8,500 Japanese in the province, 850 in the district. They might be dry cleaners, florists, bantamweight boxers,

---

10   The first Japanese immigrant arrives in Argentina in 1886, a certain Professor Seizo Itoh from the School of Agriculture in Sapporo. He takes up residence in the Province of Buenos Aires. In 1911, Seicho Arakaki is born, the first Argentine of Japanese origin (*Nikkei*). The last Argentine census (1969) records the presence of 23,185 Japanese and descendents.

acrobats. Maybe a purse maker or two with slender hands, but no murderers."

"They're tiny."

"The strange thing is he didn't escape down the shaft of the service pulley. The witnesses saw him enter and leave the room through the door."

"True," Saldías said, and specified, in a bureaucratic tone, "he didn't use his physical particularities to assist him in the crime."

Yoshio was delicate, fragile, he looked as if he were made of porcelain. Next to Durán, who was tall and mulatto, they made a very strange couple. Is beauty a moral trait? Maybe beautiful people have better character, they are more sincere, everyone trusts them, people want to touch them, see them, feel the tremor of their perfection. Besides, they were too different. Durán, with his Caribbean accent, seemed like he was always at a party. Yoshio, on the other hand, was laconic, furtive, very servile. The perfect servant.

"You saw that man's hands, right? Small and weak. What kind of pulse, what kind of heart, would he have to stab somebody like that? As if he'd been killed by a robot."

"A doll," Saldías says.

"A gaucho, good with a knife."

Croce immediately deduced that the crime must have had an instigator. Once he discarded the theory that would have solved the case at once—in other words, a crime of passion—he realized that someone else had to be implicated. All crimes are crimes of passion, Croce said, except crimes for hire. There was a call from the factory, that was strange. Luca never speaks with anyone, and even less by telephone. He doesn't go out. He hates the countryside, the quiet of the plains, the sleeping gauchos, the owners who never work and just sit under the eaves of their houses staring at the horizon, or let time pass in the shade of their balconies, go out to fuck the local girls in the shed between the bags of maize, play dice through the night. He hates them. Croce can see the tall, abandoned factory building with its rotating beacon light, as if it were an empty fortress. *The empty fortress*. It's not that he heard voices, the sentences simply reached him as if they were memories. *I know him as if he were my son*. Like lines written in the night. He knew very well what they meant, but not how they entered his head. Certainty is not the same as knowledge, he thought. It's the precondition for knowledge. General Grant's face was like a map, a footprint on the ground. A very scientific job. Grant, the butcher, with his kidskin glove.

"I'm going out for a bit," Croce said all of a sudden. Saldías looked at him, a little afraid. "You stay and keep guard, we don't want those worthless bums to come and do anything outrageous."

Luca had purchased some land outside the town, on the edge, in the deserted plains, a plot, as his father called it, and started building the factory there, as if it were the construction of a dream, a construction imagined in a dream. They had planned and discussed it when they were working in the workshop at the back of the house, in their grandfather Bruno's studio, and their grandfather had helped them, influenced by his European readings[11] and his research into the design of the ideal factory.

---

11   Bruno Belladona was very influenced by the treatise *Field, Factories and Workshops* (1899) by Prince Pyotr Kropotkin, the great Russian geographer, anarchist, and free-thinker. Kropotkin proposed that the development of communications and the flexibility of electric energy should establish the basis

Luca and Lucio used the workshop as if it were a laboratory for their technical entertainments, that's where they built their racing cars, that was their schooling, a rich-boy's hobby. Sofía seemed exhilarated by her own voice and by the quality of the legend.

"It took my father a while to understand. Because before, when they used to go out to the fields and work on the agricultural machines, he didn't have any problems with them, they'd follow the harvest about, spend long stretches of time out in the country, they'd come back dark as Indians, my mother would say, happy to have them outdoors for months, out with the harvesters and the baling machines, living the clash of two antagonistic worlds."[12]

Her father did not realize that the plague had arrived, that it was the end of Arcadia, that the pampas were changing forever, that the machinery was becoming more and more complex, that foreigners were buying up the land, that the owners of the estancias were sending their earnings to the island of Manhattan ("and to the financial paradise of the island of Formosa"). The Old Man wanted everything to stay the same, the Argentine pampas, the gauchos on horseback, even though he,

---

of a manufacturing production decentralized into small, self-sufficient units, set up in isolated, rural areas, outside the conglomeration of large cities. He defended the production model of small workshops with their large potential for creative innovation, because the more delicate the technology, the greater the need for human initiative and individual skill.

12   "Once," Sofía told him, "they took apart the engine of one of the first mechanical threshing machines and left the bolts and nuts to dry on the grass while they started looking at the blades. All of a sudden, a rhea came out of nowhere and ate the nuts shining in the sun. Gulp, gulp, went the rhea's throat as it swallowed several nuts and bolts. Then it started walking backwards, sideways, its eyes bulged out. They tried to lasso it, but it was impossible, it would run like a light, then stop and turn back toward them with such a crazy look, it seemed offended. Finally they had to chase down the ostrich in a car to recover the parts of the machine it had swallowed."

too, of course, had started to transfer his dividends abroad and to speculate with his investments, none of the landowners were born yesterday, they all had their advisors, brokers, stock transfer agents, they went wherever their capital took them—although they never stopped yearning for the peace of their homeland, the quiet pastoral customs, their paternal relationship with the workers.

"My father always wanted them to love him," Sofía said, "he was tyrannical and arbitrary but he was proud of his sons, they were going to carry on the family name, as if the last name had a meaning unto itself, anyway, that was my grandfather's thinking and then my father's, they wanted their last name to go on, as if they belonged to the royal English family, that's what they're like here, they believe in all that, even though they're all dirty-footed gringos, descendents of Irish and Basque peasants who came here to dig ditches because the locals wouldn't do it, the foreigners were the only ones willing to roll up their sleeves and dig.[13] There was an English ditch-digger, she recited as if she were singing a bolero, who claimed to be from Inca-la-perra. They must have been Harriots or Heguys, digging ditches in the fields, now they act like aristocrats, they play polo in the estancias and flaunt last names that actually came from Irish peasants and rural Basques. Everyone here is a descendent of gringos, especially my family, but they all think alike and want the same things. My grandfather the colonel, for starters, boasted that he was from the north, from Piedmont, unbelievable, he looked down at the Italians from the south, who in turn looked down on the

---

13   In the old days, they used to separate the different estancias by digging ditches between them to prevent the cattle from one to cross over into the other. This work of digging trenches in the pampas was done by Basques and Irish immigrants. The local gauchos refused to do any kind of task that meant dismounting from their horses; they considered despicable any work that had to be done "on foot" (cf. John Lynch, *Massacre in the Pampas*).

Poles and the Russians."

The colonel was born in Pinerolo, near Turin, in 1875, and he didn't know anything about his parents, or his parents' parents. One story even has it that his papers were falsified and that his real name was Expósito, that Belladona was just the word spoken by the doctor who held him in his arms when his mother died in childbirth in a hospital in Turin. "Belladona, belladonna!" the doctor had said, as if it were a requiem. And that's the name they registered him with. Baby Belladona. His own son, the first man in the family without a father. And they called him Bruno because he was dark and he looked African. No one knew how he arrived in the Province of Buenos Aires when he was ten years old, with a suitcase, by himself, and ended up in a boarding school for orphans run by the Company of Jesus in Bernaconi. Intelligent, passionate, he became a seminary student and lived like an ascetic, dedicating himself to his studies and his prayers. He could fast and remain silent for days on end; sometimes the sacristan would find him praying in the chapel by himself and would kneel down next to him as if he were a saint. He was always a fanatic, as if he were possessed, intractable. His discovery of science in his physics and botany classes, and his readings of remote, forbidden works from the Darwinian tradition in the monastery library, distracted him from his theology and distanced him—provisionally—from God. This was how he told it himself.

One afternoon he went to his confessor and expressed his desire to leave the seminary and attend the College of Exact and Natural Sciences at the university. Could a priest become an engineer? Only of souls, the priest answered, and refused his request. Bruno rejected his confessor's ban and kept appealing, but after the Head of the Company refused to respond to his petitions or receive him in person, he wrote anonymous *letters which he would leave under the pew in front of the altar. Finally, one rainy summer afternoon, he ran away from the monastery where he had lived half his life. He was twenty years old. With the little money he had saved, he rented a room in a boarding house on Medrano Street, in the neighborhood of Almagro, in Buenos Aires. His knowledge of Latin and European languages allowed him to survive, at first, as a secondary school teacher in an all-boys school on Rivadavia Street.*

He was a brilliant engineering student, as if his true education had been in mechanics and mathematics instead of Thomism and theology. He published a series of notes on the influence of mechanical communications on modern civilization and a study on the laying of tracks in the province of Buenos Aires, and before completing his degree he was hired by the English—in 1904—to direct the works of the Southern Railroads. They put him in charge of the Rauch-Olavarría Branch Line and the foundation of the town at the intersection of the old, narrow gauge from the north and the English gauge that continued as far as Zapala, in Patagonia.

"My brother grew up with our grandfather, he learned everything from him. He was an orphan too, or a half-orphan, because his mother abandoned my father when she was pregnant with Luca, as well as her older son, and ran away with her lover. Women abandon their sons because they can't stand it when they start to look like their fathers," Sofía laughed. "Who wants to be a mother when you're horny?" Smoking, the ember glowing in the dark was like her voice. "My father lives here, downstairs, he keeps us with him, and we take care of him because we know that he's been defeated on all counts. He never recovered from the psychotic decision that his wife made, according to him, to leave when she was pregnant and run away with a theatre company director who was in

town for a few months staging Hamlet (or was it A Doll's House?). To live with another and have the baby with another. Whose child was it? He was obsessed, my father. He made his wife's life impossible. One afternoon he went out looking for her and found her, but she locked herself up in her car, so he started pounding on the windows and yelling and insulting her, by the main square, with people gathering around, delighted, murmuring and nodding in approval. That's when his Irish wife left, she abandoned both sons, and erased her tracks. Around here the women run away, if they can."

Luca was raised as a legitimate son and treated in the same manner as his brother, but he never forgave his father, the one who claimed to be his father, for this indulgence.

"My brother Luca always thought that he wasn't my father's son. He grew up sheltered by Grandfather Bruno, he'd follow him everywhere, like an abandoned puppy. But that's not why he finally confronted my father, that's not why. And that's also not why they killed Tony."

6

The Inspector got in his car and headed out of town on the road parallel to the train tracks, and turned onto the highway. The night was cool, peaceful. Croce liked to drive, he could let himself go, see the countryside all around him, the cows chewing quietly, hear the even rumbling of his car's engine. Through the rearview mirror he saw night falling behind him, a few lights in the distant houses. He didn't see anyone along the highway, except for a cattle truck coming back from Venado Tuerto, which honked its horn as it passed him. Croce flicked his high beams and thought that the trucker probably recognized him, so he got off the highway and took a dirt road that also led to the lake. When he arrived, he maneuvered carefully between the willows and parked close to the shore, turned off the engine, and let the shadows and the murmur of the water wash over him.

On the horizon, like a shadow rising on the plains, was the tall building of the factory with its rotating fog light sweeping across the night. A beacon mounted on the roof made its way around and around, illuminating the pampas with gusts of light. Rustlers used this white brightness as a guide when they had to lead their herd before dawn. The ranchers in the area had filed complaints. "We won't be responsible for the peasants stealing animals from those bums," Luca always answered, and the demands would go no further.

Maybe they had killed Tony to settle a gambling bet. But no one killed over something like that around there, otherwise the entire population would have gone extinct years ago. The most anyone had done was to burn a wheat field, like the Dollans did with Schutz, the German, when he bet an entire harvest on a dice game, lost, and refused to pay. They all finally ended up in jail. It's not well thought of to kill someone because they owe you money. This isn't Sicily, after all. Not Sicily? It was like Sicily because everything was settled in silence, quiet towns, dirt roads, armed foremen, dangerous people. Everything very primitive. Workers on one side, owners on the other. Did he not hear the president of the Rural Society say at the hotel bar, just last night, that there was nothing to worry about even if elections were brought back? *We load the workers from the estancias into the trucks and tell them who to vote for.* That's how it's always been. What could a small town inspector do? Croce was being left on his own. His old friend, Inspector Laurenzi, was retired and living in the south. Croce remembered the last time they were together, in a bar in La Plata. *It's a big country*, Laurenzi told him. *You see cultivated fields, empty plains, cities, factories, but no one ever understands people's secret hearts. And that's a surprise, because we're cops. No one's in a better position to see the extremes of misery and madness.* Croce remembered Laurenzi clearly, his thin face, a cigarette always hanging from the corner of his mouth, his neat moustache. And crazy Inspector Treviranus? Treviranus had been transferred from the Capital to Las Flores and soon afterwards dismissed, as if he'd been responsible for the death of that imbecile amateur sleuth who'd spent all his time looking for Yarmolinski's murderer. Then there was Inspector Leoni, as bitter as the others, at the police station in Talpaqué. Croce had called him on the telephone because he thought his case might have originated there. Just a hunch. People from the old guard, Peronists who'd been involved in all sorts of trouble, poor Leoni, they'd killed one of his kids. There are very few of us left, Croce thought, smoking by the lake. Cueto the Prosecutor wants to throw Yoshio in jail and shut down the investigation. An open-and-closed case, that's what everyone wants. I'm a dinosaur, a survivor, the Inspector thought. Treviranus, Leoni, Laurenzi, Croce, sometimes they'd get together in La Plata to reminisce over old times. But did old times exist? Croce hadn't lost his senses yet, anyway, he was sure he was on the right track. He'd solve this case, too, and he'd do it the old-fashioned way.

He sat in his car with the engine off and smoked in the dark, looking at the light that periodically shone over the water. The light from the beacon on top of the factory seemed to flicker, but it actually rotated in large circles. Croce suddenly saw an owl shake out of its lethargy and fly with a smooth flapping of its wings, chasing the white light in a circle as if it were the herald for dawn. *Minerva's bird is confused, too, lost.* They weren't voices that he heard, the phrases just reached him as if they were memories. *The white eye of night. A superior criminal mind.* He knew exactly what they meant, but not how they got into his head. General Grant's marked face was a map. *A very scientific job. Grant, the butcher, with his kidskin glove.* Croce watched the small waves from the lake dissolve among the rushes at the shore. In the quiet, he heard the croaking of the frogs, the metallic sound of the crickets; nearby, a dog barked, and then another, and then another; a few minutes later the barking drifted and faded into the night.[14]

He was tired, but his fatigue had become a kind of sleepless lucidity. He had to reconstruct a sequence, move from the chronological order of facts to the logical order of events. His memory was an archive, his recollections burned like stars in the closed night. He never forgot anything having to do with a case until he solved it. Later everything was erased. But during the investigation, he lived obsessed with the details that went in and out of his conscience. *He arrived with two suitcases. He carried a brown leather bag in his hand. He didn't want anyone to help him with that. They pointed out the hotel across the way. Why was that fifty-dollar bill on the floor? Why did they go down to the basement?* That's what he had. And the fact that a man the size of a cat had climbed into the old service lift. His thinking was implacable, he grew exasperated, he postponed the final conclusion forever. *I don't have to try to explain what happened, I just need to make it comprehensible. I have to understand it myself, first.*

Instinct—or, better yet, a certain intimate perception that didn't quite bloom into consciousness—told him that he was about to find a way out. Whatever it was, he decided to move. He started his car and turned on the lights. Several frogs jumped into the water and a creature—an armadillo? a guinea pig?—stood frozen

---

14   People in small towns turn off the lights in their houses early in the evening, at which point everything turns gray, because the landscape under the moon is gray. The only way you know then that there is a house in the middle of the plains is by the barking dogs, one barks and then another, and then another, the barking can be heard in the vast shadows in the distance.

in a clearing, near the willow trees. Croce backed the car up a few meters, turned around, and headed into the open countryside. He drove along the edge of the Reynal Estancia until he reached the asphalt. As he drove for several leagues by the bordering fence, he saw chimango buzzards perched silently on the posts and animals grazing on the other side.

Croce followed the light from the factory, the white gusts in the sky, toward the dark mass of the building on top of the hill. The road led to the warehouse entrance for the delivery trucks. The Belladona brothers had gotten the road paved to speed up the transports that came and went from the company to the highway to Córdoba, site of IKA-Renault headquarters. But the plant had collapsed overnight. The brothers had settled the severance pay for the factory workers after the turbulent negotiations with the SMATA Union. Hounded by their debts, the demands to liquidate, and the accumulating mortgage payments, they were forced to bring production nearly to a halt. It had been a year now since the dissolution of the firm and his brother's death, and Luca had shut himself in the factory, having decided to carry on and keep working on his inventions and his machines on his own.

Croce approached the industrial complex, a row of sheds and galleries facing the parking lot. The meshed-wire fence was drooping in several places, and Croce drove in through one of the broken gates. The cement lot appeared to be abandoned. Two or three isolated lights poorly illuminated the place. Croce parked his car in front of some tracks, between two cranes. A very tall plume could be seen to the side, in the darkness, like some prehistoric animal. He preferred to enter through the back, he knew it was unlikely that anyone would open the front door for him. There was light in the windows of the upper levels of the factory. Croce made his way in through one of the partially open metal shutters and down a corridor that led to the central garage. The large machines were all quiet; several partially assembled cars were still elevated above the service pits in the assembly line; a tall pyramid of striated steel, painted brick red, rose up in the middle of the work floor; off to a side there were gears and a large, grooved wheel, with chains and pulleys to take small wagons filled with materials into the metal construction.

"Holy Mother of God," Croce yelled toward the ceiling.

"How do you do, Inspector? Do you have a search warrant?"

The happy, relaxed voice came from up above, where a heavy man leaned out from a balcony on the upper level. Nearly two meters tall, his face reddened, his eyes light-blue, Luca was wearing a leather apron and an iron mask with a glass visor hanging around his chest, and he was holding an acetylene soldering iron in his hand. He seemed jovial and pleased to see the Inspector.

"How are you, Gringo? I was just passing by," Croce said. "You haven't been to see me in a while."

Luca came down an elevator, illuminated by the light from the upper level, and walked toward the Inspector, wiping his hands and wrists on a rag that smelled of kerosene. Croce was always moved to see Luca because he remembered him before the tragedy that had turned him into a hermit.

"We can sit here," Luca said, indicating a couple of benches and a table toward the back of the garage, near a one-cylinder gas stove. Luca put a pot of water on and started preparing the *mate*.

"As La Peugeot's French friend René Queneau used to say, *Ici, en la pampá, lorsqu'on boit de maté l'on devient…argentin.*"

"I can't drink *mate,*" Croce said. "It's bad for my stomach."

"No gaucho would ever say that." Luca was having fun. "Come on, have a little bitter one, Inspector."

Croce held the *mate* gourd and drank carefully through the tin straw. The hot, bitter drink was a blessing.

"Gauchos didn't eat barbequed beef," Croce said, all of a sudden. "They didn't have teeth. Can you imagine them, always on horseback, smoking black tobacco, eating crackers, they'd lose their teeth right away and couldn't chew meat anymore. They only ate cow tongue, and sometimes not even that."

"They lived on pudding with maize and ostrich eggs, poor country folk."

"A lot of vegetarian gauchos."

They went back and forth, cracking jokes, like every time they met, until little by little the conversation became more focused and Luca grew serious. He was absolutely convinced that he would succeed. He started talking about his projects, about the negotiations with the investors, about how he was resisting his rivals and how they wanted to force him into selling the factory. He didn't explain exactly who his enemies were. Croce could just imagine them, Luca told him, the Inspector knew who they were even better than Luca did, it was the same culprits as always. *I know him as if he were my son.* Luca knew that he was completely cornered, he was fighting on his own, he didn't have any strength left, he needed funds, he had contacts in Brazil, in Chile, businessmen interested in his ideas who might advance him the money he desperately needed. He was yoked with debt, especially by his upcoming mortgage payments. "When it rains, the banks take away your umbrella," Luca said. Nobody would toss him a rope, they wouldn't give him a hand, no one in town, or in the district, or in the entire province. They wanted to foreclose the mortgage and auction off the plant, take over the building, speculate with the land. That's what they wanted. Lousy dogs! He had to pay his debts with dollars purchased on the black market and sell what he produced with dollars at the official exchange rate. He was on his own in the whole country, everyone around him, his neighbors, the dirty pigs, and the military too, had turned against him. Speculators. They'd broken his dead brother's will, that was the saddest part of it, the thorn in his heart. Lucio was naïve, that's why he had died. In dreams, at night, he sometimes saw the destruction reach the roofs of the houses in town, like in the big floods of '62. He'd be riding on a horse, bareback, under a bright moon, lassoing what he could save: furniture, animals, coffins, church saints. That's what he had seen. But he also saw a car driving through the countryside and he was sure that it was his brother, coming back to his side to help him. He saw him clearly, driving like mad, like always, pedal to the metal, rumbling through the plowed fields. Luca was quiet for a moment, a peaceful smile on his frank face, and then he added, in a low voice, that he was sure that the same people who were after him had done in Durán.

"I'd like to clear up one point," Croce said. "You called him at the hotel." It didn't sound like a question, and Luca the Gringo became serious.

"We asked Rocha to call him."

"Aha."

"He was looking for us, they said."

"But you didn't speak with him."

Rocha appeared at that point, at the door, like a shadow, under an arcade. Slight and very thin, timid, with black welding goggles pushed up on his forehead, he was smoking, looking down. He was the great technician, Luca's main assistant, his right-hand man, the only one who seemed to understand Luca's projects.

"No one picked up the phone," Rocha said. "I spoke with the telephone operator at the hotel first, she transferred me to the room, but no one answered."

"What time was that?"

Rocha was thoughtful, the cigarette hanging from his lips.

"I couldn't say...One-thirty, two."

"Closer to two or to one-thirty?"

"To one-thirty, I think, we'd finished lunch, but I hadn't slept my siesta yet."

"Good," Croce said, and turned back to Luca. "And you never saw him?"

"No."

"Your sister says—"

"Which one?" Luca looked at the Inspector, smiling. He made a gesture with his hand, as if he shooing an insect away from his face, and stood up to heat more water for the *mate*.

Luca seemed restless, as if he had started to feel the Inspector was actually hostile and maybe even suspected him.

"They say that Durán had an arrangement with your father."

"I don't know anything about that," Luca cut him off. "You

should ask the Old Man himself."

They kept talking a little longer, but Luca had closed up and barely spoke anymore. Shortly afterward he excused himself, saying he had to keep working, and asked Rocha to see the Inspector out. He placed the iron mask with the protective visor on his face and walked away, taking large steps down the glass-covered hallway toward the workshops.

The Inspector knew this to be the cost of his profession, he had to ask the questions that might help him solve the case, but no one could speak with him without feeling accused. And was he accusing him? Croce followed Rocha out to the parking lot and got in his car, certain that Luca knew something that he hadn't told him. He drove slowly through the lot toward the gates that opened out—but then, unexpectedly, the factory's reflectors shifted, shining bright white, catching Croce and holding him in its glow. The Inspector stopped the car and the light also stopped, blinding him for a moment. He sat still in the middle of the brightness for an endless instant until the lights moved on and Croce started driving his car again slowly out toward the road. In the night's darkness, with the tall light intermittently illuminating the countryside, Croce realized the terrifying intensity of Luca's obsession. He saw Luca's gesture again, his hand in the air as if shooing an insect from his face, an invisible pest. He needed money, how much money? *He carried a brown, leather bag in his hand.*

He had decided to return to town on the main road, but before he reached the station, he turned toward the corrals and parked his car in the alley behind the hotel. He lit a cigarette and smoked, trying to calm down. The night was peaceful, the only lights the streetlights in the square and a few lighted windows on the upper floor of the hotel.

Would the service entrance be open? He could see the door on the right, the railing and the stairs leading down to the basement for deliveries. It was close to midnight. The alleyway was dark. He got out of his car, turned on his flashlight, and followed the beam to the door. He used the picklock he always carried with him. The lock clicked open.

He went down an iron stairway and into the tiled hallway, past the telephone switchboard in the shadows, and found the door to the storage room. It was open. He stopped in front of the piles of unorganized items and abandoned objects. Where would they have hidden the bag? They must have come in through the service lift and looked around to see where they could hide it. Croce figured the murderer didn't know the place ahead of time, that he would have been moving quickly, that he would have been searching to leave what he was carrying. *But why?*

The storage area was a vast underground room, about fifty meters long, with vaulted ceilings and tiled floors. There were chairs off to one side, boxes to another, there were beds, mattresses, picture frames. Was there an order? A secret order, accidental. He had to look not just at the objects, but at the way the objects were distributed in the space. There were couches, lamps, suitcases piled up toward the back. Where could someone who has just come down an old, dusty service lift hide a bag? When the person came out of the chute he would be partially blinded by the light, in a hurry to go back up—by pulling on the sheave and the ropes—to the room with the dead body, and leave the room out the door and into the hallway, as the witnesses had said. Is that how it was? Croce followed the images that appeared to him like a gambler betting against the house who doesn't know what the next card will be, but bets *as if he knew*. The Inspector suddenly felt tired, without any strength. *A needle in a haystack*. Maybe the needle wasn't even in the haystack. Still, he had the strange conviction that he'd find the trace. He had to think, follow an order, track what he was looking for in the confusion of the abandoned objects.

7

Inspector Croce Manipulates Evidence, was the leading headline in the local *El Pregón* newspaper the next morning. The story contained information that shouldn't have been made public, mentioning aspects of the investigation that should have been protected by the secret nature of police activities. *Official sources confirm that Inspector Croce returned to the Plaza Hotel late last night and went down to the storage room full of lost objects, later departing with several items that might be part of the investigation.* How had the news gotten out, why were the facts presented like that? These questions no longer worried Croce. *Exclusive statements by General Prosecutor Cueto*, the newspaper said. An interview, photographs. Ever since he'd been placed in charge of the Prosecutor's Office, Cueto had been building a campaign in the press against him. As the main reporter at the newspaper—one Daniel Otamendi—had written, Croce was Cueto's *bête noir*. "I just learned that I have a rival who cares that much about me," Croce said.

Cueto didn't care about him, he just wanted to get Croce out of the way, and he knew that the key was to use the press to discredit him. The Prosecutor maintained that Croce was an anachronism, he wanted to modernize the local police force, and he treated Croce as if he were a rural cop, a sergeant in charge of a card game.

The problem was that Croce solved all his cases.

The Inspector wasn't intimidated by the leading headlines in the newspaper, but he was worried. The news of the murder of an American in the province of Buenos Aires had taken a national character. News was contagious, reporters would start flooding in like a leak through the roof of a country house.

That same morning, in fact, people had seen a reporter arriving from Buenos Aires. It was the special correspondent from the newspaper *El Mundo*. He'd gotten off the bus from Mar del Plata looking sleepy, smoking, wearing a leather jacket, had walked around a bit, and had finally gone into the Madariaga Store and Tavern and ordered coffee with milk and croissants. He was impressed by the round, white coffee mug and the foamy milk, and by the small, crispy, homemade croissants. Whenever someone from out of town arrived, people left a kind of buffer zone around him, as if everyone were studying him, so the reporter ate breakfast on his own, at the side table near the window with the bars facing out to the patio. The young man looked surprised and alarmed. At least that's the impression he gave, because he changed seats twice and was seen speaking with one of the regular customers, who leaned forward and pointed outside toward the Plaza Hotel. Then, through the window in the tavern, they saw the town's police car pull into town.

Croce and Saldías parked the car, got out, and walked along the square to the offices of *El Pregón*. They were followed at a respectful distance by the same entourage of curious townspeople and children who had taken the stranger to the tavern. The newspaper offices were on the second floor of the old Aduana

Seca building, a large area occupied by the telephone operator, the secretary, and two writers.

Everyone expected a scandal at the newspaper, but the Inspector walked calmly into the newspaper's offices, took off his hat, greeted the staff, and stopped at the editor's desk. This was Thomas Alva Gregorius, a short, myopic man who wore a woven cap—the famous Tomasito-wool caps—because he was going bald and was depressed about it. Born in Bulgaria, Gregorius's Spanish was imaginative; he wrote very poorly and only stayed on at the newspaper because he was the right-hand man for the prosecutor Cueto, who manipulated him as if he were a ventriloquist's dummy.

Croce addressed Gregorius across his desk:

"Who tells you all those stories, eh?"

"That's confidential information, Inspector. You were seen going down into the hotel basement, and come out carrying several items. It's a fact, so I publish it," Gregorius replied.

"I need some photographs from the archives," Croce said.

He wanted to check something from one of the papers from a few weeks ago. Gregorius went directly to the secretary's desk and approved the Inspector's request. The secretary looked at the myopic editor, who looked back at her through his eight-diopter glasses and winked okay.

Croce took the newspapers given to him to a back counter and leafed through them until he found what he was looking for. He began studying the details on one of the pages with a magnifying lens. It was a photograph of the horse races in the town of Bolívar. He may have been searching for certain facts and trusted that a picture would allow him to see what he hadn't been able to see when he was there in person. We never see what we see, he thought. After a while, he got up and spoke with Saldías.

"See if you can get the negative for this photograph at the lab. Talk to Marquitos, he keeps archives of all the pictures he takes. I want the negative this afternoon. We need to have this right here blown up." He drew a circle with his finger around one of the faces in the photograph. "Twelve by twenty."

The reporter from Buenos Aires walked in. He seemed half-asleep, curly hair, round glasses. He was the first reporter from a Buenos Aires newspaper to come to town since the floods of '62. He approached the front desk and spoke with the secretary, who directed him to the editor's office. Gregorius was waiting for him at the door, a friendly smile on his face.

"Ah, you're the correspondent from *El Mundo*," Gregorius said, helpfully. "You must be Renzi. Come on in. I always read your articles. It's an honor..."

Another typical small-town brownnoser, Renzi thought.

"Yes, of course, how do you do? I wanted to ask you for a typewriter and the teleprinter to send my articles, if I have anything."

"So you came because of the news."

"I was in Mar del Plata, they sent me because I was nearby. This time of year everything's flat. What's happening around here?"

"An American has been murdered. A hotel employee did it. Everything is solved already, but Inspector Croce is not convinced. He's stubborn, he's crazy. We have everything: the suspect, the motive, the witnesses, the dead body. The only thing missing is the confession. The Inspector there," Gregorius said, gesturing toward the table where Croce and Saldías were looking at the photograph in the newspaper. "That's the Inspector, the other one is his assistant, Deputy Saldías."

Croce raised his head, the magnifying glass in his hand, and looked at Renzi. A strange flare of sympathy flashed on the Inspector's narrow face. Their eyes met but neither said anything. Then the Inspector seemed to look through Renzi, as if he were made of glass, and glared scornfully at Gregorius.

"Hey, Gregorio, I need to get a blow-up of this photograph," he said in a loud voice. "I'll leave it with Margarita."

Renzi didn't like the police, in this he was like everyone else, but he liked the Inspector's face and his way of talking, his mouth slightly askew. A straight shooter, Renzi thought—not shooting straight himself, for he was using a metaphor to say that the Inspector had spoken to the editor of the newspaper as if he were some dumb neighbor and as if the secretary were his friend. And that's what they were, Renzi imagined. What they are, rather. Everyone knows everyone in these towns. When he looked up again, the Inspector was gone and the secretary was walking away with Saldías, carrying an open newspaper.

"You can set up here, then, at my desk, if you need to type anything. The teleprinter is in the back, Dorita can help you. You can use our telephone, too, if you'd like, it'll be our pleasure." He paused. "If it's possible, I would ask only that you mention our small, independent newspaper, *El Pregón*. We've been here since the times of the Indian Wars, my grandfather founded the paper to keep the agricultural producers connected. Here, let me give you my card."

"Yes, of course, thank you. I'll send something tonight, before they go to press in the Capital. I'll use your telephone now, if I could."

"Yes, yes, of course," Gregorius said. "Go on, certainly, go on," he said, leaving Renzi alone in his office.

After dealing with the long-distance operator, Renzi was able to get through to the newsroom in Buenos Aires.

"How's it going, Junior? This is Emilio, let me speak with Luna. I'm calling from this shitty little town. How's everything there? Any women asking for me? Any recent suicides in the newsroom?"

"Did you just get there?"

"I was going to call you from the bar, but you can't imagine what an ordeal it is to make a phone call from the provinces. Anyway, let me speak with Luna."

After a pause and a series of rustling, rattling noises, like wind blowing against a chicken coop wire fence, the thick voice of Old-Man Luna came on the line. Luna was the newspaper's editor.

"Come on kid, remember, we're ahead of the game here. There was a small mention on Channel 7, but we can beat everyone to the scoop on this. The town's not the story. The story's that an American was murdered out in the countryside."

"A Puerto Rican."

"Same shit." There was a pause. Renzi could picture Old-Man Luna lighting a cigarette. "Apparently the Embassy is going to step in, or the Consulate. Just imagine, what if he was killed by some guerrilla group."

"Stop kidding around, Mr. Luna."

"See if you can make something up that we can use, everything's under water around here. Send a photograph of the dead man."

"No one really knows why he came to town exactly."

"Go with that," Luna said. But, as usual, he was already onto something else, he did ten things at once and said more or less the same thing to everyone. "Hurry up, kid, we'll be going to press soon," he yelled. Then there was a strange silence, like a hollow, and Renzi realized that Luna was pressing the mouthpiece of the telephone against his body and speaking with someone else in the newsroom. He held on, in case there was anything else.

"And where am I supposed to get a photograph?" But Luna had already hung up.

Everyone at *El Pregón* was watching a television, set up on a sliding cart off to one side of the room. Channel 7, from the Capital, had requested a coaxial connection with the channel from the town. The local newscast was going to be shown nationwide. On the screen, behind the gray stripes that went up and down repeatedly, was the front of the Plaza Hotel, with the prosecutor, Cueto, entering and coming back out, very active, smiling. He was explaining, giving his version of the events. The camera followed him to the corner. There, looking directly into the camera with a smug little smile, the prosecutor concluded that the case was solved.

"Everything has been cleared up," he said. "But we have some differences with the old policeman in charge of the investigation. The issue is a procedural matter that will be settled in court. I've asked the judge in Olavarría to declare preventive custody for the accused and have him transferred to the prison in Dolores."

The channel resumed its local programming, covering the

preparations for a horse-and-duck polo match between the civilian and the military teams at the summit near the town of Pringles. Gregorius turned off the television and walked Renzi to the door of the newspaper offices.

The reporter from *El Mundo* checked in at the Plaza Hotel, rested for a while, and went back out to take a look around town and interview a few of the residents. No one would tell him what everyone knew, or what was so well known to everyone that it needed no explanation. They all looked at him sarcastically, as if he were the only one who didn't understand what was going on. It was quite a strange story, with different angles and multiple versions. Like any other, Renzi thought.

By the end of the afternoon Renzi had gathered all the available information and was ready to write his article. He returned to his hotel room, looked over his notes, and made a series of diagrams, underlining several phrases in his black notebook. Then he went down to the dining room and ordered a beer and French fries.

It was after midnight when he went back to the offices of the local newspaper, knocked on the iron shutters, and was let in by the night guard, Don Moya, who always hobbled around with an odd-looking limp, having been thrown in '52 by a horse that had left him with a bum leg. Moya turned on the lights of the empty newsroom for him, and Renzi sat at Gregorius's desk and typed out the article on a Remington with a missing *a*.

He wrote his first story in one fell swoop, looking at his notes, trying to make it what his editor Luna called a colorful article with a hook. He started with a description of the town because he realized that this would be of interest in Buenos Aires, where almost all the readers were like him, city people who thought the countryside was peaceful and boring, sparsely populated with folk who wore Basque berets, smiled like idiots, and said yes to everything. A world of simple, honest people who spent their lives working the land, faithful to the Argentine tradition of the gaucho and loyal friendships. Renzi realized that it was all a farce, in just one afternoon he had heard more mean and hostile comments than he could have imagined. In one version Durán was what is known as a carrier, someone who brings in undeclared money to negotiate, on behalf of a fictitious company, the prices for the purchase of the harvest to avoid paying taxes.[15] Everyone had told Renzi about the bagful of dollars that Croce had found in the storage room in the basement of the hotel. This was probably the main clue needed to solve the crime. The most interesting aspect, of course—as is often the case in these matters—was the dead man. Investigating the victim is the key to every criminal investigation, Renzi wrote, and to this end everyone who had interacted or had business with the deceased had to be questioned. Renzi maintained the suspense, centering the affair on the foreigner who arrived in the small town without anyone knowing why exactly. He alluded vaguely to a romance with one of the daughters of one of the main families in town.

The investigation would have to begin with those who had a motive to kill the victim. Renzi soon understood, however, that

---

15   "There are bogus societies that transport 30,000 tons of grain under the table per month. That is equivalent to 3,000 trucks. Just ten or twelve people can run such an operation. 'Some juridical reports charge $30,000 to create such a society,' several sources stated to this reporter" (Renzi's article).

everyone in town had motives and reasons to kill Tony Durán. First of all, the sisters, although according to Renzi it was strange to think that they would want to kill him. They would have killed him themselves, as several residents told the reporter. And it's true, because in this town, honestly, one of the hotel managers said, women don't hire anyone else to do their dirty work for them, they go and wipe whoever it is out themselves. At least that's what's always happened around here in crimes of passion, the interviewed reported proudly, as if defending some grand local tradition.

Renzi wrote that, according to sources, the leading suspect, a hotel employee of Japanese origins, had been detained, and that Inspector Croce had discovered a leather bag, brown, with nearly one hundred thousand dollars in fifty- and one hundred-dollar bills, in the storage room in the basement of the hotel. Apparently, Renzi added, the suspect lowered the satchel with the money from the room with a service lift used in the past to send meals up for *room service*. None of this had been officially reported, but several sources in town mentioned these facts. We note, he concluded, that officials have not confirmed or rejected these statements. The editor of the local newspaper (and Renzi took the opportunity to name *El Pregón*) has criticized the way the investigation was being carried out by the authorities. Who was the money for? And why had they left it in a storage room full of lost objects instead of taking it with them? These were the questions with which the article closed.

Renzi made a few corrections with a red pen he found on the desk, and dictated the article over the telephone to his newspaper's typist, repeating every punctuation point, coma, period, paragraph break, colon, and semicolon. The article opened with a description of the town seen from above, as if it were the chronicle of a traveler arriving in some mysterious territory. This appealed because it lent the town a concrete existence, and for once it wasn't mentioned merely as an appendix of the neighboring, larger town of Rauch.

Coming across the hills, the entire town can be seen below, from the lake from which it draws its name to the large houses on the surrounding hills.

It was a brief article, with a *spaghetti-western* title, *Yankee Murdered in Western Town*, different from the title Renzi had called in. People read it the following day, with the main events synthesized in a ridiculous order (the hotel, the dead body, the bag with the money), as if the reporter from Buenos Aires, after going around asking questions, had allowed himself to be misled by all his informants.

He seemed nervous, out of it, the night guard Moya said, adding that after hearing him dictate the story, he walked him to the door and saw him head toward the Social Club for a drink. He was accompanied at that point by Bravo, the society reporter, who suddenly appeared as if he had been awakened by the sound of the metal shutters of the newspaper offices.

Sofía was silent for a while, watching the afternoon light waning in the garden, then resumed the somewhat maddened rhythm of the story she had heard and repeated, or imagined, many times before.

"My father made himself out to be an aristocrat. That's why he sought out my mother, for her family name. She's an Ibarguren," Sofía said. "My father married for love the first time around, with Regina O'Connor,

but as I was saying before, she left him for another. My father never recovered, he couldn't conceive of anyone abandoning him or treating him with contempt. Deep down he always doubted if my brother was really his, he treated him with extreme deference, like one would a bastard. And also, unlike my brother Lucio, my brother Luca was always hostile, and this hostility became a kind of demonic pride, an absolute conviction, because when his mother abandoned them and left town, my father rescued him, and brought him back, and since then he's lived with us, at home."

Renzi stood up.

"What do you mean, where did he rescue him from?"

"He brought him home and raised him, he didn't care where he came from."

"And the theater director? Was he the father, the possible father?" Renzi asked.

"It doesn't matter, because his mother always said that Luca was my father's son, that you could tell a mile away. Unfortunately, he's your father's son, Regina used to say, you can tell right away because he's so forlorn, and a lunatic. If he wasn't his son, he wouldn't have gotten into the situation he's in now, his mother said, just about killing himself, ruining his life over an obsession."

"What is this, a melodrama?" Renzi asked.

"Of course, what did you expect? They brought him home and raised him like the rest of us, and he never saw his mother again. She finally moved back to Dublin, she lives there now and doesn't want anything more to do with us, or with this place, or her sons. The Irishwoman. My father still has a photograph of her on his desk. That woman, she was out of place here, can you imagine? She was too standoffish to be an Argentine mother, she could ride a horse better than any gaucho,

but she hated the country out here. 'What kind of shit do these shits think?' she used to say. She blamed the countryside for everything, the infinite tedium of the countryside, people wandering down the empty streets of the small town like the walking dead. Nature only produces destruction and chaos, it isolates people, every gaucho is a Robinson Crusoe riding on a horse like a shadow. Isolated thoughts, solitary, light as baling wire, heavy as a bag of maize, no one can get out, everyone's tied to the deserted fields, they head out on horseback to inspect their property, to see if the fence posts are in good shape, if the animals have stayed near the watering spring, if the storm's coming—and in the late afternoon, by the time they come back home, they've been made dumb by the boredom and the emptiness. My brother says he can still hear her curse at night, that sometimes he speaks with her, that he always sees her. She couldn't have stayed in this town, the Irishwoman. When she ran away, pregnant, my father made life impossible for her, he wouldn't let her see her other son, by court order, everyone consented to punishing her. He wouldn't let her see Lucio, she would send messages, presents, she would plead, she'd come to the house, but my father would have servants throw her out. Sometimes he'd tell her to wait in the square and he'd pass slowly by in the car so she could see her son, little Lucio looking at her through the window without waving, his eyes full of surprise." Sofía paused, and smoked pensively. *"She was pregnant with Luca (two hearts beating in one body, thump thump) and Lucio looking at her through the rear window of the car, can you picture it? Finally she left the kids and went back to her own country."*

She's putting me on, Renzi thought, she's spinning a yarn to hook me in.

"When she finally escaped forever from this damned country, as

she used to call it, she went back to Dublin, where she works now as a teacher. Every once in a while we get a letter, always addressed to her sons, written in a Spanish that gets stranger and stranger with time. No one has ever written back to her. Because her two sons have not forgiven her for abandoning them, and this served to unite them under a common sorrow. No son can forgive his mother for abandoning him. Fathers abandon their sons without any problems, they just leave and never see them again, but a woman can't do that, it's forbidden, that's why my sister and I, if we ever have children, we're going to abandon them. And they'll wave at us, standing in a square when they're small, the little kids, while we drive by in our cars with a different lover. How do you like that?"

She stopped, looked at Renzi with a smile glowing in her eyes, and served herself more wine. Then she went back to the living room and took a while. When she came back out, she was exhilarated, her eyes were shining, she was rubbing her tongue over her gums and balancing two plates with cheese and olives.

"In my family the men go crazy when they become fathers. Look at what happened to my old man: he could never get out from under his doubt. He was certain only of the paternity of my older brother, Lucio, he was the only one who obeyed his desires, except in his marriage."

Only then did Renzi realize that Sofía was going inside more and more frequently. He followed her into the living room and saw her bent over a glass table.

"What do you have there?" Renzi asked.

"Sea salt," she said, leaning forward, smiling, holding a rolled-up, one-peso bill to her nose.

"Well, well, will you look at the country girl," Renzi said. "Can I have a line?"

8

Bravo and Renzi left the newspaper offices and walked down the empty streets of the town. It was a stormy night; a warm wind was blowing from the plains. Renzi realized with disgust that he had stepped on a beetle, which made a dry crack as he crushed it under his shoe. Clouds of mosquitoes and moths flitted about the corner streetlights. After a while, a stray dog appeared in front of them, slightly deformed, its tail between its legs. A bit lame, it began to follow them with its crooked walk.

"That's the Inspector's dog, he leaves him untied and the mutt roams about all over town at night like a ghost."

The dog stayed close for a while, but finally lay down at a doorstep along the way. The two men walked on, the wind rustling the branches in the trees and raising the dust in the street.

"Here we are, Emilio," Brazo said. "This is the Club."

They stood in front of a two-story house, French style but understated. A bronze plaque announced to anyone who went close enough to read the miniscule print that this was the Social Club, founded in 1910.

"Not just anyone can come in here," Bravo said. "But you're with me, you can be my guest tonight.

"My work as the society page reporter consists of setting a high bar and keeping people on one side separate from those on the other side. My readers can't come in here, so they have to read the paper. How to cross the line; or better yet, how to make the jump from one side to the other, that's what everyone wants to know. Durán, the deceased, a mulatto, a black man really—because out in the province there are no mulattos, you're either white or you're black. Anyway, Durán, black and all, was finally able to go in."

By then the two of them had also entered the hall. Bravo greeted people he knew as they walked past the bar and took a seat at a table off to a side, near the windows, facing the gardens outside.

"Everyone is now saying that Tony had brought a bunch of money with him when he arrived. But nobody can explain why he brought it, or what he was waiting for. Americans can bring as much money into the country as they want to, they don't have to declare anything. The military set up the arrangement during the time of General Onganía," Bravo told Renzi, as if he were sharing a personal secret. "Liquid capital, foreign investment, it's considered legal. Who covers the economy at *El Mundo*?"

"Ameztoy," Renzi said. "According to him, Perón is controlled by European companies."

Bravo looked at him, amazed.

"European?" he remarked. "But that's antediluvian, from the time of the ñaupa." Like everyone in the province—as Renzi realized after his conversations and interviews from that day—Bravo used arcane words and out-of-date expressions deliberately to try to seem more genuinely from out in the country. "The freedom to move currency was imposed by the Americans as a condition to bringing in foreign investment. Now it's used to deal money under the table to make deals on the harvests."

"And that's what Durán was doing," Renzi said. "Moving money."

"I don't know, that's what people say. Don't go and cite me as a source, Emilio, I'm the town's social conscience. I say what everyone thinks but no one dares to say." He paused. "Snobbery is the only way to survive in these places," he added, and went on to explain why he was accepted in such a rarified atmosphere.

Bravo, at thirty, looked like an old man. It wasn't that he had aged prematurely, but that old age was part of his life, his face was covered with scars because he'd been in an automobile accident. He was an excellent tennis player as a youth, but his career was interrupted soon after he won a junior tournament at the Law Tennis Club in Viña del Mar, and he never recovered from his unfulfilled expectations. He had so much natural talent for tennis that people called him Stumpy—just like Carlos Gardel was called the Mute—and, like everyone with a natural talent, when he lost his gift—when he was no longer able to use his gift—he became a kind of spontaneous philosopher who looked at the world with the skepticism and clarity of Diogenes in the garbage can. He hadn't been able to accomplish anything with the gift he was given, except to win the final of that junior tournament in Chile over Alexis Olmedo, the Peruvian tennis player who'd go on to win Wimbledon years later. Bravo was forced to retire from the circuit before even entering it due to a strange lesion on his right hand that kept him from playing. That's when his decadence and old age began. He returned to his hometown, where his father, a hacienda auctioneer, got him the position at the newspaper as the society page reporter—because he still had an aura about him of having played tennis on the *courts* at a time when only the upper classes played the white sport.

"No one can imagine," he said to Renzi, after they had a few drinks and entered the stage of frank confessions, "what it's like to have a talent for something and not be able to use it. Or at least to think that one has a talent for something and not be able to use it."

"I know," Renzi said. "When it comes to that, half of my friends (and I myself) suffer the same illness."

"I can't play tennis anymore," Bravo complained.

"Usually my friends have so much talent that they don't even need to do anything."

"I understand," Bravo said. "Can you imagine how big of snobs they are here, they think of me as one of their own because I trained with Rod Laver." He paused, waiting for Renzi's smile. Bravo was rambling a bit, drinking the free whiskey he was served whenever he came to the Club. "Sometimes, when I need money," he said all of a sudden, "I go and play *paleta* against country folk who don't know who I am, and I always win. There's nothing more different from a tennis court than the walls of a Basque *pelota* game, but the key is still to see the ball, and my eyesight is just fine. I could play left-handed, with my hands tied, and I'd still win. In Cañuelas I beat Utge," he said, as if he had defeated Shakespeare in a poetry contest.

Bravo paused again, and went on, as if he felt the need to continue telling Renzi his secrets. He told him that sometimes he thought he could hear the crisp sound of a tennis ball catching the line, but that so much time had passed since his experience on the courts that it would take him a while to identify the sound. A sound that to this day still moved him.

Renzi thought again that Bravo was ranting a bit, but he was used to it. It wasn't unusual for reporters to digress and ramble when they spoke to keep from saying anything. Personal secrets and false news, that was the genre.

"You can't imagine the deals the military are making before they leave," Bravo said. "They're going to sell everything, even their tanks. Everyone here is sure that Perón is coming back and that the soldiers are going back to their barracks. They're making as many deals as they can before the tortilla is flipped over. Speaking of which, should we order something to eat? They make a Spanish tortilla here you just can't find in Buenos Aires."

Bravo ordered another whiskey. Renzi was hungry, so he took Bravo's suggestion and ordered a Spanish tortilla and a bottle of wine.

"Which wine would you prefer, sir?" asked a waiter with the face of a bird, looking at Renzi with a strange mixture of distance and disdain.

"Bring me a bottle of Sauvignon Blanc," Renzi said. "And a bucket of ice."

"Of course, sir," the waiter said, with the manners of an idiot who believed he was the son of Count Orlov.

Bravo lit a cigarette, and Renzi saw that his right hand shook. It was a little deformed, with an ugly protuberance at the wrist. Renzi thought that Bravo was using his right hand as if he were forcing himself to do so, as if he were still in physical therapy.

Renzi pictured the electrical machines, the metal clips and thin wires attached to the hand to stretch the nerves and the joints.

"Can you imagine being a society page reporter in a town like this? People tell you the news on the telephone before events occur, if you don't promise them you'll publish it, they don't do it. First they make sure it'll make the news, then the action happens," Bravo said. "Everything is arranged in here, in the Club. That woman back there, at the round table, that's one of the Belladona sisters."

Renzi saw a young redhead, tall and arrogant, leaning distractedly toward the man speaking next to her—one of those men whose heads look too small for their bodies, lending them a sinister appearance, as if their human torso ended at the face of a snake. It was the Prosecutor, Renzi recognized him from television. The young woman was speaking now, resting back in her chair, her left hand between her breasts, as if she were trying to keep warm. She's not wearing a bra, Renzi thought, the best little tits in the Argentine pampas. He saw her shake her head no, without smiling, and jot something down on a piece of paper. Then she said goodbye with a quick kiss on the cheek and walked toward the staircase leading downstairs, her gate confident and seductive.

"It started a while ago," Bravo said, and began telling the story. "Cueto got one of the first Harley Davidsons in Argentina, and when he showed up in town with the machine, all Ada Belladona wanted was to get a ride on his motorcycle. He went out with her, gave her a ride around the main square, and immediately they had an accident. Ada broke a leg, Cueto came out unscathed. He always said that the key to driving a motorcycle was knowing how to fall. That was his theory. The first thing an athlete does, he said, is learn how to fall. He asked her before she got on and she told him that she knew how to fall. But when the motorcycle grazed one of the flowerbeds on the edge of the square, the machine dragged the girl's leg along for nearly fifty meters. She wasn't left paralyzed by sheer chance, she had a cast from her hip to her toes. The work of an artist, I think they found a sculptor to do it. Aldo Bianchi or one of those, she used to say, showing off her cast, which ended in a kind of plaster sandal with the stylized form of a siren's tail. And she used it to lean on it like that. It was incredible, she was as crazy as Cueto was, that young woman, she loved to dance, and one summer night, they went to this place in Mar del Plata, Club Gambrinus. Inside, everyone asked her, What happened to you? Are you okay? She just said that her leg had been crushed by a horse and kept getting up to dance. She'd stick her white, bright leg into the ground, with that shape like the tail of a fish, and spin her body around and around the plaster cast. Like Captain Ahab."[16]

Renzi liked how Bravo told stories. It was clear he had told this one so many times, polishing it along the way, that it was now smooth as a pebble. Of course a story can always be improved, Renzi thought, absent-minded. Bravo, in the meantime, had gone on to something else, picking up again on the conjectures about Durán. He thought Tony had gotten close to the Belladona sisters to gain access to the Social Club. With them he could enter, alone they

---

16   Soon after this, Ada bought herself a Triumph 220. Since then, she rides around town on her motorcycle all the time, scaring the locals and the birds in the corrals. The dogs run after her, barking as if possessed, chasing behind her on the motorcycle.

would never have let him in.

"I would have liked to have warned Tony not to come around here," Bravo said. *He uses the pluperfect of the subjunctive*, Renzi thought. He was so tired these were the kind of thoughts that popped into his head, thoughts once typical for him, when he was in college and he used to spend his time analyzing grammatical forms and verbal conjugations. Sometimes he wouldn't understand what people were telling him because he'd get distracted analyzing syntactical structures as if he were a philologist enraged by the distorted uses of contemporary language. Recently it had been happening less frequently to him. But sometimes, when he was with a woman and he liked her way of speaking, he'd suddenly want to sleep with her because he was so excited by her use of the perfect preterit indicative. As if the presence of the past in the present justified just about any passion. In this case, it was only his fatigue and the strangeness that he felt being in that town in the middle of nowhere. When he heard the noises around him from the bar again, he realized that Bravo was telling him the story of the Belladona family, a story that seemed like any other story of an Argentine family in the countryside, but more intense and crueler.

"I'm sick of this trash," Bravo said all of a sudden, completely drunk by this point. "I want to move to the Capital. Do you think there'd be any work for me at *El Mundo*?"

"I don't recommend it."

"I'm getting out of here, for sure. I can't stand it anymore. And I don't have much time left."

"Why not?"

"I want to be in Buenos Aires when Perón returns."

"You don't say," Renzi said, waking up all of a sudden.

"Definitely. It's going to be a historic day."

"Don't get so carried away," Renzi said. He thought that Bravo wanted to be like Fabrizio, the character in *The Charterhouse of Parma* who went to Paris when he heard about Napoleon's return so he could be there to welcome the general home. When he finally goes to Paris, Fabrizio spends his time surrounded by a group of enthusiastic young men of a *seductive sweetness* who—a few days later, as Stendhal writes—steal all his money.

Then they saw Cueto walking toward them, a snooty little smile on his face.

"What do the rented consciences of our homeland have to say?"

"Join us?" Bravo asked.

Cueto had the dry, stringy, vaguely repulsive body of an older man who does a lot of exercise and maintains a kind of pathetic youthfulness.

"Just for a minute, sure," Cueto said.

"Have you met Renzi?" Bravo asked.

"You write for *La Opinión*, right?"

"No…" Renzi said.

"Ah, then you're a failure…" Cueto flashed him a knowing smile and picked up the bottle of wine. He emptied a glass of water into the bucket of ice, served himself some wine, and offered to refill Renzi's glass.

"No, I better not have any more."

"Don't ever stop drinking while you're still able to think that it's better if you don't have anymore, as my aunt Amanda used to say." Cueto savored the wine. "First rate," he said. "Alcohol is one of the few simple pleasures we have left in modern life." He looked around as he spoke, as if he were looking for someone he knew. There was something strange about his left eye, a fixed, bluish look, which made Renzi anxious. "There was an incredible news story yesterday, but of course you journalists never read the papers."

Two young guerrilla women had killed a conscript at an air force base in Morón.[17] They had gotten out of a Peugeot and walked up to the sentry box, smiling at the guard, with a 45 hidden in a *Siete Días* magazine. When the young soldier refused to turn over his weapon, they shot him dead.

"He resisted, the paper said. Just imagine if he's going to resist? He must have said, Girls, what are you doing? Don't take my rifle, they'll throw me in jail. His name was Luis Ángel Medina. He could have been from the Province of Corrientes, who knows, a little dark conscript, they were fighting for him, the women, fighting on behalf of the dark oppressed of the world, but they went and killed this one." He served himself another glass of wine. "They're cooked, both of them, they'll have to stay together from now on, right?" Cueto said. "Live in hiding in some farm in Temperley, stuffed in a hole, drinking *mate*, the two Trotskyites…"

"Okay," Renzi said, so furious that he started speaking in too-loud a voice. "Inequality between men and women ends as soon as a woman takes up arms." He went on, trying to be as pedantic

---

17   "Today the remains of the soldier Luis Ángel Medina were laid to rest in the cemetery of San Justo, having been shot to death yesterday by two women from an extremist commando group. It would have been Medina's last guard duty, since he was about to complete his military service and would have been discharged the following Friday. However, because of a routine assignment, he was destined to cover the post at which he met his death precisely on that fatal day" (*La Razón*, March 14, 1972).

as possible in his alcoholized haze. "In traditional societies, the term *nobilis*, or *nobilitas*, indicated a free person. By definition this means the right to bear arms. What happens if women are the ones who bear arms?"

"Would you look at that," Bravo said. "Everyone's a soldier! A soldier of Perón—"

"No, a soldier of the People's Revolutionary Army!" Cueto said. "They're the worst, first they go out and kill at random, then they put out a communiqué about the poor of the world."

"Ethics is like love," Renzi said. "If you live in the present, consequences don't matter. If you think about the past, it's because you've already lost your passion."

"You should write these great nocturnal truths."

"In reality," Renzi said, "the greatest sacrifice is to abide with the second ethic."[18]

"The second ethic? Too much for me. Excuse me, my dear journalists, but it's getting late," Cueto said, and started to get up.

"What we need is a female serial killer," Renzi continued. "We don't have any women who kill men serially, without a motive, just because. There should be some."

---

18   In his notes for a book on Dostoevsky (1916), speaking about political crime, G. Lukács cites Bakhtin: *Murder is not allowed, murder is an absolute, unforgivable sin. He certainly cannot be, but he must be executed.* The authentic revolutionary, like the tragic hero, faces evil and accepts its consequences. Only a crime comitted by a man who knows resolutely and beyond all doubt that murder *cannot* be sanctioned, under any circumstance, is naturally moral. In this fashion Lukács distinguishes between the first—or Kantian—ethic, which outlines responsibilities according to the immediate needs of society, and the second ethic, which focuses on transcendence. Lukács cites Kierkegaard's *Fear and Trembling* on this point: *Direct contact with transcendence in life leads to crime, madness, and absurdity* (Note by Renzi).

"For now, women only kill one husband at a time," Cueto said, still looking around the room.

He had already washed his hands of them, he was fed up with their load of ridiculous abstractions. Cueto was sitting at the table with them, but he was essentially gone.

"I'm going, too, my friend," Renzi said. "I traveled through the night to get here, I'm done in."

Bravo walked with him through the night shadows of the town for a few blocks. They stopped at the edge of the main square.

"He wanted people to see him with Ada Belladona. I don't understand," Renzi said.

"He's courting her, as they say around here. He used to be the attorney for the factory, the attorney for the Belladona family, actually. When the whole mess started between the two brothers, he split off. Now he's the public prosecutor. He'll go far."

"There's something strange with the way he looks."

"He has a glass eye, he lost it playing polo." Bravo got in his car and leaned out the window. "Were you trying to get him to bite? He's a pretty dangerous guy, you know?"

"I've been wiping my ass with dangerous guys like that ever since I can remember."

Bravo honked his horn to say goodbye, or as a sign of disapproval, and headed off toward the highway. He lived on the outskirts of town, in a residential neighborhood, up in the hills.

Renzi kept walking on his own, enjoying the cool evening. The municipal truck was watering down the empty streets, settling the dust. It smelled of wet earth, everything was peaceful and quiet. Many times, when he traveled long-distance by bus, he felt like getting out in some town in the middle of the highway and just staying there. Now he was in one of those towns and he had a strange feeling, as if his life were suspended.

But his life was not suspended. When he reached his room and started taking off his clothes, the telephone rang. It was Julia from Buenos Aires.

"You need to stop, Emilio," she said when he picked up the receiver. "Everyone's asking me about you. Where'd you go? I had to call the newspaper to locate you. Look at the hour. A letter arrived here for you, from your brother."

Renzi tried to explain that he couldn't come by to pick up the letter because he was working in a small, lousy town in the province of Buenos Aires, but he realized that Julia didn't believe him. She hung up on him mid-sentence. She must have thought that he was lying to her, that he'd taken off and holed up with some chick in a hotel somewhere, he was sure of it.

Several friends had told him that she'd been saying that he was sinking. After his father's death, which he had no intention of re-opening, he had decided to separate from Julia. But he hadn't changed his address yet, and people were still looking for him at his ex's. He would've liked to have been like Swann, who in the end discovers that he's been consumed by his desire for a woman who wasn't truly worth it. But Renzi was still so connected to Julia that six months after leaving her, just hearing her voice was enough to make him feel lost again. He loved Julia much more than he had loved his father, but the comparison was ridiculous. For the moment he was trying not to make connections between unrelated events. If he could keep everything separate he would be okay.

He looked out the window in his room toward the square. On the street he saw the lame dog, walking crooked. It moved in short jumps, until it stopped under a corner streetlight. Bravo had said it was the Inspector's dog. Renzi saw the dog lift its leg to urinate and shake its yellow fur as if it were soaked. Renzi lowered the curtain and got in bed and dreamt he was attending Tony Durán's funeral in a cemetery in Newark. It was actually the cemetery in Adrogué, but it was in New Jersey and it had old tombstones and markings near the sidewalk on the other side of an iron fence. A group of solemn women and mulattos were saying their farewells. Renzi walked up to the open grave and saw the lead coffin, shining in the sun, being lowered into the earth. He picked up a handful of dirt and threw it in.

"Poor son of a bitch," Renzi said in his dream.

When he woke up he remembered he had dreamed, but not the dream.

9

Croce had a blurry photograph of an unknown man with an outstanding warrant published in the local newspapers, but no one really understood what was going on. Even Saldías started to express his doubts, timidly. The Scribe quickly went from blind admiration to concern to suspicion. Croce didn't pay any more attention to him and, instead, left him out of the loop, ordering him to dedicate his time to typing up a report with the new theories about the crime.

That's when the prosecutor Cueto took center stage and started making decisions designed to put a stop to the scandal. He maintained that Croce's hypotheses were wildly ridiculous and served only to hinder the investigation.

"We don't know what the alleged suspect that Croce is looking for has anything to do with the murder. No one around here knows that man, he has no connection to the victim. We're living through some pretty chaotic times, but we will not allow an old country inspector to go around doing whatever he wants."

He had the state police transfer Yoshio right away to the jail in Dolores, for his own safety, as he said, while he proceeded with his own prosecutorial investigation. They hadn't found the murder weapon, but there were eyewitnesses who placed the suspect at the place and time where and when the crime had been committed. Cueto did everything necessary to close the case and label it a sex crime. In a low voice, to whoever wanted to hear, the Prosecutor assured people that the Inspector could no longer be trusted and that he had to be removed. In the meantime, Croce continued to go about town as always, waiting for some new development. No one really knew what he was thinking, or why, or why he believed that Dazai wasn't guilty.

One night, at dinnertime, Renzi ran into Croce at the Madariaga Tavern. Sitting at the table by the side window, the Inspector was eating a rump roast with French fries, drawing small figures on the paper tablecloth with a pencil while he ate. Every once in a while he'd stop moving and stare into space, holding up his glass of wine.

In his work as a reporter, Renzi occasionally covered police stories, and he'd met a number of inspectors. Most were thugs without any morals who just liked having their position on the force so they could get women to sleep with them (especially the prostitutes) and acquire an upper hand into as many shady deals as possible. But Croce seemed different. He had the peaceful air of a paisano you could trust, Renzi thought—and all of a sudden he remembered the opinion that the editor at his newspaper, Luna, had about police inspectors.

"Who wouldn't want to be an inspector?" Old-Man Luna said to him one night. "Don't be so naïve, kid. Inspectors are the real heavies. Over forty, they've already put on some weight, they've seen everything, most have a few kills under their belts. Inspectors are men who've lived a lot, they have a ton of authority, they spend their time with delinquents and political strongmen, always out at night, in cathouses and bars, getting whatever drugs they want, making easy money because everyone greases them: bookies, dealers, mafiosos, neighbors. They're our new heroes, kid. Always armed, they can get in anywhere, form a gang, knock down doors. They're specialists of evil, the damned, their job is to make sure idiots sleep at night, they do the dirty work on behalf of the beautiful. Moving between the law and the world of crime, they fly in between. Half and half, if someone changed the balance on them they wouldn't be able to survive. They're the guardians of our security. Society delegates to them the role of taking care of what no one wants to see," Luna told him. "They do politics all the time, but they never get in as politicians, when they get involved in politics it's to take down some mid-level puppet, a mayor, a representative or two, but they never go any higher. They're clandestine heroes, always tempted to run themselves, but they never do. If they did they'd be done, they'd become too visible," Luna told him that night over dinner at El Pulpito, schooling him, once again, on real life. "They do what they have to do and they endure beyond all the changes, they're eternal, they've always been there—" Luna hesitated at that point for a moment, Renzi remembered, then continued: "There's been famous police inspectors ever since the times of Rosas, sometimes they lose, like anyone else, they get killed or retired or sent to jail, but there's always another one right behind them to take their place. They're malevolent, my dear, but the level of evil in them is minimal compared to the men who give them their orders. Cops will give it to you straight, they're the ones in the trenches," Luna concluded. "So don't be crazy, just write what they tell you." I'm going to do what he said, Renzi thought, remembering Old-Man Luna's advice when he saw Croce gesturing for him to come over.

"Join me for something to eat?" Croce asked.

"Yes, sure," Renzi said. "It'll be a pleasure."

He sat at the table with Croce and ordered a strip of short ribs and a lettuce and tomato salad, without onions.

"This store and tavern was the first thing built in town. The migrant laborers used to eat here at harvest time." Renzi realized right away that the Inspector needed company. "When one is an inspector one starts to believe that one has managed to reduce the scale of death down to a personal dimension. And when I say death I mean murder. Somebody can be killed by accident," Croce said, "but you can't *murder* someone by accident. If Mrs. X hadn't walked back home yesterday, for example, and if she hadn't turned at a certain corner, could she have avoided being murdered? She might have died anyway, that's true, but murdered? If death isn't the intended goal, it's not murder. That's why there's always a decision, and a motive. Not just a cause, but a motive." He stopped. "Which is also why a pure crime is rare. If there's no motive, it's an enigma: we have the dead body, we have the suspects, but we don't have the cause. Or the cause doesn't correspond to the execution of the murder. This seems to be the case now. We have the dead body and we have a suspect." He paused. "What we call motivation could be an unseen meaning, not because it's a mystery, but because the network of determinations is too vast. We have to concentrate, synthesize, find the fixed point. We have to isolate an item of fact and create a closed field, otherwise we'll never be able to solve the enigma."

Drawing small figures on the tablecloth, the Inspector reconstructed the facts for himself, but also for Renzi. He always needed someone to speak to, someone to help him break out of his internal discourse, the words that went around and around in his head like a tune. When he spoke with someone he was forced to choose certain thoughts, it was impossible to say everything, he always tried to have his interlocutor reflect with him and arrive at his own conclusions even before him. That was how he could trust his reasoning, because someone else would have thought it with him. In this he was like everyone who was too intelligent—Auguste Dupin, Sherlock Holmes—and needed an assistant to think with him, and to keep him from falling into delirium.

"For Cueto the criminal is Yoshio and the motive is jealousy. A private crime, no one else is implicated. Closed case," Renzi said.

"It seems to me that Cueto is always saying that things that appear to be different are really the same, while I'm interested in showing that things that appear to be the same are really different. *I'll teach them differences.*[19] See?" he asked. "It's a duck, but if you look at it like this, instead, it's a rabbit." Croce drew the outline of the duck-rabbit. "What does it mean *to see* something such as it is? It's not easy." He looked down at the drawing he had sketched on the tablecloth. "A rabbit and a duck...

---

19   "I'll teach you differences" (*King Lear*, I.4).

"Things are what we know them to be *before* we see them."
Renzi didn't understand where the Inspector was going. "We see
things *according to* how we interpret them. It's called foresight: to
know beforehand, to be forewarned.[20] Out in the country, you
follow the trail of a calf, you see the footprints on the dry earth,
you know the animal is tired because the tracks are light, you
orient yourself because the birds land to peck on the trail. You
can't just randomly look for footprints, the tracker must first know
what he's looking for: human, dog, puma. Then he can see. I'm
like that too. You have to have a base first, only then can you
can make inferences and deductions. That's why you see what
you know," he pointed out, "and why you can't see what you
don't know. Discovering something is seeing what no one else
has perceived yet in another way. That's the point." Strange, Renzi
thought, but he's right. "On the other hand, if I don't think of
him as the criminal, his actions, his behavior, they don't make
sense." He paused, thinking. "Understanding," he said when he
snapped out of it, "is not discovering facts, or extracting logical
inferences, and even less constructing theories. Understanding is
simply a matter of adopting the right point of view to perceive
reality. A sick man doesn't see the same world that a healthy man
sees," Croce said, losing himself in his thoughts again, but snapping

---

20   Suppose we show the image to someone in the country, Croce said. He
says: "It's a duck," and then, all of a sudden: "Oh, it's a rabbit." He's recognized
it as a rabbit. He's had an experience of recognition. Likewise, if someone
sees me walking down the street, they'll say: "Ah, it's Croce." But one doesn't
always have an experience of recognition. The experience occurs at the
moment of changing from duck to rabbit, and vice versa. I call this method
seeing-as. Its goal is to change the aspect under which certain things are seen.
This *seeing-as* is not part of perception. It's like seeing, but it's also *not* like
seeing.

right out of it this time. "A sad man doesn't see the same world as a guy who's happy. Likewise, a policeman doesn't see the same reality as a journalist—begging your pardon," he added, smiling. "I know reporters write with the solid intention of learning about the matter later." He looked at him with a smile. Although he agreed, Renzi couldn't respond, he had food in his mouth. "It's like a game of chess, you have to wait for your opponent to make a move. Cueto wants to close the case, everyone in town wants the case to be closed, and I'm waiting for the evidence to break. I already have it, I know what happened, I saw it, but I can't prove it yet. Look." Renzi moved closer to see what Croce was looking at. It was a group of people on a horse in a photograph from the newspaper. Croce had circled the figure of a jockey. "You know what a *simile* is."

Renzi looked at him.

"It's all about distinguishing what something is from what it appears to be," Croce continued. "*Noticing* something means stopping there, in front of it." Croce stopped, as if he were waiting for something. The telephone rang then. Madariaga answered, looked at Croce, and made a cranking motion with his hand.

"A call from the police station in Tapalqué," he said.

"Aha," Croce said. "Good." He got up and walked to the counter.

Renzi saw him nod his head yes, serious, and move his hand in the air as if the person on the telephone could see him.

"And when was this?

"Is there anyone with him?

"I'm on my way. Thanks, Leoni."

Croce went up to the counter. "Add the dinner to my tab, my

Basque friend," he said to Madariaga, and started toward the exit.
He stopped at the table where Renzi was still sitting.

"There's been news. You can come along if you'd like."

"Perfect. I'm taking this with me," Renzi said, grabbing the
paper with the drawing.

Night would have to finally fall before Sofía would clear up for him—
"it's an expression"—the story of her family, between their comings and
goings to the mirror on the table in the living room with the white lines,
which gave them both a few long minutes of exhilaration and clarity, of
instant happiness, followed by a sort of dark grief which in the end Sofía
valorized by saying that it was only during those moments of coming
down— "in the comedown"—that it was possible to be sincere and tell
the truth, leaning over the glass table with a rolled-up bill to snort the
uncertain whiteness of the salt of life.

"My father," Sofía said, "always thought that his sons would marry
country girls from good families with good last names. He sent my brother
Lucio to study engineering in La Plata, because that's what he had done,
and when he got there Lucio rented a room in a boarding house on
Diagonal 80 which was run by a chronic student, a guy named Guerra.
At the boarding house, on Fridays, they'd have this young woman come
for the weekend, she rode over on a moped, the Vespa girl, they called her,
she was really nice, an architecture student, living the life, as they say.
Bimba, is the name she went by. A fun girl, she'd get there on Friday
and stay through Sunday, she'd sleep with the six students who lived
in the house, one at a time, of course, and sometimes she'd cook them
meals or sit with them and drink mate, *play cards, after doing them all.*

"One afternoon, Lucio burned his hands in an explosion in the lab at

the college and had to get his hands bandaged like a boxer, and Bimba took care of him, she looked after him, he couldn't do anything on his own because of his hands. The following week, the next time she came back on Friday, she went straight to my brother's room, changed his bandages, shaved and bathed him, spoon-fed him, and they chatted and had a great time. That same weekend Lucio asked her to stay with him, he offered to pay by himself what all the others paid together so that she would please not go with the others, but Bimba laughed and stroked his hair, she listened to his stories and his plans, and then she went off to bed with the other guys, in the other rooms, while Lucio suffered, lying on the bed, his bandaged hands in the air and his head full of horrible images. He'd go out to the patio, hear laughing, happy voices. They call Lucio 'Bear' because he's enormous and because he always looks sad, or kind of spaced out. Ever since he was a little kid his problem was always his innocence, he was always gullible, too trusting and too good. That night, when Bimba was in bed with Guerra, where she continued her rounds after Lucio, my brother could hear them laughing in bed, and he lost it. He got up, enraged, his hands bandaged, he kicked Guerra's door in and stormed into the room and knocked over the bedside table and the lamp that was on it. Guerra got up and started hitting Lucio, beating him—and my brother, as weak as he was, with his hands completely unusable, he fell to the ground right away and didn't defend himself, and Guerra kept kicking and insulting him, he wanted to kill him. At that point, Bimba jumped on Guerra, naked, and started scratching and yelling at him to leave Lucio alone, until finally they had to call the police." Sofía paused. "But the extraordinary thing," she went on, "is that my brother quit college, he left everything and came back to town and married Bimba. He brought her home, he imposed her on the family and had kids with her, everyone knows that she used to be a working girl, and my mother is the only one who won't speak with her, she's always pretended that she was invisible, but no one else cares because Bimba is wonderful, she's so much fun. My sister and I love her, she's the one who taught us everything there is to know about life, and she's the one who took care of Lucio during all these lean times and kept the house running with the few savings still remaining from the years of grandeur. My father liked her, too, she must have reminded him of the Irishwoman. Still, he was disappointed, he wanted his sons and his sons' sons to be, as he said, country men, owners of estancias, men of influence and wealth, men with weight in local politics. He could have been a governor if he had wanted to, my father, but he never wanted to get into politics, he just wanted to control it from behind, and maybe what he imagined for his sons was a future as owners of large estancias, as senators or caudillos, but his sons went in a different direction—and Luca, after their confrontation over the factory, never wanted to see him or even step in this house ever again."

Both sons had inherited from their grandfather Bruno a country mistrust and a taste for machines. They started working in his company at a very early age. "My grandfather," Sofía said, "when he retired from the railroad, he was a representative for Massey Harris. They expanded the workshop behind the house, on Mitra Street. That's how it all began. You must have heard the legend of the neighborhood chicken coop..."

"Yes," Renzi said, "they welded at night, with the blowpipe, and the chickens from next door watched the whole time, dazzled by the light, maddened and drunk, their eyes like gold coins in the dark. They'd jump around, the chickens, clucking, stunned by the whiteness of the welding machine, as if an electric sun had come out at night..."

"Drugged," Sofía said. "Cluck, cluck. The chickens doped by the glare, when they put a corrugated fence up to keep in the glow from the welding blowpipe, the chickens became desperate, they'd climb the wire of the coop looking for the whiteness, they had withdrawal symptoms. I remember seeing that light when I was a girl, too, crisp as glass. We used to go to the workshop all the time, we lived with the machines, Ada and I. My brothers made us the most extraordinary toys that any girl has ever had, dolls that could walk on their own, or dance as if they were alive, with gears and wires connected to a tape recorder, dolls that talked in Argentine slang, they'd make them look like showgirls, which would drive our my mother crazy. Once they made me a Wonder Woman that could fly, she'd circle above the patio like a bird, I'd guide her with a fishing reel, I could make her go around in the air, red and white, with stars and stripes, so beautiful I could barely breathe. My sister and I adored our brothers, we followed them everywhere, they used to take us to the dances with them (my sister with Lucio, me with Luca), my sister and I wearing high heels and make-up, pretending we were a couple of night girls from town out with our boyfriends, we'd go to the dances in the area, the neighborhood clubs, the dance floor they set up on the paleta courts with the colorful lights and a band on a platform playing tropical music, until our mother intervened and ended the party right then and there—that party anyway."

10

They headed out of town in Croce's car, at midnight, on a side road that bordered the district line, toward Tapalqué. They drove across the countryside, avoiding the fences and the still animals. The moon was occasionally covered by the clouds, so Croce would use the searchlight attached to his side of the car, a bright bulb with a handle that could be adjusted by hand. All of a sudden, in the illuminated circle, they saw a rabbit, paralyzed by fear, white, motionless—like an apparition in the middle of the dark. Caught in the light beam, it was a target in the night[21] that they quickly left behind. They drove for several hours, bumping along because of the pits in the road, staring at the silver lines of the wire fences under the stars. Finally, turning off at a wooded path, they saw a glow from the lighted window of a country house in the distance. By the time they reached the source and were getting close to the small house, dawn was starting to break on the horizon, turning everything a pinkish hue. Renzi got out and opened the gate so the car could enter and go down a narrow road surrounded by bushes.

---

21   Ten years after the events narrated in this story, on the eve of the Malvinas War, Renzi saw in *The Guardian* that English soldiers were equipped with infrared glasses that allowed them to see in the dark and fire at targets in the night. As he read this, Renzi remembered that night in the country with the paralyzed rabbit in the beam of the searchlight from Croce's car, and realized that the war was lost before it had begun.

A peasant was sitting on a bench under the house eaves, drinking *mate*. A patrol officer was dozing off nearby, leaning back against a tree.

The sorrel was in the field next to the house, covered with a plaid blanket, and one of its legs was bandaged. The man on the bench was the horse's keeper, an ex-broncobuster named Huergo or Uergo, Hilario Huergo. A dark gaucho, tall and thin, he smoked and smoked as he watched the two men approach.

"How do you do, Don Croce?"

"Cheers, Hilario," Croce said. "So, what happened here?"

"A misfortune," he spoke, and smoked. "He asked me to come," he said. "When I got here he had already done it." He kept smoking. "Yeah," he said, pensively. "In his religion it's allowed."

"No, you're not allowed to kill," Croce said.

"Have respect for him, Inspector. He was a good person. He had the one misfortune. No one feels pity for the guilty," he stated after a while.

Croce paced back and forth. Like always, he was postponing the moment when he would have to go in and see a dead body. He peeked in and came back out.

"He said something to you about the American," Croce said.

"He left a letter, I haven't opened it. It's where he put it, by the window."

The house had a packed, dirt floor and was lit by a dim lamp, fading with the light of dawn. There was a stove to one side, unlit. On the other side, lying on a foldout bed under a woven blanket, was el Chino Arce. On a mat next to the deceased, Hilario had put a few weeds in a pitcher. A country wake, Renzi thought. A locust jumped out of the pitcher, rubbed its eyes with its antennas, and jumped on el Chino's yellowish face. Renzi shooed it away with his handkerchief, and the insect hopped off toward the stove. In the dead man's hands, as if it were a holy card, Hilario had placed a photograph of the jockey sitting on his horse on the runway before a race at the track in La Plata.

"He used a shotgun. He was so short he was able to lean the barrel against his mouth and shoot standing up," Hilario said, with a strong country accent. The shotgun was off to one side, resting carefully against the leather seat of a small stool.

They uncovered the dead man and saw that he was wearing country trousers, a flowered shirt, and a scarf around his neck. He was a yellow gaucho, all dressed up, his right foot bare with a gunpowder burn on its big toe. They could have killed him and made it look like a suicide, with the shotgun and all, Croce thought. Maybe he was choked, he added in his thoughts, but when he removed the scarf from the dead man's neck, Croce saw that there were no marks there, except for the shot on the roof of his mouth where his brains had been blown out. That was probably why Hilario had put a scarf there, to cover the site of the wound.

"He killed himself there," Hilario said, "standing next to his little foldout bed, and I fixed him up. He wasn't a Christian, you know, that's why I covered the Virgin."

In the letter el Chino left the horse to Hilario, asking him to take care of it, and feed it fresh alfalfa and run it every day. He reminded Hilario to tend to the horse's recovering broken leg, the horse wasn't supposed to walk on rocks or wet ground. There was no mention of who had hired him to kill Durán. The letter implied that he had done it to buy the animal, but it didn't say who had told him what he was supposed to do, or why he had killed himself.

"He was very bitter," Hilario said. "Neurasthenic."

The word, spoken by this man, sounded like a definitive diagnosis.

The jockey, then, had been paid to kill Durán, but he had only taken as much money as he needed to buy the horse. He was scared, when he saw his photograph in the newspaper he thought he would be found out. He had been on the run, but in the end he had holed himself up in that partially abandoned country house and ended it all.

"He was a good person, rough but straight. He had the one misfortune. I'll tell you what happened."

The three men sat down as if they were keeping vigil, Hilario prepared a few *mates*, and they drank in a circle. So hot and bitter that Renzi burned his tongue and barely said anything the whole night.

"I was a broncobuster, first in La Blanqueda, then here in Tapalqué, until one afternoon they came with a station wagon to pick me up because word had gotten around that I was good at taming colts, I get along with horses, so they came and hired me for the Manditeguy stud farm. Race horses, or for polo. Delicate horses, very sensitive. If a horse isn't tamed right," he said, "it develops bad habits, and later when it runs it'll do all sorts of crazy things."

"Yes, you're right about that," Croce said.

"Aha," Hilario said. "Yes, that's right, but it's hard to do. That's what I was born for," he went on. "You have to get along with the animal. There's no one left who really knows how to tame a horse, Don Croce. Beating and whipping them, that won't get you anywhere. El Chino was very admired. The Menditeguy had brought him in because they'd seen him racing when he trained in Maroñas, in the Oriental Republic, he was the best. He didn't say much, but he knew how to sit on a horse, very light, very proud. Horses pick up on things like that, animals can tell right away what the rider is like. He and *Tácito* understood each other as if they'd been born together, one on top of the other, but then the misfortune happened and I was the only one who could step in. It took me six months to get the horse so el Chino could ride him again, even though he was light as a feather and gentle as a girl."

This is going to take all night, Renzi thought, already half asleep. At one point he had the feeling that he had dreamt that he was in bed with a woman, someone like the Belladona sister he'd seen at the Club. A redhead. He had always liked redheads, so it could have been another woman, Julia even, whose hair was also red. He didn't see her face, only her hair. She was naked, he was looking at her from behind, she was leaning over to tie a black shoelace at the ankle. *I'll put on my high heels so you can check out my ass*, the girl said in the dream, turning toward him. I must have asked her to walk around the room, he thought all of a sudden, waking up.

"He killed him for the horse. That's why he did it, to save the horse. The rancher from Luján, the Englishman, he was going to sell him off, to breed him, he was going to send him out to pasture, el Chino wouldn't have been able to ride him anymore. Where could he get so much money from? He thought he was lost, he was going crazy. It's all business now, they don't use horses any-more, except to race or play polo, or for the girls in the estancias to go out for a ride. A handler, just imagine, a man who knows how to lasso, halter horses, bullocks like Blind-Man Míguez, just to name one, there's none left, no one needs them anymore."

"Who came to see him?"

"I don't know, he went to town and met a man who's not from around here, I wasn't there when he set it up. One day he just showed up with the money. I didn't find out how. He'd come, he'd go, drink a few quick *mates*, have a smoke, he was all worked up, he wanted to lose weight so he could ride the horse without the horse realizing that anyone was even on him. He started taking pills around then, Actemin, the kind of garbage that jockeys take to keep from eating, because they always have problems with the scales. El Chino wasn't usually like that, he was always light as a frog, but now he didn't want to weigh anything at all, he didn't want to put any extra pressure on the sorrel because of its broken leg." He tells it all tangled up, Renzi thought, as if we already knew what he was talking about, or as if we had been there. There was a moment of silence. Hilario, like any good storyteller, left blanks and didn't spell out the connections. "He was such a high-quality three-year-old racehorse," he went on, "that even the price that el Chino paid for him was fair, high as it was. Very unusual too, because of the bad leg." Renzi realized that he'd fallen asleep again and had missed part of the story. It was strange being there, sitting in that room with the dead man, the dim lamp lit even though it was already daylight, the burnt smell from the small stove to heat water, it all kept making him sleepy. Anyway, everything the man was saying was about the horse, up one side and down the other, as if he were putting together a puzzle, Hilario the gaucho.

"*Tácito*, whose father's father was *Congreve*, fast as a light. In his debut at Palermo he got the fastest time any horse has ever gotten in a thousand-meter debut. Better than *Penny Post*, better than *Embrujo*, better than all of them. To el Chino's merit, I would add, because a horse runs with the courage and the brains of its jockey, especially when it first debuts and doesn't have any experience yet. He had a unique style, el Chino did," he said. "He'd lean forward from the very beginning of the race, as if he was already at full speed from the start. Well, you know," he added, as if they knew, "he won his first five races, then the misfortune. We had the accident at the San Isidro Stakes, with the colts."

There was another silence. Renzi, thinking that he liked Hilario's use of the plural, felt as if he was going to fall asleep again, but strangely the extended silence woke him up.

"What year was that?" he asked, just to say something.

"1970. That was the San Isidro Stakes of 1970."

Renzi wrote the date in his small notebook, trying to shake the feeling of being under water. He thought he had fallen asleep and that in his sleep he had murmured something and that, in his dream, he had sleepwalked to the car so he could lie down in the backseat. But no, he was still there.

"The difference between a good jockey and a great one is courage. A jockey has to decide if he and his horse can squeeze through an opening of a certain size, without knowing before entering if it will be big enough. El Chino tried to slide between the posts and got caught. It happened at the bend by the hill, they were coming around in a group, he tried to pass on the inside but got pressed into the fence and the horse broke its leg. El Chino didn't get killed by sheer luck, he was laid out on the track. The other horses ran over him but he survived, unscathed." Renzi liked that the man used that word, unscathed. "El Chino's horse was on the ground, breathing heavily from the pain, foaming, its eyes wide with fear. El Chino petted him and spoke to him and didn't leave his side until the ambulance arrived. It was his fault, he tried to pass on the inside when there wasn't enough space, he rushed it, apparently the horse hesitated but of course it pushed through anyway when el Chino urged him on. He was very noble, that horse. They took him to the stables and laid him down on the grass and the veterinarian said that he had to be sacrificed, but Chino went crazy and wouldn't allow it. Those hours when they went back and forth trying to decide if they were going to finish off the horse were so intense that el Chino's life *and* character were altered. He stayed by his horse and convinced the doctors that he'd take care of him, and they cured him. He stayed with his horse the entire time, by the time they took him back to the farm el Chino was a changed man, by the time they took him back he was already the man you see lying there now: resolved, hobbled by a fixed idea, the only thing he wanted was for the animal to run again, and he did it. It was a metamorphosis, a metempsychosis between man and horse," Renzi heard, and he thought that he had fallen asleep again and that he dreamed that a gaucho was using these words. "That's what I mean when I say that it wasn't that anyone convinced him to buy the horse. He simply believed that he had to. Neither the buyer nor the seller, the animal itself seemed to tell him, and el Chino believed it with such determination it was impossible for anyone to argue with him, even less to refuse him." Renzi thought he was still dreaming. "And that," Hilario said, "is not because he was an exceptional jockey, as he could have been if he'd kept racing on the best racetracks, he already had terrific statistics that first season. No. It was because an affinity of the heart developed between man and animal, to such an extent that if el Chino wasn't there the horse wouldn't budge, it would just stand still and not let anyone else come close or feed him, much less ride him. First, he managed to save him, then he managed to get him to start walking again, then he started riding him, and slowly he taught him to race again, on three legs just about, because it can barely set its front left leg down. It's lame in one leg, but it runs so fast you can't even tell how bad off it is. Soon el Chino started pushing him to do short distances and finally he raced him again, not in the big racetracks of course, but in the country races, with the illusion of seeing him remain undefeated, even if its step was uneven and it ran with a gangly style, it was still always faster than any other horse. He'd win and bet and save his winnings, he wanted to save enough money to buy him, but he never could because the Englishman, the rancher from Luján, set such an impossible price, it was like one of those English jokes no one understands. At least six times its value, and he'd threaten to have him sent to the stud farm for breeding, to take him out of action, so el Chino did what he did to get the money and buy the animal. By the time you found out about him, Inspector, he was already lost. He came to see me, he asked me to take care of the horse because he knows me and he knows that I know how to treat the horse, and he left him with me. That night I had gone to town to have a drink and when

I got back he'd already done it. He knew I'd take care of the horse, that's why he left him to me, and that's why he came to my house to kill himself. Someone offered him the money, someone who knew his story, and he went and did it. I know there's no excuse for killing another man, but I'm explaining it to you, Inspector, so you'll understand his actions—even if that doesn't justify them." Hilario paused for a longer time, and stared out into the countryside. "He disappeared for a few days and when he came back, he had the horse with him. I didn't see how, he told me he'd won some bets and had gotten the money that way. He didn't tell me how he did it. As if once he'd done it, it didn't matter anymore how he'd done it. He left him to me, and now I'm not sure what I'm going to do with him. Because the animal is very intelligent, he understands that something's happened, he hasn't moved in over twenty-four hours."

They remained quiet, looking at the horse, grazing out in the field. Near a spring, off to the side, an *evil light* appeared between the bushes, a bright phosphorescence that seemed to burn like a white flame in the plains. It was a lost soul, the sad presence of a spirit dragging its livid brightness along. The men watched in respectful silence.

"Must be him," Hilario said.

"The skeleton of a gaucho," the officer said in a low voice, from a distance.

"Just the bones of some animal," Croce said.

They said their goodbyes and got back in the car. Renzi learned years later that the countryman Hilario Huergo, the horse tamer, had ended up in the twilight of his life working with el Chino's horse, *Tácito*, in the Rivero Brothers Circus. Huergo the Gaucho, as he would then be known, came up with an extraordinary number, which they performed as the circus toured around the countryside. He'd mount the sorrel and they'd raise them up to the heights of the tent with a system of pulleys and harnesses, to make it look as if they were floating in the air. The animal's legs rested on four iron discs covering only the rings of its hooves, and since the wires and the sheaves were painted black, it seemed as if the man was riding up to the sky on the back of the sorrel. When they got to the very top, everyone would look on in silence, and Huergo the Gaucho would whisper to the horse and look down into the darkness and the clear circle of sand on the ground below, small as a coin. Then they'd set off a round of colorful fireworks and up in the heights, dressed all in black, with a tall-brimmed hat and a pointed beard, Huergo would look like Lucifer himself riding on the majestic horse. They always did the same fantastic number, the same man who'd been a great broncobuster, motionless now on the sorrel, up above everything, with the wind flapping in the canvas of the tent—until one night some sparks from the fireworks hit the horse in the eye and the frightened animal reared up on its hind legs, and Huergo held on to the reins, knowing he wouldn't be able to set the horse back down on the iron rings. Then, as if it were all part of the number, Huergo took off his hat and waved his arm up high, and he came flying down and crashed into the ring below. But this happened—rather: Renzi was told about it—many years later. That night, when they got back to town, Renzi noticed that Croce looked grief-stricken, as if he blamed himself for el Chino's death. He'd made a number of decisions that had led to a series of events, which he hadn't been able to predict. Croce was pensive on the way back, he spent the entire drive moving his lips, as if he were talking to himself, or arguing with someone, until finally they reached town, and Renzi said goodnight and got out at the hotel.

11

The news that Croce had found Durán's murderer, dead in a small house near Tapalqué, surprised everyone. It seemed like another of his acts of conjuration that lay at the foundation of his fame.

"The witnesses saw a small, short man go in and out of the room, slightly yellowish, and they thought it was Dazai," Croce explained. He reconstructed the crime on a blackboard with maps and diagrams. This is the hallway, here's the bathroom, this is where the witnesses saw him come out. He drew an x on the board. "The murderer's name was Anselmo Arce, he was born in the District of Maldonado, he trained in the racetrack in Maroñas and made it as a jockey in La Plata, he was an excellent rider, very much valued. He raced in Palermo and in San Isidro, but he got in trouble and ended up racing country races in the Province. I have the letter, here, where he confesses what he did. He killed himself. He wasn't murdered, we presume he committed suicide," Croce concluded. "We've discovered that they used the hotel's old service lift to lower the money. We found a fifty-dollar bill on the floor there. It was a crime for hire; the investigation remains open. What's important, as always, is what happens after the crime is committed. The consequences are more important than the causes." He seemed to know more than he was saying.

According to Croce, a hired killing was the greatest innovation in the history of crime. The murderer doesn't know the victim, there's no contact, no connections, no relationship, all traces are erased. This was such a case. The motive was being studied. The key, he had concluded, was to locate the instigator. Finally, he handed out a copy of the jockey's letter, written in a neat and very clear hand. It was a piece of paper from a notebook, actually an old sheet from one of those large ledgers used in the estancias. On top, in round, English cursive, it said *Debits* and *Credits*. Good place to write a suicide note, Renzi thought. When he turned the sheet over, he saw a few notes written in a different hand: *tether 1.2, crackers 210, herb for* mate *3 kg, ox halter*—there was no number after that last item. At the bottom of the list was a sum for the total. He thought it was strange that they had photo-copied the back of the page, too. When one tries to solve a crime, everything eventually makes sense, the investigation slows over irrelevant details which, at first, don't seem to play a role. The bag in the storage room, the fifty-dollar bill on the ground, a jockey who kills for a horse. *I'm afraid I've disgraced myself over a man I don't know. I also take this opportunity to note that I'm responsible for two other deaths, a policeman in Tacuarembó, in the Oriental Republic of Uruguay, and a cowhand in Tostado, in the province of Santa Fe. Every man has his faults and I have plenty of my own. My last will is that my horse be given to my friend, Don Hilario Huergo. I hope I may have better fortune in the next world as I give myself to the Lord. Goodbye, My Country, Goodbye my friends. My name is Anselmo Arce, everyone calls me el Chino.*

"Country folk are all psychotics, they ride on their horses all day long, lost in their own thoughts, and kill whoever crosses them," the reporter who covered Rural News for *La Prensa* said, laughing. "One time a gaucho fell in love with a cow, what can I say? Some guy from Corrientes, he ended up following the cow around everywhere."

"You should have seen the small country house where he died," Renzi said. "And the wake without any people, just the horse out in the field."

"Oh, he took you with him," Bravo said. "You better watch out, or you'll end up writing *The Cases of Inspector Croce*."

"That wouldn't be so bad," Renzi said.

The next day, Cueto filed a court order to requisition the evidence from Croce. Croce replied that the case was closed, but that the remaining evidence couldn't be turned over to the Prosecutor until the motive of the crime had been determined. That a new case should be opened to seek out the instigator. The murderer had been found, but not the originating cause. Cueto immediately decreed what he called a preventative measure and demanded that the money be deposited at once with the court.

"What money?" Croce said.

For days this was a joke that everyone in town repeated. Everyone used the phrase as a default. Regardless of the question asked, the answer was always:

What money?

In any case, Croce refused, he defied the summons to hand over the money, using as a shield the need to keep crucial aspects of the investigation in the hands of the police. His idea was to wait until the owner of the money showed up for it. Or until someone showed up to claim it.

He was right, but he wasn't allowed to carry out his plan because they wanted to smother the affair and shut down the case. Maybe Yoshio had left the bag filled with the money in the storage room of the hotel, Cueto argued, because he planned to go back and get it once everything calmed down. If the murderer had taken the money for himself, the case would be closed. If it could be proven that the money was destined for someone else, the affair remained open.

At this point Cueto convinced Saldías to turn against Croce. He intimidated him, he made promises, he bribed him—no one ever knew how exactly. Whatever the case, Saldías issued a statement in which he declared that Croce had the money hidden in a closet, and that the Inspector had been behaving strangely in recent weeks.

Saldías betrayed him, that was the truth of it. Croce had loved him like a son (of course Croce loved everyone like a son, because he didn't really know what that feeling was like). People remembered that there had been some tensions and some differences about procedures, and of course Saldías was part of a new generation of criminology. Even if he admired Croce, the Inspector's investigative methods were not, to his way of thinking, proper or sufficiently "scientific"—which is why, he said, he agreed to give a statement about Croce's irregular behavior and his eccentric methods. He doesn't use proper criteria in his investigations, Saldías declared. He was probably looking for a promotion and needed Croce to be retired. And that's what happened.

Cueto made a number of comments about old country police-men and a new redistribution that fell under his judicial over-sight, and everyone in town understood, with a certain amount of sadness, that things didn't look good for Croce. Soon an order came from the Province's Chief of Police and Croce was moved into retirement. Immediately Saldías was appointed as the new Municipal Inspector. The money that Durán had brought to town was requisitioned and sent to the court in La Plata, the Capital of the Province.

After Croce was retired his behavior became even more bizarre. He shut himself up in his house and stopped doing the things he always used to do: no more morning rounds ending in the Madariaga Tavern, no more walks through town, no more being the main presence at the police station. Luckily, everything in the house where he'd always lived was in order, so they couldn't evict him until the inquiry was complete. People saw him in his yard at night, but no one knew what he was doing. He'd walk around in the dark with his little mutt, which would whine and bark as if it were asking for help.

Madariaga came by one afternoon to say hello but Croce didn't want to see him. He came out wearing an overcoat and a scarf and waved and made other gestures with his hands, which Madariaga didn't understand very well. Croce seemed to be trying to say, with hand signals, that he was okay and that they should stop bother-ing him. He locked the front door to the house and Madariaga, outside, was unable to go in after him.

After this Croce started writing anonymous letters. He wrote them by hand, altering his handwriting slightly, as he'd probably seen criminals do at some point. He'd leave them secretly on park benches in the main square, under a few pebbles so the wind wouldn't blow them away. He had the facts, he knew what had happened. The letters spoke repeatedly about the Belladona brothers and the factory. The anonymous notes became famous in town, everyone very quickly found out what they said and started speculating about their origin. *They want Luca to be thrown out of the building of the factory so they can sell the plant and build a commercial center there*, the letters said, in short, with slight variations. So the versions about Luca resurfaced, that he had called Tony, that Croce had gone out to see him, that he owed a lot of money. The stories flowed like water sneaks under the door in a flood. A few times the town had flooded when the nearby lake had overflowed. Now, the anonymous letters and the gossip were having the same effect. Several days passed before anyone said anything and then, one afternoon, when Croce showed up and started handing out his letters to people as they were coming out of church, they put him in the asylum. There might not be a school in a town like this, Croce said, but there's always a mental hospital.

Renzi listened as he ate dinner at the hotel restaurant. Everyone talked about the case, spinning different theories and reconstructing the events in their own way. The dining room was big, with tablecloths on the tables, floor lamps, all laid out in a traditional style. Renzi had published several articles supporting Croce's position about the case, and the turn of events had confirmed his suspicions. He didn't know what would happen next, he might have to return to Buenos Aires, he was being told by his newspaper that the story had lost interest. Renzi was thinking about this, eating a shepherd's pie and slowly finishing off a bottle of El Vasquito wine, when he saw Cueto enter the room. After saying hello to several of the customers and receiving what appeared to be pats on the back and congratulations, he walked over to Renzi's table. Cueto stood next to the table, without sitting, and spoke to him almost without looking at him, with his condescending and snobbish attitude.

"Still around here, Mr. Renzi." He used the formal address to let him know that he came to talk to him about a serious matter. "The case is solved, there's no need to keep going over it. It'll be better for you if you leave, my friend." He threatened him as if he were doing him a favor. "I don't like what you write," he told him, smiling.

"I don't either," Renzi said.

"Don't stick your nose where it doesn't belong." He was speaking now with the careless, cold tone that thugs use in the movies—which, according to Renzi, had taught everyone in the countryside to sound worldly, like wise guys. "It'll be better for you if you leave—"

"I was thinking about leaving, actually. But now I think I'll stick around a few more days," Renzi said.

"Don't get cute with me. We know exactly who you are."

"I'm going to quote this conversation."

"As you wish," Cueto smiled at him. "I'm sure you know what you're doing."

He walked toward the exit, stopped at another table to greet people there, and left the restaurant.

Renzi was surprised, Cueto had taken the trouble to come over and intimidate him, it was very strange. He went to the counter and asked to use the telephone.

"It's like a UFO," he explained to Benavídez, the newsroom secretary at *El Mundo*. "There's a bag full of money, it's really a weird story. I'm staying."

"I can't authorize that, Emilio."

"Don't fuck with me, Benavídez, I have a scoop here."

"What scoop?"

"They're putting the screw on me."

"So?"

"Croce's in the mental hospital, I'm going to see him tomorrow."

It sounded confusing when he tried to explain it, so he asked to speak with his friend Junior, in charge of special investigations. After a few jokes and long explanations, Renzi convinced Junior to let him stay a few more days in the town. The decision was a good one, because all of a sudden the story changed—and so did his situation.

The light in the cell went out at midnight, but Yoshio couldn't sleep. He was lying still on the mattress, trying to remember as precisely as possible every detail of the last day that he was free. He carefully reconstructed the events, from Thursday at noon, when he accompanied Tony to the barbershop, to the fatal moment on Friday afternoon with the loud knocks on his door when they came to arrest him. He could see Tony sitting on the nickel-plated chair, covered with a white towel, facing the mirror, and López lathering his face. The radio was on, "La oral deportiva" was playing, the broadcasters recapping the latest score lines, it must have been two o'clock. Yoshio realized that reconstructing every detail of that day would take him an entire day. Or maybe more. You need more time to remember than to live, he thought. For example, that last day, at six in the morning, he was sitting on one of the benches in the station and Tony was showing him a dance step that was very popular back in his country. *The Crab Dance*, it was called. With great agility, Tony would move backwards in his white shoes, keeping the rhythm, dancing backwards, his heels together, his hands on his knees. It had been a very happy moment. Tony moving to the beat of an imaginary song, leaning forward, his elbows out as if he were rowing, moving back elegantly. They were in the empty train station, dawn had already broken, the sky was very clear, blue, the tracks shone in the sun. And Tony smiled, a little agitated after his dance. They liked going to the station because it was usually deserted and they could imagine that they might take a train and go somewhere, anytime. All of a sudden, a dead bird fell on the platform. With a dry, muffled *plop*. Out of nowhere. From the immense empty sky. It was a very clear day, peaceful and white. The bird must have suffered a heart attack mid-flight and fallen dead on the ground. An ordinary bird. Not a hummingbird, which can fly in place in front of a flower, miraculously, flapping its wings in such a frenzy that they die, sometimes, because their heart fails them. Not a hummingbird, nor one of those featherless pigeons seen on the ground sometimes, the ones that take a while to die, opening their red beaks, their necks featherless, their eyes enormous as if they were the thirsty mouths of tiny Argentine babies. It was a *chingolo*, a rufous-collared sparrow, perhaps, or a *cabecita negra*, a hooded siskin, lying there dead, its body intact. The strangest thing was that a flock of similar birds started to circle overhead and squawk and fly lower and lower over the dead bird. The birds' joint horror before one of their own species, dead. It was a premonition, maybe, his mother could read the future in the flight patterns of migratory birds, she'd move like a frightened sparrow, her small feet under her blue kimono. She'd go out to the patio and watch the swallows flying in triangle formation and announce what they could expect that winter.

Yoshio was unable to organize his memories in the order in which the events had occurred. The sound of the water in the pipes, the muffled complaints of the prisoners in the nearby cells. He had a nearly physical awareness of the tomb in which he was buried and of the anxious murmur of the dreams and nightmares of the hundreds of men sleeping between those walls. He could imagine the corridors, the barred doors, the different blocks. From the patio he could hear the strumming of a guitar and a voice singing a few lines. *From the school of pain I have drawn my lessons / From the school of pain I have drawn my lessons...*

Yoshio felt sick, he heard voices and singing because he'd suddenly stopped smoking opium. He remembered the pipe he'd calmly prepared and smoked, laying on his tatami that last morning. He'd fallen asleep to the quiet sweetness of the flame burning on the tip of the bamboo pipe. When you're on the drug, giving it up seems easy, but when you're sick with withdrawal, your entire body burns and you'll do anything for it. Had he been able to reduce his whole life down to a single decision, it would be to quit the drug. He wasn't an addict, but he couldn't quit. He was afraid they'd tempt him by promising him a fix and forcing him to sign the confession that the Prosecutor had shown him several times.

It was already written out, it said that he confessed to killing Durán. He was able to get codeine pills in the prison, he took them whenever he felt as if he were dying. It was like a burning, although the word didn't do justice to the pain. He was obsessed with the thought that his father might think that his job at the hotel was a woman's job, that he'd betrayed the traditions of his race. His father had died a hero. He, on the other hand, was lying in that pit, moaning because he did not have his opium. If he'd done his job dressed as a woman, he thought all of a sudden, maybe they wouldn't have accused him and he wouldn't be in jail now. He could see himself dressed in a blue kimono with red flowers, rice powder on his face, his eyebrows plucked, taking small, little steps as he slid down the hallways of the hotel.

Tony's death hurt Yoshio more than his own fate. *An owner next door*, he heard the man singing in the distance. *The neighbor next door / they killed one of his workers / they put the blame on me / and did me in at the trial.* Everyone in jail was innocent. That's why Yoshio refused to speak with the other prisoners. He'd had his visit by the court-appointed lawyer assigned to his defense. One afternoon they took him from his cell and escorted him to the office of the prison warden. The lawyer—a fat, unshaven, dirty-looking man—didn't bother to take a seat, he seemed in a hurry to tend to other, more important matters. Yoshio, handcuffed, wearing prison garb, listened, dispirited. "Look, mister, it'll be better for you if you make a deal and accept the terms, your sentence will be shorter that way. This is the offer from the Prosecutor's office. If you sign, you'll be out in a few years, otherwise they'll accuse you of premeditated murder and intended malice, and you'll get stuck with life. There's not much choice in the matter, all the evidence and the witnesses are against you. It won't be much fun for you if you don't make a deal, my dear." He was telling him for his own good, but Yoshio refused. So he was sent to a block with prisoners awaiting their sentences, and of course no one had done anything more since he'd been put in there. And now he was in hell, waiting, hearing the voice of someone who seemed to be singing in a dream. *A prisoner doesn't know which way / the scales will tip, / but waiting makes no sense / this much I know: / any man who enters here / leaves all hope behind...*

Yoshio lit a match and with the match he lit a candle resting on a tin jar. The light flickered off and back again. In the semi-darkness he searched for a small hand-mirror, a woman's item that they let him keep on the pretext that he needed to shave, although he never needed to shave. He had it for his secret vices. Lying on the bed, he looked at his lips in the mirror. A small, womanly mouth. He began to masturbate, looking at himself. He moved the image very slowly. His face reflected back to him in fragments, white skin, plucked eyebrows, he stopped on his ice-cold eyes. He barely needed to touch himself, he felt as if another were looking at him, devoted, servile...

"We barely saw them until we finished high school, because by that point they'd already opened the factory and it was far away from town, and we'd gone to study in La Plata. That was in 1962. My grandfather used part of his wealth to buy the land, near the provincial highway, in an area that wasn't anything then, but it's worth a fortune now. My grandfather died before the factory was finished, my brother kept building

and working as if he was keeping a promise to a dead man.

"Right away they started making money, growing and expanding, towards the end they had almost a hundred workers at the plant, they paid the best wages in the Province, the Belladona Brothers. They went to Cincinnati to buy some expensive machinery, the latest of the latest, and that was the beginning of the end. Suddenly everything started to collapse, the government devalued the peso, the economic policies drastically changed course. The interest on their debts in dollars became impossible, and my father, to save him, as he said, took a shortcut, he tricked one of his own sons, I should say. To save the investment—again, as he said—my father convinced Lucio to set up a public corporation and to negotiate away the preferred stocks, until my brother lost control of the company. One night my brother came to the house with a gun, looking for my father, he wanted to kill him."

"Yes, yes. I heard about that."

"He was blind with anger," Sofía said. "He was looking for my father, he wanted to kill him," she repeated, and got up again and walked around the balcony, anxiously. "He howled like a hungry wolf, poor thing...[22]

---

22   Croce found Luca crouched next to the closed gate outside the large Belladona house, waiting for the right moment to go in and kill his father. The Old Man had turned the outside lights on, locked all the doors, and called the police. The Inspector went up to Luca, very relaxed, as if he was just running into him by chance. Even though he was very wound up, Luca was so respectful and so polite that he said hello to the Inspector and started talking to him about lost oxen, one hand behind his back, hiding the gun. *You're going to keep fighting with him, whether you kill him or not*, Croce said to him all of a sudden. Before long he'd talked him down. Luca wanted to hand the gun over to Croce, but the Inspector told him that it wasn't necessary. *Whether or not you give me the gun now, you can still kill him later.* The two hypotheticals that Croce mentioned and his show of trust were enough to finish calming Luca down. He got back in his car and nervously backed away from the house. When he drove by the lake Luca threw the gun in the water, "so he wouldn't be tempt-

"Some men," she went on, "can survive anything, the worst catastrophes, any suffering, you could say, because they have an absolute conviction and an unbelievable amount of sympathy. A light deep in their eyes that shines on everyone around them, an ability to inspire feeling—no, no, it's not feeling. Understanding. That's how Luca is. Anyone else who'd faced what my brother had to face would have caved in, but not him. It's something else, he's obsessed, he can block out the world and keep pursuing the light of perfection until in the end, eventually, he hits up against reality. Because reality is what muzzles you," she said. "Reality waits for you and reins you in. Luca got into debt, he took a mortgage out on the plant, but he didn't let them sell the factory. He fought against bankruptcy, he started doing whatever he could."

"He shut himself up in the factory."

"He went to live in the factory—it was the light of all his illusions, his hope for survival—and he never came out again."

---

ed by the Devil."

12

The mental hospital was well outside the town, in a circular arrangement originally used as a convent. Standing on its own at the end of the road leading to the bluff, it looked isolated, rising over the hill, near the lake and the sown fields to the west, like a mirage in the deserted plains. There was a stone wall around the property, lined with broken glass, and a tall door with iron spikes. Renzi walked in and across a large lawn. As he advanced up the graveled path, he looked at the whitewashed trunks of the trees, barer and taller the closer he got to the building. Finally, he reached the large front door, and after a while an orderly let him in. The rooms for the women were toward the back; in the men's block there were only three patients.

Croce sat on an iron bed secured to the floor, leaning back against a mattress that he had rolled-up, dressed in a gray robe that made him look older. He wore a wool cap on his head and his eyes were bloodshot, as if he hadn't been sleeping. Behind him, two other patients stood and faced each other. They seemed to be playing some kind of silent game, with hand and finger signs.

It took Croce a moment to say hello. At first Renzi thought that he didn't recognize him.

"Saldías sent you," he said. It sounded like a question, but it was a statement.

"No, not at all. I haven't seen him," Renzi said. "How are you, Inspector?"

"Not good." He looked at Renzi as if he didn't remember who he was. "I think I'll stay here for a few days, get some rest, then we'll see. Every once in a while you need to spend some time in the nuthouse, or in jail, to understand what this country is all about. I've already been in jail, years ago. I think I'll take a break here now." He smiled, a sparkle in his eyes. "They suspect dementia."

Renzi had brought him two packs of Avanti cigarettes, a can of peaches in their own juice, and a rotisserie chicken from the Madariaga Store and Tavern. Croce put everything in an apple-crate he had pushed up against the wall, which he was using for storage. Renzi saw that inside he had a shaving brush, soap, and a razor without blades.

"Listen, kid," Croce said. "Don't pay any attention to what people say about me in town. I can just hear those idiots talking." He touched his forehead with his finger and smiled a smile that lit up his face. "Did you see my little notes? I've written two more." He looked inside the rolled-up mattress and took out two sealed envelopes. "Mail these for me, will you?"

"But there's no address on them."

"It doesn't matter, drop them in the mailbox in the main square. I'm going to get those shits. And that Judas, Saldías, what do you make of him? To think I actually liked him. I must be some kind of idiot. He accused me of drawing conclusions that weren't scientific enough. So I ask him: 'What do you mean by that?' And he answers: 'They're not deductions, it's all intuition.'" Croce smiled mischievously. "Fools, the bunch of them. But I'm not complaining, if you complain in here you never get out." He lowered his voice. "I unlocked a laundering scheme that was being used to transfer secret funds to open channels, so they could keep everything. That's why Durán was killed, to redirect the money, or to squirrel it away. It's older than Methuselah. But the dollar bills were unmarked and I declared it all, and they're not going to forgive me for that. If you find a clean hundred thousand dollars and don't take it, you're made out to be dangerous, they know that you can't be trusted. Same thing happened to el Chino Arce, he only took what he needed, he left the rest behind in that bag with the abandoned luggage. And when he saw the trouble coming his way, he had to kill himself, poor kid, he got involved with some real heavies. Now they're waiting for me to do the same thing, but I'm going to get them. Instead of writing posthumous letters, I'm writing my last letters." He smiled. "They're all addressed to the judge. There's nothing worse than being a judge. Much better to be a cop, although I'm sorry about that, too. I spent my life ridding the Province of all the political caudillos and ended up more alone than Robinsón," he said, placing an accent on the last syllable of Crusoe's name, as if he were trying to rhyme the end of a line. "One time, in the town of Azul, I sent an Italian to jail for killing his wife, but he turned out to be innocent, the woman had been killed by some random drunkard. He spent six months in the penitentiary, that man, and I've never been able to forget him. When he got out, he seemed lost, he never recovered.

Another time I mowed down this little thief in Las Lomas, he'd locked himself in a country house with a hostage, a farmer who cried like a little baby, I used a mattress as a cover and charged in, killed the thief with one shot, poor kid—and the farmer, the hostage, he got out just fine, except that he'd messed himself. That's what happens. We live in pain and shit. My father was an Inspector and he went mad, my brother was killed in '56, I'm an ex-Inspector and here I am. One time I was so desperate I went into a church, I had gone to Rauch with a rustler, the guy begged me to let him go, he said he had two baby boys, what can I tell you? I left him in the prison and went for a long walk, I couldn't get that gaucho out of my head, he carried a photo of his two little darlings with him, that's what he called them, his little darlings. So I crossed the street and walked into a church, and that's where I made a promise that I hope I'll always be able to keep." He paused, thinking. "I don't know why I remember those things, certain ideas stick in my head, like hooks, they don't let me think properly." He stopped again, his expression seemed to change. "I came here," he said, with a wicked look in his eye, "because I want Cueto to think that I'm out of circulation. You have to help me." He lowered his voice even further and gave him some instructions. Renzi jotted down a few things. Since Renzi didn't know anything about anything, he might be able to discover something—that was Croce's theory. Before, you had to know what was going to happen before it happened, now it was better to go in blind and see what came out of it, he said. Then he got distracted looking at the other patients.

The two men came over and stood near the Inspector's bed,

in the middle of the room, making gestures as if to ask Renzi for a cigarette. They would bring two fingers to their mouths and pretend they were smoking.

"In here," Croce said, "a cigarette is worth one peso in the morning and five pesos at night. The price goes up every hour you don't smoke. They're going to offer one to us, say no, thank you, and give them one of yours." They came closer to Croce's bed, the whole time pretend-smoking in the air with their fingers.

Renzi gave them a cigarette and the two men started smoking it right away, taking turns, standing near them. The fatter of the two broke a one-peso bill in half and gave half of it to the other for a drag of the cigarette. Every time they took a smoke they would give the other patient half of the bill, and when they exhaled they would take the other half of the bill back. They paid with half a bill, took a smoke, exhaled, accepted half of the bill, the other would smoke, blow out the smoke, they would pass the half-bill back, the other would smoke—and the cycle accelerated and went faster and faster as the cigarette was consumed. The end of the cigarette forced them to speed up to keep from getting burned and, finally, when it was barely an ember, they threw it on the ground and watched it go out. The last one to smoke from the cigarette demanded he be given the other half of the bill back. They started screaming at each other until an orderly appeared at the door and threatened to take them to the showers. Then they sat down facing the wall, each on a different bed, their backs to each other. Croce greeted Renzi with joy, as if he'd just realized that he was there.

"You've read my letters." He laughed. "They're dictated to me."

He pointed up to the ceiling. "I hear voices," he said, very softly. "Poets talk about that, it's like a tune in your ear that tells you what to say. Did you bring paper and pencil?"

"I did," Renzi said.

"I'm going to dictate something to you. Come on, let's take a walk."

"If I walk I can't write."

"You stop, you write, we keep walking."

They walked around the men's block, from one end to the other. Sirs, Croce dictated, I've returned to inform you that real estate speculation—but he stopped, because one of the other patients, the thin man with the pockmarked face, had stood up and come over and started walking with them, matching his step to Croce's. The other man also came over and followed their pace exactly, as if they were all marching together.

"Careful with this one," the thin man said. "He's a cop."

"He thinks he's a cop," the fat man said. "He thinks he's a police inspector."

"If he's an inspector, I'm Carlos Gardel."

"The jockey murderer should have hung himself from a bonsai."

"Exactly. Hanging like a little cake toy."

Croce stopped next to a barred window and grabbed Renzi by the arm. The other two patients stopped with them and kept talking.

"Nature has forgotten us," the fat man said.

"There is no nature anymore," the thin man said.

"No nature? Don't exaggerate. We breathe, we lose our hair, our freshness."

"Our teeth."

"And if we hang ourselves?"

"But how can we hang ourselves? They took our shoelaces, they take away the sheets."

"We can ask this young man for his belt."

"Belts are too short."

"I'll tie the belt around my neck and you can pull my legs."

"And who would pull me?"

"True, a logical dilemma."

"Sir," the thin man said, looking at Renzi. "I'll buy a cigarette from you."

"You can have one."

"No, I'll buy it," the thin man said, and handed him half a one-peso bill.

Immediately the fat man gave Renzi the other half of the bill for another cigarette. The two men stood to the side and began a different routine, one which they had apparently also repeated many times before. They took turns smoking their cigarettes, crossing their arms to hand their cigarette to the other's mouth. When the thin man blew out his smoke, the fat man would wait until he was done and then he would smoke and exhale, blowing rings. The two men smoked back and forth in this manner, without pausing, in a continuous chain. Hand, mouth, smoke, mouth, smoke, hand, mouth. They stood side by side and raised their hands to bring the cigarette to the mouth of the other, who would in turn smoke facing forward. The routine was repeated until the cigarettes were smoked down to their ends. They came back with the butts and sold them to Renzi, who returned each their half of the one-peso bill. With a few leftover crumbs of flour they had stashed in an old cookie tin, they made a paste and stuck the two halves of the bill back together until they had the whole peso again. Then they each laid down on their bed, face up, motionless, their arms crossed and their eyes open.

Croce resumed speaking with Renzi, softly.

"They're brothers, they say they're brothers," he said, nodding toward the two patients. "I live with them, here. They know who I am. Outside I would have been killed, like Tony was killed. I'm waiting to be transferred to Melchor Romero. My father died there. I used to go visit him, he'd tell me about a radio that had been installed inside his head somehow, On the inside of my skull, he used to say. Now I believe I can hear the same music."

Renzi waited while Croce sat down again, facing the window.

"Listen carefully. Cueto wanted to redirect the money, the Old Man was right about that, but Luca didn't want anything to do with it, he doesn't even want to see his father, he almost killed him one night, he blames him for the collapse of the factory, the Old Man sold the shares and when Luca found out, he went over with a gun. He blames him for the collapse." Croce suddenly grew quiet. "You better go now, I'm getting tired. Help me with this." They stretched his mattress out and Croce lied down. "It's not bad, no one can mess with you in here."

The thin man came over.

"Say, will you trade me this bill for a new one?" he asked, and handed Renzi the bill stuck together with the paste. Renzi handed him another one-peso bill and put away the repaired bill, with one half of Mitre's (or was it Belgrano's?) face upside down. The thin patient looked at the new bill, pleased.

"Let me buy a cigarette from you," he said.

Renzi's pack was nearly empty, he only had three cigarettes left. The fat man came over. Each took a cigarette and they split the third one in half, carefully. Then they split the new one-peso bill in half and started smoking and passing the half-bill back and forth. Pass the half-bill, smoke, pass the half-bill, smoke. They did everything in a very neat manner, without any hesitation, following a perfect order. Croce, lying on his bed, had fallen asleep.

Renzi walked outside. It was almost nighttime, he had to hurry if he wanted to catch the last bus back to town. Croce seemed to have entrusted him with some kind of task, as if he always needed someone to help him think clearly. Someone neutral who could be sent into reality to gather facts and clues, from which he could later formulate his conclusions. He could come visit him every afternoon and discuss with him what he'd found in town, while Croce could make his deductions without having to leave the place. Renzi had read so many detective novels that he already knew how the mechanism worked. The detective always has some-one with whom to discuss his theories. Now that Saldías was no longer around, Croce had fallen into a crisis, because when he was alone, his own thoughts were the end of him. He was always rebuilding a story that wasn't his. He doesn't have a private life and if he's given a private life, like now, he loses his mind. He goes out of his mind, Renzi heard himself say as he was getting on the bus heading back to town.

The houses on the outskirts were like all the houses in the low neighborhoods on the edge of any town or city. Handwritten signs, partially finished construction sites, kids playing ball, tropical music sounding from the open windows, nearly antique cars barely crawling along, country folk galloping on horseback on the ditch along the cobblestone road, a cart with empty bottles and cans pushed by a woman.

When the bus entered the town, the landscape changed and became a mock-up of suburban life, a series of houses with yards out front, windows with security bars, trees on the sidewalks, packed dirt alleys. Finally, coming onto the main road, which was first cobblestoned and then paved, the two-storied houses, the entry hallways with the tall doors, the television antennas on the roofs and terraces. The center of town was also the same as that of other towns, with the central square, the church and the municipality building, the pedestrian block with the shops and the music stores and the small markets. This monotony, this endless repetition, was what the people who lived there probably liked.

Renzi imagined that he, too, could move to the country, dedicate himself to his writing. Take walks around town, go to the Madariaga Store and Tavern, wait for the newspapers that arrived on the afternoon train, leave his useless life behind, become somebody else. He was in a state of waiting, he felt that something was about to change. Maybe it was his own feeling, his false wish not to return to the routine of his life in Buenos Aires, to the novel he'd been writing for years without success, to his stupid job at El Mundo, writing reviews or going out into reality every once in a while on special assignment to investigate some crime or plague.

Night had fallen over the house. They were still sitting on the chairs, out on the back porch, mostly in the dark—except for a small lamp behind them, in the living room—looking out over the peaceful back gardens and the lights beyond. After a while, Sofía got up and put a Moby Grape album on the turntable and started to move, dancing in place to "Changes."

"I like Traffic, I like Cream, I like Love," she said, and sat down again. "I love their band names and I love their music."

"I love Moby Dick."

"I'm sure you do. Take your books away from you and you'd be buck-naked. My mother's the same, the only time she's relaxed is when she's reading. As soon as she stops reading, she's a nervous mess."

"Crazy when she doesn't read, not crazy when she reads."

"See her over there? See that light across the yard?"

There was a guesthouse across the back gardens with two large, lit windows, through which one could see a woman, her white hair pulled back, reading and smoking on a leather armchair. She looked as if she were in another world. All of a sudden she took off her glasses, reached back with her right hand without looking to grab a blue book from a bookshelf out of sight. She put the page up against her face, then put her round glasses on again, settled back in the tall armchair, and kept reading.

"She reads all the time," Renzi said.

"She's the reader," Sofía said.

13

Renzi spent several days in the Municipal Archives going over documents and old newspapers. Every afternoon he'd go to the hall, cool and peaceful, while the rest of the town slept their siesta. Croce had given him several facts to look up, as if he'd assigned him a task that he couldn't do himself. The history of the Belladona family unfolded from the very origins of the place. Renzi was most impressed by the articles he read about the inauguration of the factory, in October 1961.

The director of the Archives helped him find what he was looking for, assisting him the moment she learned that the Inspector had sent him. Croce, according to her, withdrew to the asylum every so often to spend some time there, resting, she said, as if it were a resort in the mountains. The woman's name was Rosa Echeverry and she had a desk in the middle of the always-empty hall. She showed Renzi around the shelves, the boxes, and the old catalogues. She was blond and tall, wore a long dress, and used a walking stick with cheerful indifference. She'd been very beautiful and still moved with the confidence that beauty had granted her. It was surprising to see her limping, then, her kindness and happiness didn't seem to match the hardness of her pain-riddled hips. People in town said that she took morphine—small, greenish glass vials that she had delivered from La Plata, and which she picked up every month at the Mantovani Pharmacy with a prescription from Doctor Fuentes. She cooked it up herself, apparently, first opening the vials with a small serrated knife that she kept especially for this purpose, then boiling the needles in the metal box with the syringe.

She lived on a second story in the same building were the Archives were housed, in a vast attic accessed by an internal staircase. Whenever Renzi turned to look at her, she always seemed to be working on crossword puzzles in old numbers of the magazine *Vea y Lea*, or watching the canary she'd put by the back window, which was allowed to come out of its cage and peck at the spines of the bound documents.

"There's not much to do here, the readers have been dying off," she told him. "The advantage of this place is that it's more peaceful than the cemetery, even if the work is the same."

Rosa had studied history in Buenos Aires and had started teaching in a school in the town of Pompeya, but she married an estancia auctioneer and came back to town with him. Soon afterward her husband died in an accident and she ended up buried in the Archives, where no one ever came to look for anything.

"Everyone thinks they remember what happened," she said. "No one needs to find anything out from a place like this. We have a good library here, too," she added. "But in the end, I'm the only reader in here, you know. I don't follow an alphabetical order, please don't confuse me with Sartre's Autodidact," she boasted. "But I do have a system." She read a lot of biographies and memory books.

Slowly, she told Renzi her story, and he felt that a certain complicity was established between them from the beginning—a certain instant sympathy that sometimes arises between people who have just met—and that Rosa would help him find what he was looking for. People said that she was or had been Croce's lover, and that they'd sometimes spend weekends together. She invited Renzi to take a look about the place and took his arm as they walked under the awning and into the courtyard.

"One day, my dear, you're going to write a book about this town. Believe me, I know. A novel, a feature story, something you can sell to buy clothes for your kids and take a vacation with your wife. And when you do, you'll remember me, what I'm telling you. There was a family war here," she said. The most interesting thing, according to Rosa, was that the battles were always personified by specific individuals, actual men and women with faces and names who didn't know they were fighting a war. Countrymen and women who thought they were simply involved in normal family disputes or arguments among neighbors. Argentina's political history moves on the ground while events happen above like a flock of swallows migrating in winter. The residents of the town represented and repeated old stories without knowing it. Now what they had to talk about was the whole affair of the lawsuit over Luca's firm. Tony's death seemed connected to the abandoned factory. Rosa spoke with a high, serene voice, like a schoolteacher, with a touch of irony, to let Renzi know that she didn't believe everything she was saying, but enough sincerity to give her work as town archivist significance.

She saved newspapers, magazines, flyers, documents, and many family letters that people left over time. "I have, for example, an archive with all of the town's anonymous letters." It's the most important genre, she said, the annals of the worst slander of the Argentina pampas. They started the same day that the Archives were founded. You could write a history of the town just with those anonymous letters. New messages arrive all the time, they tell of intrigues, reveal secrets, and are written in the most diverse ways—with words cut out from newspapers and glued on notebook paper, or written in a shaky handwriting, probably with the opposite hand, to conceal things not worth concealing, or with old Underwood or Remington typewriters that skip a letter, or in letters printed as flyers in some small press somewhere in the Province. These documents were kept in brown boxes in a special section of the Archives, on their own shelf. She showed him the first one ever received—stuck to the door of the church on a Sunday in 1916—and read it out loud as if it were an edict.

Dear neighbors: The legislators of the Province are not defending the countryside. We must go and get them out of their houses and demand an explanation. It's easier to deceive a multitude than an individual. Sincerely, an Argentine

According to Rosa, Croce had taken up the tradition of writing anonymous letters to let people know he was dissatisfied with the turn of events and with the shady dealings of the prosecutor, Cueto. Like other times, whenever he was in the absolute minority, he had withdrawn to the local asylum and calmly begun sending his anonymous messages with his elaborate theories about events.

On several occasions Rosa had placed ads in the area newspapers asking for people to donate their collections of family photographs to the Municipal Archives. She also arranged to acquire the archives from the English railroads, the sessions of the Rural Society, and the minutes from the Automobile Club containing the records of the construction of the roads and highways in the area.

"No one else cares about these ruins, it's just me," she said, and showed him a series of well-organized and clearly-labeled boxes with negatives and developed photographs and old Kodak plates. "I've always been waiting for someone to come and dig through these remains, to give my work meaning."

Several photographs, grouped in a series, showed various images of the area. Construction workers, white scarves tied with four knots on their heads, building an enormous house that would become the old quarters of the La Celeste Estancia; a photo of El Moderno Bar, with a side room used as a movie theater (Renzi was able to see the sign advertising the movie they were showing that day with a magnifying glass: Jacques Tourneur's *Nightfall* — *Al caer la noche*); a snapshot taken at harvest time with a row of laborers walking up a plank toward the freight cars with bags swung over their shoulders; several old photographs of the train station with silos, "bird-of-prey" grain augers, and waterwheels in full activity, and in the back a threshing machine pulled by horses; an image of the Madariaga Store and Tavern when it was just a cart outpost.

"If you look at the photographs, you'll see that the town hasn't really changed. It's gotten worst with time, but overall it's still the same. What happened is that the highway drove all the wealth westward. The factory, for example, is far from here, but the entire town lived off of the factory when the crops started losing their yield. And that's why the firm is under dispute, because that land on the hill, near the highway—that land is worth a fortune."

Renzi spent a few hours looking through the material. He was able to trace how the Belladona wealth had been amassed. In the middle of the modern history of the town was the business that Luca Belladona had built, with the help of his older brother, Lucio, under their father's condescending and skeptical eye. An unbelievable building of architectural rationalism, ten kilometers outside the town, in the hills, especially striking in the middle of the countryside, like a fortress in the desert.

"Luca designed it himself," she said. "And you could already tell—or one should have already been able to tell—that he was in a different reality. He spent a fortune. It's an extraordinary building, so modern that many years later, amid the decadence and the paralysis, it still hasn't lost its strength. He drew up the plans, he spent months redoing parts of the windows and the gates because the angle of the hinges was off. It was the most modern car manufacturing factory in Argentina at the time, much more modernized than the Fiat plants in Córdoba, and Fiat in Córdoba was on the industry forefront."

They had the photographs from the different stages of the building process. Renzi followed the process as if he were observing the construction of an imaginary city. First you could see the empty vastness of the plains, then the large holes in the ground, the concrete and iron base foundations, the great wooden structures, the glass galleries along the ground level, the abstract structure of the beams connecting the walls (which looked like a chest board from above), and finally the walled building, with the tall, sliding doors and the endless wrought-iron railings.

Among the documents and newspaper articles, Renzi found a long statement by Lucio Belladona from the day of the inauguration of the plant. They had started from nothing, going around the countryside to repair agricultural machines during the harvests[23]—the first mechanical threshing machines, the first steam combine reaper machines—and eventually set up a workshop behind their house. It was there that they started building racecars, working with light coupes, small and resistant, that competed on open highways and dirt roads throughout the provinces. It was the grand time of the Touring Car Racing Series, normal cars, customized, touched up by mechanics, with production engines—the first V8's, the 6-cylinder Cadillac's, the Betis cars—at the top of their power, the "spherical" fuel tanks always installed at the center of the automobile, the fenders like wings, the reinforced frames and aerodynamic body designs. Soon they became famous throughout the country, the Belladona brothers appeared in newspapers and the magazine *El Gráfico* with Marcos Ciani or with the Emiliozzi brothers, always next to the fastest cars. They moved up in the field of national mechanics (copy-adapt-graft-invent), becoming great innovators. In the mid-1960s they signed the first contract with Kaiser Motors in Córdoba to make prototypes for experimental cars.[24]

---

23 "I remember there were twelve horses per harvester, six bouncers tied to the front and six to the back. The horses knew the sound that the engine made when it was struggling against a tough row of wheat, when the throttle sped up, and they'd stop and wait until the sound of the engine would go back to normal, at which point they'd take off again of their own accord. As if the horses were living instruments" (Lucio Belladona).

24 The factory built so-called *Concept Cars*, automobiles designed as models

Renzi followed the storyline, he studied the newspaper clippings, the photographs, the smiles of the brothers working under the open hoods of the cars. In 1965 they traveled to the U.S. and, in Cincinnati, purchased very large guillotine shears and folding machines. Their situation became complicated by a sudden devaluation of the peso, from one day to the next the dollar in Argentina was worth twice as much as it used to be.

From that moment on, the newspaper articles and the court archives started portraying Luca as a violent man, but the violence lay in the circumstances of his life rather than in the particularities of his character. He was the only man known in the town—or in the district, or in the whole province, for that matter, as Rosa clarified, with some irony—who had latched on to any kind of dream. Better yet, Luca was attached to a fixed idea, and his stubborn determination for that idea led to his catastrophe. People distrusted him. They considered his decision not to sell an attitude that explained all the misfortune that had befallen him. It explained, too, that he ended up isolated and alone in the deserted factory, like a ghost, never leaving or seeing anyone. He had endless confidence in his project. When it failed, or when he

---

to be later tested and line-produced. With an order from Chrysler, they formulated the prototype of the Valiant III. They built the *Vans* for Škoda Auto, new jeeps, sports cars. Many cars you see on the street today, they were the first to build them. They worked for the branches of Fiat and Kaiser Motors in Córdoba. Headquarters would send them the characteristics of the vehicle they wanted developed. They would conceptualize and build it, piece by piece. The engine, the frame, the upholstery, the windows, the wheels, the bodywork, the paint rectification and final adjustments, everything. Each car was valued somewhere between $100,000 and $150,000. It would take them six to eight months to build one. The cars could be driven out of the factory when finished.

was betrayed, he felt empty, as if he'd lost his soul.

The decline was not the result of a process or something that happened slowly over time, however, but an act of negative illumination. A single moment that changed everything. One night Luca arrived at their offices in the center of town unannounced and found his brother negotiating with a group of investors planning a takeover of the factory. They had prepared a contract to establish a corporation through public shares,[25] everything behind Luca's back, because they were trying to assume control of the company. There were all sorts of clashes. The workers occupied the plant, demanding that the source of their jobs be maintained, but the State intervened in the conflict and decreed the closing. That's when Luca decided to take out a mortgage on the factory, to deal with the debt, refusing to negotiate and insisting that he would continue with his projects. Since then he has lived there, without seeing anyone, in a battle to the death with his father and the town leaders.

"Luca doesn't want to accept things as they are. I can understand that," Rosa said. "But at a certain moment this became a problem for everyone, because the town was divided over the issue and anyone allied with Luca had to go into exile—let's just say it like that. And he was left alone, convinced that his father had tried to sink him.

"He resisted and kept control of the factory, which just about

---

25   The process is classic. An investment fund (*a hedge fund*) buys 51% of the shares. Once the company is under their control, the board of directors votes a structural dividend over the capital to recover their initial investment. Technically, it is called the emptying out—or laundering—of a company (*Wash and wear system*).

stopped producing anything. He stayed there, in the half-empty plant, working on his machines, trying at all costs to save the property, which is worth millions. They want to expropriate the factory, subdivide the land and the premises into smaller plots, there's a lot of money at play, they have a project that's already been approved and announced in the papers.[26] There are several lawsuits against him, but Luca fights on. The way I see it," Rosa said, "Durán's death is connected to this affair. Why did he come here with so much money in dollars? Some say he came with the money to save the plant, others maintain that he came to bribe officials and use the money to buy the factory and throw Luca out. That's what they say."

Renzi wrote the facts in his black notebook and, with Rosa's help, followed the trace of the carry trade in the finance company assets and the official balance of the money markets. The bonds circulated from one place to another and were traded on Wall Street. In this fashion, they reached an investment firm[27] from Olavarría,

---

26   "*A little history*. The first major enclosed commercial center, the South-dale Shopping Center, near Minneapolis (in the U.S.), was built in 1956. The Great Commercial Center consists of a vast, central area (the 'mall') and a large market at the far end of the gallery that anchors the Center. The Center offers everything 'under one roof,' allowing customers to shop regardless of the weather, always avoiding parking problems, and bringing clients together in one large, single space, with heating and air-conditioning, and many different locales to purchase quality products and brand names. The Center also becomes a recreational area for the entire family. The project scheduled to be built in our town, already presented to the military administrator, would be the first of its kind in Argentina" (*El Pregón*, August 2, 1971).

27   "The term *carry trade* refers to speculation of assets used to guarantee loans. The rescue mortgages have much higher interest rates than standard market rates, and the fees for the middlemen are notoriously high. In such cases, the loan might be sold two or three different times and form part of direct financial transactions through the purchase of bonds and assets securitization. The investment fund prevents the mortgage from being settled and

in which one of the main investors was Doctor Felipe Alzaga, an estancia owner in the area. Apparently they had purchased the bonds from the underwriting of the factory's mortgage and the decision was theirs to make. There was nothing illegal, Renzi was even able to record the information and all the numbers of the register of the investment fund at the branch office of Banco Provincia: Alas 1212.

Rosa showed him other figures and facts, leading him into the secrets of the conflict. But Renzi had the feeling that it wasn't the papers or Rosa's story that would permit him to understand what had happened, but the mere fact of being in town. The places were still there, nothing had changed, the town was like a stage set, even the attitudes seemed to repeat the story. "Right here, where we are now, is where everything started," Rosa said, and made a gesture with her arms as if she were showing him the past.

The building of the Municipal Archives was Colonel Belladona's old house when he founded the town and first built the train station. The English had sent him there because he was considered trustworthy, he came from Italy as a child and he, too, had a tragic story. "Like everyone, if you look at their life close enough," she said. They called him Colonel because he had volunteered to fight in the Italian Army in the Great War and had been decorated and promoted.

The collection of documents in the library was very thorough, there was an archive of the history of the factory from the initial

---

overwrites the speculative interests to the initial loan. They do this without allowing for the possibility of paying off the mortgage, in the meantime speculating with the pay-off date. Many assets are thus transferred into the power of large financial entities" (*El Cronista Comercial*, February 3, 1971).

plans to the filing for bankruptcy. Luca took care of the factory archive himself, personally, he was always sending in announcements and documents so they would be saved, as if he'd already imagined what was going to happen.

"He trusts me," Rosa said, a little later. "Because I'm part of the family, and he only trusts family, in spite of the catastrophe. My mother is Regina O'Connor's sister, the boys' mother, we're first cousins."

According to her, something was about to happen. The past was like a premonition. Nothing would be repeated, but what was about to happen—what Rosa imagined was about to happen—had been forecast. There was an air of imminence, like a storm you can see on the horizon.

All of a sudden she asked him to excuse her. She walked toward the back, where the birdcage was, with the canary outside the cage. She sat at a small desk near the staircase and, after using a benzene lighter to heat a metal container to boil the needles, and after cutting open a small vial with a small penknife, she raised her dress and gave herself an injection on her thigh, looking at Renzi with a peaceful smile.

"My mother sometimes forgets a book she's reading on a chair out in the yard. She hardly ever goes outside, she always wears really dark glasses because she doesn't actually like the sunlight, but still sometimes she'll sit and read by the plants in the yard, in springtime when it's especially nice, and when she reads she murmurs under her breath. I've never been able to tell if what she's doing is repeating what she's reading or if she's speaking to herself in a low voice—like I do, too, sometimes—because

her thoughts rise as they say to her lips, so maybe she's speaking to herself, who knows, or maybe she's humming some song, she's always liked to sing, when I was a little girl I loved my mother's voice, I'd hear it from the back of the house when she sang tangos, there's nothing more beautiful or more moving than a young, lovely woman—like my mother—singing a tango by herself. Or maybe she's praying, maybe she's saying some prayer under her breath, asking for help when she reads. Whatever the case may be, she moves her lips when she reads and they stop moving when she stops reading," Sofía said. "Sometimes she falls asleep and the book falls off of her lap, and when she wakes up she seems afraid and quickly goes back to 'her lair,' as my mother calls the place where she lives—and that's when she forgets the book and doesn't dare go back for it."

"And what does she read?" Emilio asked.

"Novels," Sofía said. "They arrive in large packages every month, my mother orders them on the telephone, she always reads everything by a writer she's interested in. Everything by Giorgio Bassani, all Jane Austen, all Henry James, all Edith Wharton, all Jean Giono, all Carson McCullers, all Ivy Compton-Burnett, all David Goodis, all Aldous Huxley, all Alberto Moravia, all Thomas Mann, all Galdós. But she never reads novels by Argentine writers; she says those stories, she already knows."

14

Old Man Belladona's large house was on top of a hill, behind a eucalyptus grove. To get there, you had to walk up a path that wound through the trees. Renzi had hired a car in town; when he let him out at a turn in the road, near the path that led to the electric fence and the entrance gate, the driver told him how to walk up to the house. The large house had its name carved in wrought-iron lettering: Los Reyes. Before Renzi reached the fence, a security officer with a tired-looking face came out, communicated on a walkie-talkie with someone inside the house, and after a while opened the gate and let him in. Renzi waited in a large hall, with tall ceilings and windows facing the gardens, and paintings and photographs on the walls above leather couches, all of which made the place seem like the waiting room of a public building.

After a while a maid appeared, looking more like a nurse, and took Renzi into an elevator and up to the second floor. She left him by an open door that led into an enormous living room with barely any furniture. Toward the back Renzi saw a tall and imposing heavy man waiting for him, standing. This was Old-Man Cayetano Belladona, the Engineer.

"Bravo told me you wanted to see me," Renzi said, after they sat on two oversized chairs placed against one of the walls.

"And Bravo told me that you wanted to see me. So the interest is mutual," the Old Man laughed. "That doesn't matter, what matters are the articles you're publishing in that newspaper in the Capital. Anyone who reads them is going to think that our town is a war zone. You cite unnamed sources, and like any reporter who says his sources are confidential, this means you're lying."

"Can you cite that opinion?" Renzi asked.

"I don't like those stories about my family," the Old Man said, as if he hadn't heard him. "Or your far-fetched theories about why Anthony brought that money." He doesn't beat around the bush, Renzi thought, taking out a cigarette. "You can't smoke here," the Old Man told him. "And this is not an interview, I just wanted to meet you. So don't take any notes, and don't record any part of what we say."

"Right," Renzi said. "A private conversation."

"I'm a family man at a time when being a family man doesn't mean anything anymore. I protect my right to privacy. I'm not a public person." He spoke with extreme calm. "Journalists like you are destroying the little that we have left of solitude and isolation. You gossip and you slander. And you scream about freedom of the press, which for you just means the freedom to sell scandals and destroy reputations."

"So, then?"

"Nothing. You asked to see me, and here you are," he said, and pressed a button; a bell rang faintly somewhere in the house. "Would you like something to drink?"

"I was told that I could speak frankly with you."

"You're a friend of Croce's, so you're a friend of mine," the Old

Man said. "Even though we've been distanced for a while. He's sick, they've told me."

"Admitted to the madhouse."

"Well, I barely leave here anymore." The Old Man made a gesture that included the entire mansion. "In a sense, I'm admitted too and this, you could say, is my clinic. My wife and daughters live with me, but we could imagine that they have also been committed, and that they think that they're my wife and daughters in the same way that I think that I own this place. Isn't that right, Ada?" the Old Man said to the young woman who entered the room.

"Of course," she said. "The people who help and serve us are actually nurses and orderlies who play along when we say that we belong to an old family that founded the town."

"Perfect," the Old Man said, as his daughter pulled up a low glass table on rubber wheels—with a bottle of Glenlivet and several tall, cut glasses—and started serving whiskey. "These country towns are closed in like chicken coops, isolated from everything, and people sometimes say a bunch of nonsense just because they're bored. I'm sure you can imagine. And now that there's been a crime, everyone's going on about Tony, going round and round adding their bit to the story. I'd like to put an end to the merry-go-round. The best thing for my family is no news. You can write whatever you'd like, but I'd like you to know what we think."

"Of course," Renzi said, "but without quoting this conversation."

"Would you like to serve yourself?" the Old Man said. "This is my daughter."

The young woman smiled and settled into a chair in front of them.

There was no ice; whiskey straight up, Italian style, Renzi thought. The girl was the young woman he'd seen in the Club, wearing a pair of jeans now and another thin blouse without a bra. She had a ring with a large emerald that she spun on her finger as if she were winding it up. She looked as if she was in a bad mood, or had just gotten out of bed, or was about to collapse, but without losing her sense of humor. Every once in a while a lock of hair would fall over her eyes like a curtain, blocking her sight for a moment, or the top button of her blouse would come undone, revealing her breasts (beautiful and tanned by the sun). When she raised an arm you could see the hair in her armpits (also Italian style). Everything seemed to be part of her style, or of her idea of elegance. All of a sudden, in the middle of a sentence, she dropped the ring with the green stone in the whiskey glass.

"Frickin', I say," she said. "It's swimming on me."

Unflustered, she fished the ring out of the whiskey with her long fingers, and after cleaning it with her tongue—in a slow, circular motion that it took Renzi a while to forget—she put it back on her finger. As if what she was about to say was related to her action to save the emerald, she told him that she wanted to thank him for not mentioning the stupid stories circulating in town about the relationship between her sister, the deceased, and her. His discretion is what had made them think that Renzi's intentions weren't all bad, or at least that he didn't intend to fall into the usual superstitions that people had in town. Country folk, she told him, get all excited ("horny") telling perverse stories—which never actually take place the way people imagine. He must know, of course, that after undertaking much research attempting to identify the defining characteristics of the gaucho of the pampas, anthropologists had been unable to isolate any specific, identifying traits, other than those of being naturally selfish and believing in imaginary illnesses. The young woman referred to country towns as if she were speaking about another world that was not her own. But what most caught Renzi's attention was that when she spoke she emphasized certain words, stretching out the vowels, as if she were counting the syllables in a line of poetry. It was one of those self-conscious, personal mannerisms that in some women constitutes the nature of their language, in the same way that a special timbre is always audible in blank verse—blank verse, Renzi said to himself in English—in the iambic pentameter of Elizabethan drama. The woman underscored certain archaic and very Argentine words in each phrase, as if sticking long pins into live butterflies, to show she was a country girl from a good family. Or as if she were having fun with that. Renzi got a bit lost in his internal digression about modes of speech. When he started paying attention again, the conversation had taken a different turn.

"The stories about Tony are all wrong, including the one about his death being the result of the crime of passion that everyone is talking about. We have nothing to say." Daughter and father took turns speaking, complementing each other as if they were a duo. "Sometimes," the Old Man said, "he used to come visit me at night. Let me tell you, he was an exile, he was forced to abandon his country, with his family, because he believed in Puerto Rican independence. His family had always supported Albizu Campos, they never considered themselves citizens of the United States. You know who Albizu is, right? He was a kind of Puerto Rican Perón."

"Better than Perón."

"It's no great merit to be better than Perón," the girl said, to her father's pleasure.

"Of course, it's like saying that someone sings better than Ataúlfo Gómez."

"He was a nationalist leader in Puerto Rico who confronted the United States."

"And he wasn't from the military."

"He was an intellectual who studied at Harvard."

"Even though he was a mulatto. The illegitimate son of a black laundress and a white land owner."

The father and daughter were having fun, as if Renzi wasn't there, or as if they were putting on a show for him. So he could see how a traditional family interacts, except there was something strange about the game, a couple's understanding between father and daughter that seemed a bit overacted.

"I liked speaking with him," the Old Man said. "He had integrity. He thought it was strange that there should be so much land in the hands of so few people in this country. I explained to him that it was one of the results of the Indian Wars, that they gave land to the army officers as far as their horses could ride.[28] Five

---

28 One of the most widely disseminated stories in the countryside, the legend has it that after the Campaign of the Desert, the State divided the lands taken from the Indians and distributed it to the officers using a method entirely in line with Argentine traditions. The individual would gallop as far as his horse could go, and the rider would be given the land he had managed to cover, galloping, without stopping. Commonly the soldiers would ride the Indians' extraordinary horses, which could run for days on end, in long, smooth gallops, without tiring. If one keeps in mind the facts about the distribution of land in the country, it is difficult to believe the extension of that solitary ride. In 1914, half of the Argentine extension—the five provinces of the wet

million leagues were handed out to thirty families, I told him one day. When he calculated it out, comparing the pampas to the size of the island of Puerto Rico, he laughed. I liked his way of speaking, and I know why he came here. But he was on a road to perdition," the Old Man added suddenly, "and no one could stop it. Just like my children, on parallel and divergent roads."

"I'm sure no one knows what you're talking about, Father," Ada said.

"You think that Yoshio killed him."

"I don't think anything. That's what the police say."

"That's not Croce's theory," Renzi said.

"But who would imagine that they would hire a jockey and have him dress up as a Japanese night porter to go in and kill Anthony? It's inconceivable, even in this country. That's not how things are done around here."

"And how are things done around here?"

"Different," the Old Man said, smiling.

"Less baroque," the girl clarified. "And out in the light of day." She stood up. "If you need me, let me know," she said, and said goodbye. Only then, as he saw her walk away, did he realize that she was wearing high heels and that her jeans were very tight, as if she wanted to shock her father in this fashion, or entertain him.

"I'd like to get your thoughts on the situation with the factory."

"My son Luca is a genius, like my father was," the Old Man seemed tired. "But he doesn't have any common sense. I've helped

---

pampas—was occupied by gigantic estancias in the hands of very few owners. And nothing has changed since then. According to the latest estimates from the National Agricultural Census, in 1969: 124 million hectares, with 59.6% of the total land in the hands of 1,260 owners (2.5% of the total population).

him in every way possible."

By that point the Old Man was basically speaking to himself, with the tone of an owner reprimanding his foreman because he's let insects into the hacienda. He went back to the beginning.

"I'm sick of this whole affair, I'm tired of journalists, of the police, I don't want to hear any more stories about my family or about my children. That young man was very dear to me, Tony, he was a lucky boy until he somehow came here, to die in this desert." The Old Man stopped and served himself another whiskey. "I've had what's called a cerebrovascular incident, a brain hemorrhage, and I shouldn't drink, but when I don't drink I feel even worse. Alcohol is the fuel of my life. Listen, young man, they want to confiscate the factory, the military does, and when Perón comes back it's going to be the same, because Perón's a military man too. We've owned this place since its foundation and now they want to take everything away, their plan is to speculate with the surrounding lands. At a certain point my son confronted me, he's turned away from me, he's always been set in his ways, determined to have it his way, but he has every right to keep his factory empty if he wants to, he should be able to use it like a *paleta* court if he felt like it, or a pigeon house, whatever, he's paid his debts and he's going to cover the mortgage, but they want to get a hold of his loan and confiscate the plant. It's not a State loan, it's a loan from a private bank, but they want to expropriate it. Look, see?" he said, looking through some papers and showing him a cutout from the newspaper. "The business owners are behind it, they want to build a commercial center there. I hate progress, I hate this kind of progress. The countryside should be left alone. An enclosed mall! As if this were Siberia." Suddenly the Old Man grew quiet. Then he put the palm of his hand on his forehead, and resumed his monologue. "There are no values left, only prices. The State is an insatiable predator, it pursues us with its confiscatory taxes. For those of us—for me, I should say—who live in the country, away from the chaos, life is harder all the time, we're surrounded by large floods, by large taxes, by new commercial roads. Like my ancestors were surrounded by the Indian hordes who were always raiding them, now we're surrounded by a State Indian horde. Every once in a while, we get a drought in this area, or hail, or locusts, and no one protects the interests of the countryside. To keep the State from taking everything, we're supposed to trust their word, to follow the old customs, no checks, no receipts, everything by word, honor above all, but there are two economies at play, a double bottom with an underground where money circulates. Everything to avoid state expropriations, the confiscatory taxes on rural production, we can't pay those rates. Buenos Aires should be an independent nation, like in the time of Mitre. Buenos Aires on one side, the thirteen ranches on the other. Or is it fourteen now?" He paused again, looking for something in the pockets of his jacket. "There's a lot of real estate speculation in the area, they want to use the factory as a base for a new project of urbanization. The town already seems obsolete to them. I'm going to prevent it. Here, take a look. I sent for that money for my son, it's part of his inheritance, from his mother." He handed Renzi a withdrawal receipt from Summit Bank in New Jersey, for $100,000. "I wanted to make amends with my son. I wanted to help him without him finding out. But the son of a bitch inherited his Irish mother's pride." He paused for a longer stretch. "I never imagined anyone would die."

"You never imagined..."

"And I don't know why they killed him, either."

"Who's doing all those business deals, Mr. Belladona?"

"The same black rabble as always," he said. "Anyway, enough for today. We'll continue some other time." He pressed the button again, and a little bell sounded somewhere in the large house. Almost at once the door opened and a young woman entered, identical to the other but dressed differently.

"I'm Sofía," she said. "Come on, let's go, I'll see you out." She covered her father with a blanket and patted him gently on the head. The Old Man had dozed off. Then she and Renzi walked out. "I know you," she said when she closed the door behind them. They were in a side room, a kind of office, looking over the gardens. "We met a long time ago, in a party in City Bell, in Patricio's house. Zip zap. Touché. I studied in La Plata too."

"That's impossible. How could I forget someone like you?"

"I was in Agriculture School," she said. "But I used to go over to Humanities sometimes, listen in on some of the classes, and I was good friends with Luciana Reynal, her husband is from around here. Don't you remember? You wrote a short story about that night."

Renzi looked at her, surprised. He'd published one book of stories, years ago, and it turned out that this girl had read it.

"It wasn't with the story from that night," he managed to say. "I can't believe that I could forget someone like you..."

"A party in City Bell. And you killed Luciana off, how silly, she's perfectly alive, still getting laid all the time." She looked at him, seriously. "And now you write a bunch of poppycock for the paper."

"I've never heard that word. Poppycock. Is it a compliment?"

Her eyes were a strange color, her pupils would suddenly expand and cover her irises.

"Give me a cigarette, will you?"

"And how is she?" Renzi asked. It's what they had in common, he hung on to keep the conversation alive.

"I haven't the faintest idea. And of course her name wasn't Luciana, that's what she told people because she didn't like her real name."

"Right, her name was Cecilia."

"Her name is. But I haven't seen her in years. She used to come here in the summer with her husband. One of those idiots who plays polo all the time, she wanted to study the philosophy of Simone Weil, can you imagine? And she also had some kind of adventure with you, I'm sure she told you she was going to leave her husband."

"I loved her," Emilio said. They remained quiet for a moment. She smiled at him. "What do you do?" he asked.

"I take care of my father."

"Other than that?"

Sofía looked at him, but didn't answer.

"Come on, let me show you where I live. We can talk a while longer."

They walked down a hallway and came out on the other side of the house. An open back porch faced a lawn and gardens. On the other end of the yard there was a guesthouse with two large windows, lighted up.

"We can sit here," Sofía said. "I'll get some white wine."

They had grown silent. A nocturnal butterfly flickered around the light with the same determination with which a thirsty animal approaches a puddle. Finally it hit against the lighted lamp and fell to the ground, partially singed. An orangish splash of dust burned for a moment in the air, then dissolved like water in water.

"In the summer I get very skinny," Sofía said, looking at her arms. "I live outside. When I was a little girl I forced myself to sleep out in the fields with a blanket, under the stars, to see if I could overcome my fear of being out there. Because Ada didn't want to, she's afraid of insects, she prefers the winter."

Sofía walked back and forth along the edge of the porch with a soft smile on her face, distant and peaceful. Like all very intelligent women who are also beautiful, Renzi thought, she considered her beauty to be annoying because it gave men the wrong idea about what she was really like. As if wanting to refute what he was thinking, Sofía stopped in front of him, grabbed his hand, and brought it to her chest.

"Tomorrow I'll take you to meet my brother," she said.

PART II

15

From a distance the building looks like a fortress, rectangular and dark. In recent months the Industrialist—as everyone here calls him—has reinforced the original structure with steel planks and wooden partitions, and he's had two guard towers raised at the southeast and southwest corners of the factory. These turrets look over the plains that extend for thousands of kilometers toward Patagonia and the end of the continent. All the transoms, glass roofs, and windows are broken and haven't been replaced because his enemies would simply break them again. The same goes for the outside lights, the bulbs of the street lamps, which someone has smashed by throwing rocks at them—except for a handful of the tallest lamps, still on that late afternoon, soft and yellow in the twilight. The outside walls are covered by torn, re-glued posters and political graffiti, all seemingly repeating the same slogan—*Perón Returns*. Written in different styles by a variety of groups, the posters all show the same smiling face ready as always to come back from anything, they all claim and celebrate the imminent return—or hope for return—of the General Juan Domingo Perón. Flocks of pigeons fly in and out of holes in the walls and the broken windows, and circle above the premises; below, stray dogs bark at each other, or lie in the shade under the trees along the broken sidewalks. Luca hasn't been outside the factory in months, to avoid seeing the landscape and the decrepitude of the outside world. He remains indifferent to everything outside the plant. Echoes and threats reach him, still, voices and laughter and the sound of cars speeding by on the highway, near the fence, on the other side of the factory's parking areas and loading zone.

After ringing the bell several times outside the locked, chained front iron door, and after leaning through a broken window and clapping their hands trying to get someone's attention, they were finally received by Luca Belladona himself. Tall, polite, oddly dressed in very warm clothes for the time of year—with a large, black leather cardigan, a gray flannel pair of pants, a thick, leather jacket, and Patria boots—he asked them to come directly up to the main offices. They could visit the factory plant a little later, he told them. They walked down a gallery, where the enclosing glass was broken and dirty, and there were phrases and words drawn along the inside walls, too. Things Luca had written there, he explained, things he couldn't afford to forget.

There was a layer of green covering the ground, in the interior courtyard, a smooth pampa of herbs as far as the eye could see. Luca would empty his *mate* and dump the herbs out the window from his study above. Or, sometimes, when he walked back and forth along the balconies, he'd change the herbs in his *mate* and dump the old ones into the interior opening of the building while he heated up water for a new one. Now he had a natural park with pigeons and sparrows fluttering above the green mantle.

His bedroom was upstairs, in the west wing of the building, close to one of the old meeting rooms, in a small space that used to be a filing room. It had a foldout bed, a small table, and several cupboards with papers and medicine bottles. Luca chose the room so he wouldn't have far to go when he undertook his calculations and experiments. He could just stay in that wing of the factory, walk down the hallway, and go downstairs to his office. Sometimes, he told them all of a sudden, when he got out of bed and walked down the hallway in the morning, he'd write whatever dream he remembered on the wall, because dreams fade and are forgotten as easily as we breathe, so they have to be written wherever you are when you remember them. The death of his brother Lucio and his mother running away were the central themes that appeared—sometimes successively, other times alternatively—in the majority of his dreams. "They form a series," he told them. "Series A," he said, showing them a chart and several diagrams. When the dreams moved on to other subjects, he'd write them in another section, under a different key. "This is Series B," he said. He repeated that in recent days he'd been dreaming mostly about his mother in Dublin and his dead brother.

There were phrases in ink on the walls, words underlined or circled, arrows relating "one word family" to another.

He called Series A *The Process of Individualization*, and Series B *The Unexpected Enemy.*

"Our mother couldn't stand her children being more than three years old, as soon as they turned three, she abandoned them." When his mother found out about Lucio's death, she almost traveled back to Argentina, but they had dissuaded her. "She was desperate, apparently, which surprised us, because she'd abandoned our brother when he was three years old, and she abandoned us, too, when we turned three. Extraordinary, isn't it?" he asked, the small crooked mutt looking up at him sideways, its tail wagging with tired enthusiasm.

It was extraordinary. When their mother had abandoned them, their father had gone out to the street with a hammer in his hand, wearing only an overcoat, and he'd started pounding on their mother's car—which meant that he *loved her.* The townspeople had looked on from the sidewalk by the main road, as the Old Man climbed on the hood of the car like a madman and struck the car repeatedly with the hammer. He wanted to throw acid on her, he wanted to burn her face off, but he didn't go that far. His wife had left him for a man whom his father considered better than him—besides, his father didn't want to have problems with the police, everyone knew what the Old Man was involved in, starting with his wife, who left him because she didn't want to be his accomplice, or be forced to denounce him.

"Pregnant with *me*," Luca said, going back to the first person singular. "The other man raised me for three years after I was born, as if he was my father, and I don't even remember him. Not even his face, just the voices I could hear from the stage, he was a theater director, you know? But eventually she left him, too, moved to Rosario, then to Ireland, and I had to go back to my family house, that's how it was, legally, since I have the same last name as the man who claims to be my father."

Then Luca told them that he'd been looking for a secretary that week, not a lawyer or a simple typist, but a secretary. In other words, someone who could write down what he was thinking and what he needed to dictate. He smiled at them, and Renzi

confirmed again that Luca—like a Russian *starets*, or like peasants—spoke in the plural when referring to his projects, and in
the singular when talking about his own life. On the other hand,
he said that he ("we") had accepted that he ("we") would be
appearing in court to request that the money that his father had
sent from his mother's inheritance be turned over to him. He had
all the documents and records necessary to file the claim.

"We had to hire someone who could take dictation and type
up the proofs that we'll be taking to court to reclaim the money
that belongs to us. We don't want lawyers, we'll file the lawsuit ourselves, under the law of the defense of inherited family
patrimonies."

Right away he started talking about Cueto, the prosecutor.
According to Luca, Cueto had been the company's *trusted* attorney in the past, only to betray and drive them into bankruptcy.
Now Cueto wanted to use his political post—to which he had
risen through raw ambition, under the umbrage of the current
powers—to confiscate the plant and the land it was on. Their plan
was to keep the factory and build what they called an experimental center for agricultural exhibitions, in collusion with the area's
Rural Society. But first they'd have to litigate in district court, in
the provincial and national courts, and even in the international
tribunals, because Luca was ("we are," he said) willing to do whatever it took to keep the factory up and running. It was an island,
as he saw it, in the middle of an ocean of peasants and ranchers
who cared only about fattening their cows and pulling riches from
a land so rich that any ol' fool could toss a handful of seeds, stand
back, and watch his profits grow.

He was excited about the possibility of *getting out* of his own field for once, and taking a trip into town to defend himself before the law. He walked around the room as he spoke, in a state of great unrest, imagining every step of his defense. He was certain that a secretary would help him expedite his ability to prepare the necessary documents.

So he placed an ad on x10 Rural Radio for two consecutive days, he told them, announcing the opening for a private secretary. Several men showed up from the countryside, hats in hand, calm, bowlegged, horse-riding men, their faces darkly tanned but their foreheads white at the line of their hat brim. They were muleteers, herdsmen, horse tamers, out of work because of the recent concentration of the large estancias that was driving small farmers, tenants, and seasonal laborers to search for new jobs. Honorable men, as they said, who'd understood the word secretary as someone who can keep a secret. They'd come and applied for the position, ready to swear, "if it came to it," that they could keep as quiet as the grave. Because, naturally, "they knew our story and our misfortunes," Luca explained. They risked coming to the factory and were willing not to say a single word that they weren't authorized to say. In addition, of course, they'd also do the necessary work, as they told him, turning both ways, looking at the walls and windows, expecting to see the corral where the animals might be, or the land they'd be expected to farm.

Two others arrived and applied as tiger hunters. Puma hunters, actually. First one with scars on his face and hands. Then a short, chubby man with clear eyes, skin pockmarked like dried leather, and only one arm. Both said they could track and kill a puma without a firearm, using just a poncho and a knife—even the one-armed guy, the man without a left arm, who everyone called Lefty. If there were any pumas left to kill, that is, and to kill by hand, as these hunters had always done, heading out at dawn through the grasslands to track the fattened tigers that lived off of the calves from the large ranches. The hunters went to the estancias and the farms looking for work, offering their services. They showed up at the factory, wary and distrustful as a puma that's gotten lost at night and finds itself, in the morning, walking on the cobblestones of a town's main road, sullen and alone.

But that wasn't it. He wasn't looking for a puma hunter, or a foreman, or an axeman—none of the things you might need in an estancia. He was looking for a technical secretary, someone who knew the secrets of the written word, someone who could help him face the vicissitudes of the battle in which he saw himself implicated, the long war he was waging against the rough forces of the region.

"Because in our case," Luca said, "we're talking about an actual military campaign, we've secured victories and suffered defeats. Napoleon's always been our main point of reference, basically because of his ability to react in the face of adversity. We've studied Napoleon's campaigns in Russia, and have found more military genius there than in his victories. That's right. There's more military genius in Waterloo than in Austerlitz, because in Waterloo the army didn't want to retreat. *It didn't want to retreat*," Luca repeated. "Napoleon opened the front to the left, and his reinforcement troops arrived ten minutes too late. This delay, caused by natural causes (large rains storms), was Napoleon's greatest act of genius.

Everyone studies that defeat, in every military academy, it's worth more than any of his victories."

Luca stopped and asked if they knew why crazy people, everywhere in the world, always saw themselves as Napoleon Bonaparte. Why, he asked, whenever someone needs to portray a madman, why do they draw someone with a hand tucked into his vest and a bicorn hat on his head? It was true, wasn't it? A quick sketch of Napoleon, that was the universal way to draw a madman. Had anyone thought of that? Luca asked. I am Napoleon, the *locus classicus* of the classic madman. But, why?

"We'll leave that one stewing," he said with a sly look in his eye, and escorted them down the hallway and into his office. To return to the question of the secretary, which they had left "pending," he said.

Although the main office was luxuriously furnished, it was much deteriorated, with a layer of gray dust on the leather chairs and the long mahogany tables, moisture marks on the carpets and walls, the windows all broken, and white splotches of pigeon shit on the floor. The birds—not just pigeons, but also sparrows, ovenbirds, chingolos, and even a carancho—would come in through the roof, land on the iron crossbeams along the roof of the factory, and fly in and out of the building, sometimes building nests in different places of the edifice—all apparently without being seen by the Industrialist, or at least without being considered of sufficient interest or importance to interrupt his actions, or his speeches.

Luca had to place another ad, this time on the Church radio station, he told them, the parish station actually, x8 Radio Pius XII.

Several sacristans and members of the Catholic Action applied, as well as a few seminary students who needed to spend a period of time in civilian life. These latter revealed a certain indecision that Luca noticed right away, they were like children, willing to collaborate, charitable, but reluctant to move into the factory with the exclusive dedication that the Industrialist would've demanded of them. Until finally, after interviewing a number of applicants and fearing that he wouldn't find anyone, a pale, young man showed up who immediately confessed that he'd left the priesthood before being ordained. He said that he'd come to doubt his faith and that he wanted to spend time in the secular scene, as his confessor, Father Luis, had advised him. These were his words. And there he was, dressed in black, wearing his white-banded collar ("clergyman") to prove he still carried with him "the mark of God," as he told him. Mister Schultz.

"That's why we hired him, because we understood that Schultz was, or would be, the right man for our legal task. After all, is justice not based on belief and the written word, like religion? There's legal fiction, just like there are sacred stories, and in both cases we believe only what's told right."

Luca told them the young secretary was in one of the offices now, organizing their correspondence and typing up the nighttime dictations, but that they'd be able to meet him soon. Luca needed a secretary who'd be trustworthy, a believer, a convert in a sense. He needed a fanatic, someone willing to serve a cause. He had a long conversation with the candidate, whom he finally selected, about the Catholic Church as a theological-political institution and as a spiritual mission.

In these times of disillusion and skepticism, with an absent God—the seminary student had told him—truth resides in the twelve apostles who saw Him when He was young and healthy, in full use of His faculties. One should believe in the New Testament because it was the only proof of the vision of the embodiment of God. In the beginning there were twelve apostles, the seminary student had said—and *one traitor*, we added. This made the seminary student blush, Luca told them, he was so young that the word *traitor* had some kind of sinful, sexual connotation for him. The idea of a small circle, of an exalted and loyal sect, *except* with a traitor infiltrated at its core, an informant who's not foreign to the sect, but constitutes an *essential* part of its structure—this was the true organizational form of any small society. One must act knowing that there's a traitor infiltrated in the ranks.

"Which is what we *didn't* do when we organized the board (with twelve members) that went on to direct our factory. We stopped operating as a family business and became a corporation with a board. That was our first mistake. As soon as they stopped working solely within the confines of the family, my brother and father started to waver and lose confidence. Faced with a series of economic crises and the onslaught of the creditors, they succumbed to the siren song of that vulture Cueto, with that little perpetual smile of his, and his glass eye. The songs of sirens are always signs of risks to be avoided, the songs of sirens are always precautions warning us not to act, that's why Ulysses put wax in his ears, to avoid hearing the *maternal* songs that warn us about life's risks and dangers, the ones that paralyze us, destroy us. No one would ever do anything if they had to avoid all the unforeseen risks of their actions. That's why Napoleon is the hero of all madmen and of all failures, because he took risks, like a gambler who bets everything on the cards he has, loses, and plays the next hand with the same courage and spirit as if he'd won. There're no contingencies and there's no chance, there're only risks and conspiracies. Luck is operated from the shadows. We used to attribute our misfortunes to the wrath of the gods, then to the fatality of destiny, but now we know that in reality the only things we really have are conspiracies and secret maneuvers.

"*There's a traitor among us,*" the Industrialist told them, smiling. "That should be the basic operational sentence of every organization." Luca gestured toward the street, toward the grafitti and posters on the walls outside the factory. "That's what happened to us, because there was a traitor inside our family business who took advantage of the family's well-being to *squeal,*" he said, again using a metaphor that revealed his origins, as was his habit. Or at least his birthplace.

Luca told them that there were two contradictory tendencies in the teachings of Christ—according to the seminary student—one in conflict with the other. On the one hand, we have the illiterate and dejected of the world, the fishermen, artisans, prostitutes, and poor peasants upon whom the Lord bestowed long and clear parables. For the meek He had not concepts or abstract ideas, but stories and anecdotes. In this line of teaching, arguments were made through narratives, with practical examples from everyday life, which were thus opposed to the intellectual generalizations and abstractions of the men of letters and the philistines, the eternal readers of sacred texts, the interpreters of the Book.

Was He literate? What did He write on the sand? An undeci-pherable mark, or an actual word? Did He have God's absolute knowledge and did He know all the libraries and all the writings, and was His memory infinite? Christ didn't forecast a good end for the priests and the rabbis and the erudite men at all. To the poor in spirit, rather, to the wretches of the earth, to the humble and the oppressed, was destined the Kingdom of Heaven.

In the other line, the idea was that only a small group of the initiated, an extreme minority, can lead us to the high and hidden truths. This initiated circle of conspirators, who share the great secret, however, act with the conviction that there's a traitor among them. They say what they say, they do what they do, knowing they're going to be betrayed. What is said can be interpreted in several different ways, even the traitor doesn't trust the explicit meaning, the traitor is not quite certain what he should or should not denounce. This is how we can understand how this young, Palestine preacher—a bit of a night owl, strange, who's aban-doned His family and speaks to Himself and preaches in the desert; a healer, a fortune-teller, a layer of hands who in His opposition to the occupying Roman forces foretells of a future kingdom—all of a sudden proclaims that He is the Christ and Son of God (*You have proclaimed it*, he said). This theological-political version of the eccentric community, the seminary student said, according to Luca, was the classic structure of a secret sect that knows there's a traitor in its ranks, and protects itself by using a language suffused with hidden meanings.

On the other hand, they may have been a sect of mushroom eaters. This would explain why Christ withdraws to the desert and visits with Satan. Those Palestine sects—the Essenes, say—ate hallucinatory mushrooms, they're at the base of all ancient religions. They walked around the desert hallucinating, speaking with God, hearing angels. One could think that the consecrated host was nothing other than the image of a mystical communion tying the initiated of the small group together, the seminarian added in an aside, Luca told them. *Eat, flesh of my flesh.*

Mr. Schultz, Luca's secretary, was more apt to trust the second line of teachings. The tradition of a "convinced minority": a nucleus of faithful, formed activists who are able to resist persecution and are united together by a forbidden substance—imaginary or not—with texts full of secret allusions and hermetic words, as opposed to a rural populism that speaks in the local Spanish with the conservative sentences of so-called popular knowledge. Everyone in small towns takes drugs, in the pampas of the Province of Buenos Aires or the pastures and farmlands of Palestine. It's the only way to survive the elements in the countryside, the seminary student said, according to Luca, adding that he knew as much because he'd heard all about it in the confessional. In the long run, everyone confessed that you couldn't live in the countryside without taking some kind of magical potion: mushrooms, distilled camphor, snuff, cannabis, cocaine, mate spiked with gin, yagé, cough syrup with codeine, Seconal, opium, nettle tea, laudanum, ether, heroine, dark pipe tobacco with Rue leaves, whatever you can get in the provinces. How else do you explain gauchesque poetry, *La Refalosa* by Hilario Ascasubi, the dialogues of Chano and Contrera by Bartolomé Hidalgo, *Anastasio el Pollo* by Estanislao del Campo? All those gauchos, high as a kite, speaking in rhymed verses through the pampas… *That's the law of the land, the man on top does what he wants / The shadow of the tree and its milk is always a menace.* That's what town pharmacists are for, with their prescriptions and concoctions. Isn't the apothecary a key figure of rural life? A kind of general consultant for all ailments, always available, waiting in the doorway at night, ready to deal in milk of the cow and a range of banned products.

The seminary student and Luca understood each other right away, because Luca thought of the restructuring of the factory as if it were a Church in ruins that needed to be re-founded. In truth, the factory had been born from a small group *(my brother Lucio, my grandfather Bruno, and us)*, and in those small groups there's always one person who turns away and sells his soul to the devil. Which is what happened with his older brother, the Oldest Belladona son, Lucio, who everyone called Bear. His half-brother, actually.

"He sold his soul to the devil, my brother, influenced by my father. He made a pact, he sold his shares to the investors, and we lost control of the firm. He did it in good faith, which is how all crimes are justified."

Only after the *betrayal*, and after the night that Luca ran out half-crazy and had to hide away for a few days—isolated in the Estévez Estancia, in the middle of the countryside—only then was he able to stop thinking in traditional terms, and dedicate himself instead to building what he now called the objects of his imagination.

People accused him of being unreal,[29] of not having his feet

---

29   "More unreal, and more illusory, was the economy. Luca was shocked by the announcement made by U.S. President Richard Nixon, on the evening

on the ground. But he'd been thinking, the imaginary wasn't the same as the unreal. The imaginary was the possible, that which is not yet. This projection toward the future contained—at the same time—both what exists and what doesn't exist. Two poles that continually change places. And the imaginary was this changing of places. He'd been thinking.

From the window, in that room on the second floor, you could see the back gardens and the guesthouse where the mother lived. Old Man Belladona would be in one of the rooms downstairs with the nurse who took care of him. Renzi turned toward Sofía on the bed. She was sitting up, naked, smoking, leaning back against the headboard.

"And your sister?"

"She must be with the Vulture."

"The Vulture?"

"She's seeing Cueto again."

"Man, that guy is everywhere."

"She feels uneasy when she's with him, uneasy, annoyed. But she goes out with him every time he calls."

Cueto was arrogant, according to Sofía, super-adapted, calculating, and he gave the impression of being empty: an ice cube covered by a shell of social adaptation and success. He was always doing his best to

---

of August 15, 1971, regarding the end of the convertibility of dollars into gold—the *Gold Exchange Standard* created by the Genoa Conference of 1922. The decision was meant, according to Nixon, 'To protect the country against speculators who have declared war on the dollar.' From that moment on, according to Luca, everything had been 'a cesspool' and—*he'd been thinking*—financial speculation would soon start to predominate over material production. Bankers would impose their norms and abstract operations would dominate the economy" (Report by Mr. Schultz).

compliment Ada, while she, for her part, never hid her disdain for him; she made fun of him in public and laughed at him, no one understood why she didn't stop seeing him. Why she stayed with that man, as if she didn't want to leave him.

"Cueto is the biggest hypocrite of all the hypocrites, a born charlatan, an opportunist. Ugh, yuck."

Sofía was jealous. It was curious, strange.

"Ah... And that bothers you?"

"Do you have a sister? Do you?" Sofía asked, irritated. "Have you ever had a sister?"

Renzi looked at her, amused. She'd already asked him. He appreciated having a brother who was unbearable, because this had disillusioned him of the belief that family could be anything but a burden. He was surprised to see Sofía nested to her genealogical tree like a Greek immortelle.

"I have a brother, but he lives in Canada," Renzi said.

He sat up on the bed next to her and began caressing her neck and the upper part of her back, in a gesture that had become a habit for him in his life with Julia. This time, too, Sofía seemed to calm down, with the caress that wasn't for her, because she rested her head on Emilio's chest and started murmuring.

"I can't hear you," Renzi said.

"She was just a girl when she first went with Cueto. It's like he left his mark on her. She's fixated on him. Fixated," she repeated, as if the word were a chemical formula. "I wish I'd lost my virginity first, instead of her."

"What?" Renzi said.

"He seduced her... But I didn't let her get married, I took her away on a trip."

"And the two of you came back with Tony."

"Aha," she said.

She'd gotten up, wrapped in the sheet, and was now at the marble night table chopping up the cocaine with a razor blade.

16

When he had his nervous breakdown, nearly a year ago, Luca went to hide out in a country house, where he spent the nights on the front porch—with a lantern as a nightlight, and the sounds of the crickets and the distant barking of the dogs until the singing of the roosters at the break of day—reading Carl Jung. He concluded that the *process of individuation* in his life was embodied or expressed in a universe that he was trying to unveil. He'd lost his way and was now jumping through a ploughed field looking for the road.

When his brother betrayed him, Luca wandered around the roads, aimless, lost. He'd shown up that afternoon at their company's town offices without telling anyone he was coming, and had surprised his brother in an unannounced meeting with the new shareholders and Cueto, their factory's lawyer. They wanted to hand majority control and decision-making power of the board over to the intruders. He feared, his brother, with the rise in the dollar, and with the government's exchange policy, that they wouldn't be able to pay off the debts they'd acquired in Cincinnati. That was where they had purchased the large power tools—a giant steel guillotine shear and an enormous folding machine—which they could see down below, on the floor of the factory, if they leaned over edge of the balcony where they were now walking.

When he saw Luca enter unexpectedly into the offices, Lucio smiled with that smile that had connected them for decades, an intimate expression between two inseparable brothers. They'd worked together their whole life, they understood each other without having to say a word—but in that moment everything changed. Luca had left to go to Córdoba to ask for an advance from the head offices of IKA-Renault, but he'd forgotten some papers and had come back to get them, when he walked into the secret meeting. *Oh, evil.* He realized right away what was going on. He didn't speak to the intruders, didn't even look at them. They were sitting calmly around the table in the conference room when Luca entered. They looked at him in silence. He felt that his throat was dry, burning with the dust from the road. "Let me explain," Lucio said. "It's for the best." As if his brother had lost his head, or was under some kind of spell. On one side of the table, Cueto, the hyena, was smiling, but Luca only blew up when he saw that his brother was also smiling like that, blissfully. There's nothing worse than a naïve idiot who does something wrong thinking that it's for the best, and smiles, angelically, proud of himself and his good deeds. "I saw red everywhere," Luca said. He charged toward his brother, who was tall as a tower, and knocked him out of his chair with one punch. Lucio didn't defend himself, which only made Luca angrier. Luca finally stopped and left his brother on the ground. He didn't want to disgrace himself. He walked out, his head spinning, his life in shambles. He understood that his father must have convinced Lucio, that he must have frightened him first and then forced him to listen to—and accept—Cueto's advice.

The next thing he knew, Luca was in his car, driving down the highway, because driving always calmed him down, helped lull his mind. He eventually went to the Estévez Estancia, but he didn't remember what happened between walking in on the meeting and pulling into the country house. Later they told him that Inspector Croce found him prowling outside their family house with a gun in his hand, looking for his father, but he didn't remember any of that. He remembered only his car lights illuminating the fence of the Estévez residence, the caretaker opening the gate for him and letting him through, reminding him which road to take up to the house. He spent several days sitting on a wooden chair, on the porch, staring out at the countryside. He smoked, drank *mate*, looked at the road surrounded by the poplar trees, the gravel on the road, the birds flying in circles and, beyond, the empty pampas, always quiet. Vague voices reached him from the distance, strange words and screams, as if his enemies had found a way to drive him mad. A few white, liquid lightning bolts flashed in the sky, burning his eyes in the dark. He saw a storm building on the horizon, the heavy clouds, the animals running to take refuge under the trees, the endless rain, a thin blanket of wetness on the grass. His body seemed to suffer strange transformations. He started wondering what it would be like to be a woman. He couldn't get the idea out of his head. What would it be like to be a woman at the moment of coitus? It was a very clear and crystalline thought, like the rain. As if he were lying on the ground, out in the country, and had started sinking into the mud, a viscous feeling on his skin, a warm moisture. Sometimes he'd fall asleep and wake up with the light of morning, find himself sitting on the wooden chair on the porch, not thinking anything at all, like a zombie in the middle of nowhere.

One evening, during those days on end that were all the same, in his breakdown in the country house, he went inside to look for a blanket and found a book that he'd never heard of. The only book he found and was able to read during all those days and days of isolation in the Estévez Estancia. A book he found in an old, country wardrobe, one of those with mirrors and tall doors—in which one hides as a child to listen to the conversation of the adults—while he was searching through the winter clothes. He saw the book all of a sudden, as if it were alive, as if it were kind of a vermin, as if someone had forgotten it there, for us, for him. *Man and His Symbols* by Carl Jung.

"Why was it there, who had left it? That doesn't matter. When we read it, though, we discovered what we already knew, we found a message directed personally to us. Jung's *individuation process*. What's the purpose of an individual's entire oneiric life? That's what the Swiss Master had asked himself. Jung discovered that the dreams that a person dreams in his life all follow an order, which the Doctor called a dream plan. Dreams produce different scenes and images every night. People who aren't very observant probably never realize that a common thread runs through their dreams. But if we observe our dreams carefully, Jung says, over a set period of time (one year, for example), and we write the dreams down and study the entire series, we'll see that certain contents emerge, disappear, and come back again. *These changes, according to Jung, can be accelerated if the dreamer's conscious attitude is influenced by the proper interpretation of his dreams and their symbolic content.*

This is what Luca found one night looking for a blanket in an old country wardrobe in the Estévez house, as if it were a personal revelation. He discovered Carl Jung by chance, and this is how he was able to understand and later forgive his brother. But not his father. His brother was possessed. Only someone who's possessed can betray his brother and sell himself to strangers, and let them take over the family business. His father, on the hand, he was lucid, cynical, and calculating. In secret, for days and days, he had devised a trap—with Cueto, *our legal advisor*—to convince Lucio to sell his preferred stocks to the intruders and hand majority control over to them. In exchange for what? His brother committed the betrayal, terrified of the economic unknown. His father—on the other hand—thought like a man from the countryside who always goes in for a sure thing.

In his isolation, Luca understood the misfortune of men tied to the ground. He achieved what he called *a certainty*. The countryside had destroyed his family, they were unable to escape, as his mother had done, unable to run away from the empty plains. His older brother had known, for example, the happiness of having a mother.

"But before I was born," Luca said, using the first person singular, "my mother was already fed up with country life, with family life, she'd started secretly seeing the theater director who she'd leave my father for, when I was in her belly. My mother abandoned my brother, who was three years old, left him playing out on the patio, and escaped with a man who I will not name, out of respect. She left with the theater director and with me inside of her, when I was born the two of them were living together. But later, when

I too turned three, she abandoned me (like she had abandoned my brother) and moved to Rosario, to teach English for Toil & Chat, and then she moved back to Ireland, where she lives now. I always dream about her," Luca added, later, "about my mother, the Irishwoman."

Sometimes, in his dreams, he felt that a certain *suprapersonal* force was interfering in an active, constructive fashion, as if it were following a secret design. This was why he'd been able to build, in recent months, the objects of his thoughts as realities, and not just as concepts. To produce what he thought directly, thinking not just ideas, but real objects.

For example, a few objects that he'd designed and built in the last few months. There was nothing else like them, no previous models. The precise production of the objects of his thoughts that did not exist before being thought up. The exact opposite of the countryside, where everything exists naturally, where *products* are not products but a natural replica of previous objects, reproduced in the same manner, time and time again.[30] A field of wheat is a field of wheat. There's nothing to do, except plough a little, pray for rain, or for the rain to stay away—the earth takes care of everything else. Same thing with the cows: they walk around, graze, sometimes they need to be dewormed, have someone make an incision if they get a grass obstruction, herd them to the corral. That's all. Luca considered machines, instead, to be very delicate instruments.

---

30   "Democritus, in Antiquity, already pointed out that: *Mother earth, when made fruitful by nature, gives birth to harvests that serve as food for men and beasts. Because what comes from the earth must return to the earth, and what comes from the air must return to the air. Death does not destroy matter, it breaks up the union of its elements so they may be reborn in other forms. Very different from industry, etc…*" (Report by Mr. Schultz).

The machines were there to assist in bringing about new and unexpected objects, each more complex than the one before. He thought he could find, in his dreams, the steps necessary to carry on with the company. He walked ahead in the dark, looking for the configuration of a specific plan in the continuous series of his oneiric materials, as the Swiss Master called it. He liked the idea of them as materials—that one could work with them, as one works with stone, or chromium.

"What we write on the walls is the debris of memory. It's never the dream exactly as we've dreamt it. It's the remains, rather, like the wreckage and gears that survive a demolition. We're using metaphors here, of course," he said.

Often it was only an image. *A woman in the water with a rubber bathing cap on her head*. Sometimes it was a phrase: *It was quite natural for Reyes to join our team in Oxford*. He'd write these remains and later connect them to earlier dreams, as if they were all part of the same story, discontinuous fragments that needed to be put together. He always dreamt about his mother, he'd see her with her red hair, laughing, on the dirt patio facing the street—and he wasn't satisfied until he could find a natural way to integrate all the images. It was intense work, taking up a large portion of every morning.

The writings on the walls were a tapestry of phrases connected with arrows and diagrams, certain words underlined or circled, connections established, with figures and sketches, and fragments of dialogue. As if a painter were working on the wall, trying to compose a mural—or a series of murals—by copying hieroglyphics in the dark. It looked like a comic strip, actually,

a black-and-white cartoon, including dialogue balloons and draw-
ings assembling a plot.

His hope, then, was to record all his dreams for a year to be able
to finally intuit the direction of his life, and then act accordingly.
A plan, the unexpected anticipation of what was to come. He'd
understood, at last, that the expression *it is written* referred to the
results of these recording operations and the interpretation of the
materials supplied by personal archetypes and a collective unconscious. His dreams—he'd later confess—were hermetic anticipa-
tions of what was to come, the discontinuous elements of an oracle.

"As if the world were a spaceship and we were the only ones
who could see the flashing lights and hear the sounds on the
bridge and the conversations of the crew and the orders spoken
by the pilots. As if only with our dreams could we discover the
plans for the trip, and redirect the ship when it's lost its way and
is about to crash. We're still using metaphors here," he said. "A
simile, but also a *literal truth*. Because we work with metaphors
and analogies, with imagined worlds and with the concept of
equal to, we look for equivalences in the absolute difference of
the real. A discontinuous order, a perfect form. Knowledge is not
the unveiling of a hidden essence, but a connection, a relationship, a similarity between visible objects. That's why I," he added,
switching back to the first person singular again, "can only express
myself with metaphors."

For example, the observation deck, which was the opening from
where you could see the lights of the bridge and hear the distant
voices of the crewmembers. He wanted to transcribe what they
said. Another reason why he needed a secretary, to help him copy

everything down. And also why his table of interpretations was designed to read all of his dreams at the same time.

"Come, take a look," he said.

"That's why I got separated," Renzi said.

"How strange."

"Any explanation will do."

"And what were you doing?"

"Nothing."

"What do you mean, nothing?"

"Writing a novel."

"You don't say."

"A man meets a woman who believes she's a machine."

"And?"

"And nothing. That's it."

"The problem is always what you believe you experience, or what you believe you think," Sofía said after a while. "That's why one always needs help to be able to stand it all, a potion, some kind of miraculous concoction."

"The power of life, not everyone can stand it."

"Of course, there's a crest, a narrow pass, you fall—Plop."

"I completely agree."

Renzi dozed off. The night lamp, covered with a silk scarf, gave off a softened reddish light.

"In two, no, in three years," Sofía said, looking at and counting with the fingers of her hand, "I'm going to get pregnant. I'll be really big. It'll be interesting." She was laughing. "I want to have a child who turns twenty-five in the year 2000."

Luca took them to a small room next to the study—his work-room, as he called it[31]—which looked like a laboratory, with magnifying glasses and rulers and compasses and drafting tables and photographs from the different stages of the construction of multiple devices. On one of the desks, to the side, there was a cylinder with a number of small, brown, wooden tablets—like Venetian blinds, or the mechanical assembly of a series of small Egyptian tablets—each filled with handwriting tiny as fly legs. They were miniature blackboards, on which Luca wrote words and drew images, in different colored pencils, related to his dreams. "The dreams that have already been told are the ones that get transferred to the tablets, in miniature," he said. The engraved plates could be moved by a series of nickel-plated gears, *like the flapping of a bird's wings*. This made the words change places, allowing different readings of the phrases, at once simultaneous and successive. *My mother in the river, her red hair tucked into a rubber bathing cap. "It was quite natural," she said, "for Reyes to join our team in Oxford."* This was just one example of a preliminary interpretation. His mother, in Ireland: had she traveled to Oxford? And those Reyes, how should they be understood? As the kings, the *reyes*, or as the Reyes family?

---

31   "He works uninterrupted, for many hours on end, at night and in the afternoon, never allowing himself any slowdowns, with great effort, through great fatigue. He demonstrates unbreakable confidence in the 'immensurable value' of his work. He never lets himself be brought down by the difficulties and he never admits the possibility of failure for any of his endeavors. He does not accept the least bit of criticism, he has absolute confidence in the destiny in store for him. For these reasons, he does not care about recognition. 'We are concerned with praise and recognition in the *exact measure* to which we are unsure about our work. But he who, like us, is sure—absolutely sure—of having produced a work of great value, has no reason whatsoever to care about recognition. Such a person, like us, will feel indifferent to all worldly glory'" (Report by Mr. Schultz).

The question was: what does it mean to put different elements in relationship to each other and thus articulate and construct a possible meaning—and how should this be done?

This was the other filing room. Luca had decided to remove the filing cabinets, as he had done in the filing room upstairs, and placed a folding cot in place of the cabinets here, too, creating another resting place exactly like the one upstairs. Not only was it the same, Luca explained, it actually occupied the same, exact location, one on top of the other, in a perfect vertical axis.

"We sleep here, facing a specific direction, always facing the same direction. Like the gauchos who used to ride into the deserted plains and put their saddles in the direction they were supposed to be going, and sleep like that, too, to keep from getting lost in the middle of the countryside. To keep from losing their way, the direction of their route." After many months of experimenting, Luca realized that it was essential for everything to be exactly the same when he slept at night, every night—even if he slept in different rooms in the factory, wherever his activities might leave him at the end of the day—so the dreams would continue repeating themselves without major alterations.

At that point, a man in overalls appeared, lean, very meticulous-looking. Luca introduced him as Rocha, his main assistant and mechanical technician. Rocha had been the leading machinist in the plant, and Luca had kept him on as his principal consultant. Rocha smoked, looking down, while Luca praised his skills as an artisan and his pinpoint accuracy in all technical calculations. Rocha was followed by Croce's dog, the small mutt that came to visit him, as he said, and to which he spoke as if it were a person.

The dog was the only living creature of whose existence Rocha seemed to take any notice, as if truly intrigued by it. The dog was twisted, crooked. It had some kind of strange ailment or injury that kept it from walking straight, making it lose its sense of direction. So Croce's dog moved diagonally, as if an invisible wind kept him from walking in a straight line.

"This dog you see here," Rocha said, "it comes up to the factory from town, it always walks crooked, it even goes around and around in circles when it gets disorientated. But still, somehow, it makes it all those kilometers from there to here in two or three days. It'll stay with us for a while and then, just like that, one night it'll leave and go back to Croce's house."

His older brother's unexpected death, in an accident—Luca said all of a sudden—had actually saved the factory. Two months after the dispute, Lucio called him on the telephone, came to get him in his car, and was killed on the road. What is an accident? A malevolent byproduct of chance, a detour in the lineal continuity of time, an unforeseen intersection. One afternoon, standing in the same place where they were now, the telephone—which almost never rings—rang. Luca decided not to pick it up. He walked outside, but came back in again because it was raining (again!). In the meantime, Rocha, without anyone having asked him to do so, had picked up the telephone, as if it'd been a personal call. Rocha was so slow, so deliberate and tidy in everything he did, that Luca had time to walk out of the factory and walk back in, at which point Rocha was able to tell him that his brother was on the phone. He wanted to speak with him, Lucio, he wanted to tell Luca that he was coming by to pick him up in his new station wagon, so they could go get a beer at Madariaga's Tavern.

Luca had been unable to foresee his older brother's death because he hadn't been able to fully interpret his dreams yet, but Lucio's death was part of a logical line that he was trying to decipher with his Jungian-machine. The event was the result of an axial shift, and Luca was trying to understand the chain that had produced it. He could go back to the most remote times to identify the precise instant when it was produced, an imprecise succession of altered causes.

Luca couldn't stop thinking about the moment right before his brother's phone call.

"We stepped out," he said. "We were here, where we are now, and we stepped out, but when we saw that it was raining we came back in to get a raincoat, and then my assistant, Rocha, a special-ized lathe operator and the best machinist in the factory, told me that our brother was on the phone, and we stopped and went back to answer the call. We could've simply not answered, if we'd gone out and not come back in to get our raincoat."

That night his brother had called him on a whim, he told him that he'd just thought of it, that he was coming by the factory to pick him up to go get a beer. Luca had stepped out when the telephone rang, but he came back in because of the rain. Rocha, who was about to hang up the telephone and had already told Lucio that Luca was out, saw Luca walk back in, and told him that his brother was on the line.

"Where were you?" Bear asked him.

"I went out to get the car, but I saw that it was raining and came back to get my coat."

"I'm on my way to pick you up, let's get a beer."

They spoke as if everything was the same as always, as if their reconciliation was a done deal. They didn't need to explain anything, they were brothers. It was the first time they'd see each other after the incident of the meeting with the investors in the company offices.

Lucio came to pick Luca up in the Mercedes Benz wagon that he'd purchased a few days earlier. It had an anti-radar system to help avoid speed traps. Lucio used the car to visit a girlfriend in Bernasconi, he could make the trip in three hours, get laid, and be back three hours later. "My kidneys, don't get me started," Bear said. Then he said that with the downpour it would be better to take the highway and get off at the Olavarría exit. Then, at the exit, on the roundabout, he got distracted.

"Listen, little brother," Lucio started to say, turning his head to look at him. At that instant, at the bend of the road by the Larguía fields, a light shined on them, appearing brightly out of nowhere in the middle of the rain. It was the high beams of a semi. Lucio sped up, which saved Luca's life, because instead of hitting them straight on, the truck grazed the rear of the station wagon. Lucio was crushed against the steering wheel. Luca was thrown from the car, but he landed safely in the mud by the side of the road.

"I remember it as if it were a photograph. I can't forget the image of the light beaming on my brother's face, he'd turned to look at me with an expression of understanding and happiness. It was 21:20 hours, 9:20 pm, my brother sped up and the truck only hit the back of the station wagon, we spun around and I was thrown out into the mud. After my brother was killed,

I saw my father at the burial, that's when he offered me the money from our family inheritance, he had deposited it in an undeclared account in the United States for us. My sister Sofía was the one who intervened so he'd give us the part of the inheritance that corresponds to us, from my mother. This is what we're going to explain at the trial, even if it puts into doubt our father's integrity. Anyway, everyone here knows that's how it is, everyone deals in foreign currency.[32] He agreed to send us what we needed to pay off the mortgage and recover the deed to the factory."

Tony's death was a confusing episode, but Luca was sure that Yoshio wasn't the murderer. Luca shared Croce's theories. He was sure that they'd cede the money to him without any problems as soon as he showed the court the papers and the certified withdrawal statements from Summit Bank.

"Let's go downstairs and see the installations," Luca said.

"My mother says that reading is thinking," Sofía said. "Not that we read and then we think, but rather that we think something and then we read it in a book as if it were written by us, although it's not written by us. Rather, someone in another country, in another place, in the past, writes it like a thought that hasn't been thought yet, until, by chance, always by chance, we find the book that clearly expresses what had been, confusingly, not yet thought by us. Not every book, of course, but certain books are destined for us, certain books seem like objects of our own thoughts. A book for each one of us. To find it, there must be a series of accidentally interrelated events, until in the end you see the light you're looking for, without

---

32   "I am too curious and too clever and too proud to behave like a victim" (Dictated to Mr. Schultz).

even knowing you were looking for it. In my case it was the Me-Ti, *or*
The Book of Changes. *A book of maxims. I love the truth because I'm
a woman. I trained with Grete Berlau, the great German photographer
who studied in the Bauhaus, she used the* Me-Ti *as a photography
manual. She came to the college because the Dean thought that an agricultural engineer should learn with pinpoint accuracy to distinguish the
different kinds of grasses that grow on the estancias. 'In the countrysides
nobody sees a ting, therre's no borrderrs therre.[33] To see you must cut.
Photogrraphy is like trracking and raking.' That's how Grete spoke, with
a heavy accent. I remember one time she put me and my sister together
and took a series of photographs, and for the first time you could see how
different we were. 'You can only see what you have photogrraphed,' Grete
used to say. She was friends with Brecht, she'd lived with him in Denmark.
They said she was the Lai-tu of the* Me-Ti.[34]

---

33   "The pampas presents a privileged medium for photography because of
the distances, its folding effects, and the intense plenitude lost in the non-
space of visual deprivation" (Note by Grete Berlau).

34   Two years after the events recorded in this story, on January 15, 1974,
Grete Berlau drank one or two cups of wine before going to bed, and there,
lit a cigarette. There was a fire, and she suffocated in the burning room. She
may have dozed off while she was smoking. "We have to do away with the
habit of speaking about things that cannot be said by speaking," was one of
the sayings of Lai-tu that Brecht recorded in the *Me-ti*, or *The Book of Changes*.

17

They walked down the interior stairwell and into the main part of the factory, where they toured the industrial plant and were surprised by the elegance and spaciousness of the building.[35] The indoor garage was nearly two blocks in length, but it looked like a place that had been suddenly abandoned, right before some imminent disaster. A general paralysis had fallen over the steel accumulated there, much like a stroke leaves a man—who has drunk and fornicated and lived life to the fullest until the fatal instant when, from one second to the next, an attack immobilizes him forever—dry and lifeless.

Frozen assembly lines; a stretched-out section of upholstery with the dyed leather and the seats waiting on the floor; rims, wheels, stacked tires; a shed, its door and windows covered with canvases; inside the shed, metal sheets and cans of paint; tools and mechanical pieces, wheels, pulleys, and small measuring instruments on the floor of the garage; tires with Stepney wood crossbeams; Hutchinson pneumatics; a Stentor horn; an ingenious turbine to inflate tires, activated by the output from the

---

35   Surface area covered: Main nave: 3,600 m². Underground level: 1,050 m². Offices: 514 m². Conference rooms: 307 m². Total surface covered: 5,501 m². Land for future expansion: 6,212.28 m². Total: 11,713.28 m².

exhaust pipe; a *cigüeñal* crankshaft with its strange bird-name; a long workbench with adjustable bench vices, optical apparatuses, and gauging devices. The feeling of sudden abandonment was like a cold draft coming off the walls. The steel guillotine shear and the Campbell automatic folding machine, both purchased in Cincinnati, were in perfect condition. Two partially assembled automobiles had been left elevated above the service pits in the middle of the garage. Everything seemed to be in a suspended state, as if an earthquake—or the gray, viscous lava of an erupting volcano—had frozen the factory during an average workday, at the precise moment of its freezing. *April 12, 1971.* The calendar with naked women from a tire shop in Avellaneda, the old wooden box radio plugged into the wall, the newspapers covering the broken glass windows: everything pointed to the exact moment when time had stopped. A blackboard hanging by a wire still had the call to assembly from the plant's internal commission. There was no date on that, but it was from the time of the conflict. *Fellow workers, there will be a general assembly tomorrow to discuss the situation of the company, the new conditions, and our battle plan.*[36] The electric clock on the back wall had stopped at 10:40 (but was it am or pm?).

After a while they were able to discern the signs of Luca's more current activity. Spherical and curved objects set up on the floor, like animals from a strange mechanical bestiary; a device

---

36 There were meetings, marches, protests, but they didn't get any support. The people from the countryside would come by on their horses to see the acts, they'd say hello by touching their hats with the tip of their riding crop, and ride on. "Gauchos don't go on strike," Rocha said. He'd been the delegate for the internal commission. "If they have a problem, at most they kill their boss, or they take off. They're more self-sufficient than the Virgin."

with wheels, gears, and pulleys, which seemed recently finished, painted in bright red and white paint; a small bronze plate that read: *The wheels of Samson and Delilah*; the diagrams and plans for a monumental construction, fragmented in small, circular models, laid out on a drafting desk. A garage where one hundred workers were once employed, now occupied by a single man.

"We have resisted," Luca said, then switched to the second person singular. "No one helps you," he said. "They make everything difficult. You get taxed before you've even produced anything. This way, please."

He wanted to show them the work to which he'd dedicated his recent efforts. He led them on a path between connecting rods, batteries, and stacked tires, through an alley formed by large containers, and to an opening near the back where they saw an enormous steel structure rising in the air. It was a conical construction, six meters tall, made of grooved steel, resting on four hydraulic legs, painted with a dark, brick-red antioxidant paint. It looked like a stratospheric device, a prehistoric pyramid, or like the prototype of a time machine, maybe. Luca called this unsettling conical contraption *The Viewer*.

You could only enter *The Viewer* from underneath, by sliding through the tubular legs. Inside, once you stood up, you found yourself in a triangular metal tent, tall and serene. The interior contained stairs, a glass elevator, stretched platforms, and small, grilled windows. The device culminated in a glass eye at the top, two meters in diameter, surrounded by metal corridors. It could be reached by climbing the spiral staircase that led up into the control room, with its large windows and rotating chairs. The view from the top was circular and magnificent. In one direction, according to Luca, you could see the entire *celestial sphere*. In the other, by using a mechanical arm to adjust a series of mirrors set up as square cells, you could also look out over the deserted pampas. In the distance, toward the south of the province, the moon reflected off of the surface of the lakes, in turn surrounded by flooded fields that formed an extended yellow vastness across the plains. Closer in were the sown fields, the animals scattered in the prairies, and the roads intersecting on the slopes near the large estancias. Finally, crowded at the foot of the hills like a sandbank, you could just make out the roofs of the tallest houses in town, the main street and square, and the railroad tracks.

In front of the chairs there was a board with electronic instruments to fine-tune the positioning of the mirrors and make slight oscillations to the pyramid. Luca had placed three Zenith television sets above the steel walls, attached by clamps, and he'd connected them with a complex network of cables and movable antennas. The screens, when they were turned on, were tuned to simultaneous channels. On them, you could follow three different images at the same time.

"We considered calling this machine *The Nautilus*, but it's actually the replica of a spaceship, not a submarine. It's an aerial machine; it produces changes in the perspective and viewpoint of what one comes to see. It's a sign of the times: a stationary vehicle that brings the world to us, instead of us having to go to the world."

It had taken him nearly a year to build the pyramid, all the instruments, and the accompanying guides. He took advantage of the technology available in the factory's garage to fold the large sheets of metal. The seamless carapace of the machine, formed without any soldered joints, was the work of a watchmaker.

"It's not finished yet. It's not finished, I don't think we'll have it finished before winter."

He was haunted by the idea that the factory might be confiscated the following month, when the mortgage payment was due. He had received a letter from the courts with a date for a reconciliation hearing, but he'd postponed it because he didn't think that he was ready.

"We received the telegram inviting us to parley a week ago. They didn't use that word exactly, but that was the meaning of it. They want us to sit down and negotiate, they want to discuss the fate of the confiscated funds. We'll see what they propose. For the moment we've postponed the date. We didn't write directly to the judge, but to his secretary. We sent him notice that our company needs more time and that we were requesting an extension. They send telegrams or cablegrams, we only write letters." He paused. "Our father has interceded. My father has interceded, even though I didn't ask for his help."

"Do you know what this is?" Renzi asked, showing Sofía a piece of paper with the code Alas 1212 on it.

"Looks like an address."

"A finance company."

"At my brother Lucio's funeral, my father decided that he was going to get the money to Luca, even though they weren't speaking to each other."

"And Tony brought it for him."

"The funds belonged to the family, they were in an account that the

Old Man had abroad, in dollars, he couldn't transfer it legally. Or he didn't want to."

"He sold his soul to the devil."

Lying sideways on the bed, propped up on her elbow, a hand on her face, Sofía started laughing.

"Achalay! Man, you live in the past." She touched him with her bare foot. "I wish I could make such a deal with the devil, my little dove. You don't know how quickly I'd take off. But what I'm offered is never that convincing."

"My father helped me with the money, but I didn't ask for it, he saw me at the cemetery, at Lucio's funeral. I didn't ask him for anything, I'd rather die first. He advanced me my inheritance, but I don't want anything to do with him." Luca started pacing around the garage as if he were alone. "No, I can't ask my father for anything, ever." He couldn't ask the person responsible for all his misfortune for help. That's why at first he hesitated, but there were larger issues at stake. He stopped his pacing. "While I'm able to keep the factory operational, my father can have his rationale and I can have mine, my father can have his reality and I mine, each separate. We will succeed. The money is legal, it was brought in *surreptitiously*, but that's secondary, I can pay the back taxes and the fines to the Tax Office once the capital is acquired. If necessary, I have the official statements from my father and my sisters, and from my mother in Dublin, to prove that the money belongs to the family. It's joint assets—and that's how I'm going to pay off the mortgage. I'm one step away from finding a process for the lighting, my observatory needs just a few final touches. I can't stop now." He lit a cigarette and smoked, lost in his thoughts. "I don't trust my father, he's hiding something, I'm sure the prosecutor is working for him. If I'm not mistaken, this is why I have to be very clear. I don't understand his reasons, my father's, and he doesn't understand the *unfathomable* humiliation that he subjects me to by having to accept that money to save the plant. The factory is my whole life.[37] This place is made with the stuff of dreams. *With the stuff that dreams are made of.* I must be true to this directive. I'm sure that my father wasn't responsible for that young man's death, Tony Durán. That's why I've accepted what belongs to me, from my mother's inheritance."

This was going to be the basis for his case in the trial. The factory was his great work, it was already built and had proved its effectiveness, so why liquidate? Why make it dependent on loans? He thought these arguments would convince the court.

He was going to bet his life at the trial. Luca had a cause, a sense, and a reason to live—and this was all that mattered to him. This fixed idea kept him alive, he didn't need anything else, just a little *mate* to make his hot, bitter infusion to have with some crackers, and occasionally to be able to pet Croce's dog. He was absorbed in his own thoughts for a while, then said:

"We have to leave you now. We're very busy, our secretary will see you out." Barely waving goodbye, he headed to the staircase and climbed to the upper levels of the plant.

---

37   "Sometimes Luca hears the mocking laughter of a group of children. Are they laughing at him? He hates children, their voices, their *metallic* laugh, the little childish monsters. The *neighbors* are watching, they send their children *to observe*. His fate has been to be celibate, a true non-father, the anti-father, nothing natural, everything *made*, and thus rejected and persecuted" (Report by Mr. Schultz).

The secretary, a young man with a strange look about him, accompanied them to the front door. As they walked toward the exit he told them that he was worried about the trial, which was actually a reconciliation hearing. The offer from the prosecutor Cueto had arrived. Rather, Cueto had communicated to them that he had an offer about the money that Luca's father had sent him through Durán.

"Luca didn't want to open the envelope with the offer from the court. He says he prefers to go in with his own arguments, and not know those of his rival ahead of time."

The secretary seemed alarmed, or maybe that was his normal demeanor. A bit detached, there was a strange, shy air about him. He walked down the corridor, a few steps behind them, and said his goodbyes at the door. When they crossed the street, Renzi looked back and saw the dark mass of the factory and a single light illuminating the windows of the upper rooms. Luca was looking down from behind the glass, smiling, pale as a specter, following them from the white above, in the middle of the night.

They heard noises from the entrance downstairs. Sofía sat up, motionless, anxious and alert.

"She's here," she said. "It's her, Ada."

They heard a door and then a few steps and a soft whistling, someone had entered whistling a melody. And nothing else, except for window shutters being closed in one of the rooms down at the end of the hallway.

Sofía looked at Emilio then, and moved closer to him.

"Do you want me to... I can call her..."

"Don't be silly," Renzi said, and embraced her. Her body temperature

was incredible, soft skin and very warm, with beautiful freckles like a golden archipelago drifting down, disappearing into her red pubic bush.[38]

"I was kidding, dummy," she said, and kissed him. She finished getting dressed. "I'll be right back, I want to see how Ada is doing."

"Call me a taxi?"

"Really?" Sofía said.

---

38   When she lay down on a white sheet on the grass to sunbathe, the chickens would always try to peck the freckles on her torso...

18

When Renzi went back to visit Croce at the asylum, he found him alone in his block. As he crossed the lawn, the fat man and the thin man, who'd been transferred to another section of the hospital, approached Renzi and asked him for cigarettes and money. Off to the side, sitting on a bench between the trees, he saw another of the admitted patients—a very gaunt man, with the face of a corpse, wearing a long, black overcoat—masturbating, looking up toward the women's rooms on the other side of the gated fence. On the upper level of that building, Renzi thought he saw one of the women leaning out the window with her chest bare, making obscene gestures while the man watched her with a lost look in his eye, touching himself between the folds of his open coat. Did they pay for that? Renzi wondered.

"Yeah, they pay," Croce said. "They send money or cigarettes to the girls so they'll stick their tits out the windows upstairs."

In the vast, empty room with the beds undone, Croce had set up a kind of desk using two old fruit crates. He sat, facing the window, taking notes.

"They left me alone. It's better this way, so I can think and sleep in peace."

He seemed calm. He'd put on his dark suit and was smoking his small cigar. His bag was all packed up. When Renzi told him that Luca had accepted the summons from the court, Croce smiled with the same mysterious look as always.

"That's the news I was waiting for," he said. "Now the matter will be settled."

He jotted a few things in his notebook, behaving as if he were in his own office. Croce confused the noises he heard through the window—voices, murmurings, distant radios—with the sounds of the past. He thought the footsteps and the creaking noise in the corridor, on the other side of the door, were the footsteps and rubber wheels of the girl who came around the offices in town with the coffee cart. But when he got up he saw it was the nurse with the medicine, a white liquid in a small plastic cup that Croce drank in a single swig.

Renzi gave him a summary of his investigations at the Archives. He'd followed a series of clues in the newspapers and found that the transactions led to a ghost finance company from Olavarría that had purchased the factory's mortgage to appropriate the assets. Apparently, the banking code or the legal name was Alas 1212.

"Alas? So Cueto is behind it."

"The name that appears is that of a certain Alzaga."

"Of course, that's his partner."

"This is what's at stake," Renzi said, showing him the cutout he'd found in the Archives. "They're also speculating with the land. The Old Man is opposed."

"Good," Croce said.

Cueto, who was once the family lawyer, commandeered the operation to appropriate the shares for the new corporation.

Everything was done under the table, which is why Luca blamed his father—with good reason, for the Old Man trusted Cueto and didn't realize until some time later that Cueto was the black monk of the story. But now it seemed that the Old Man had distanced himself from Cueto.

"And the trial? Luca doesn't know what's in store for him."

"But he knows what he wants," Croce said, and started elaborating a new hypothesis based on the information that Renzi had just brought him. Of course they wanted to keep the money from reaching Luca, but the crime was still an enigma. *The Intrigue*, Croce wrote on a piece of paper. *The factory, a Center, the surrounding land, the speculation with the real estate.* He sat still for a moment. "You have to be able to think like the enemy," he said all of a sudden. "Someone who acts both like a mathematician and a poet, someone who follows a logical line but at the same time associates freely. A mind that builds syllogisms *and* metaphors. The same element enters into two different ways of thinking. We're facing an intelligence without limits. What in one case might be a simile, in the other is an equivalence. Understanding a fact hinges on the possibility of seeing the connection. Nothing is worth anything in and of itself, everything is worth something in relationship to other factors, but we don't know what the other factors are. Durán," Croce said, and drew an ex on the paper, "a Puerto Rican from New Jersey, a U.S. citizen, meets the Belladona sisters in Atlantic City"—Croce drew two exes on the paper—"and comes here after them. Did the girls know or did they not know what was happening? That's the first unknown. They have dodged the question, as if they were protecting someone. The jockey was the executor: he served as a substitute for another. They may have murdered Tony for no reason at all, just to keep anyone from investigating the real reason. *A diversionary tactic.*[39] They killed him to divert our attention elsewhere," he said. They had the dead body, they had the suspects, but the motive was of a different order. This seemed to be the case. A diversionary tactic, he wrote, and handed the paper to Renzi.

Emilio looked at the piece of paper with the underlined phrases and the checks and exes, and understood that Croce wanted him to reach the same conclusions as he had. This way he could be certain that he'd hit right on target.

Croce found a repeating mechanism: the criminal tended to resemble the victim so as to erase his tracks.

"They leave a corpse to send a message. It's the structure of the mafia: they use bodies as if they were words. And that's how it was with Tony. They were trying to say something. We know the cause of Tony's death, but what was the reason?" Croce remained quiet, looking at the bare trees through the window. "They didn't have to kill him, poor Christ," he said after a while.

He seemed nervous and tired. It was late afternoon and the block he was in was entirely in shadows now. They went outside to walk in the park of the asylum. Croce wanted to know if Luca was relaxed. He was betting everything on that lawsuit, he wished he could help him, but there was no way to help him.

"That's why I'm here," he said. "You can't live without making

---

39   Croce had intuitively understood the basic thought process. The evidence was known a priori, no empirical discovery could invalidate it. Croce called this method of deduction *playing it by ear*. And he wondered: Where's the music when one plays it by ear?

enemies, you'd have to lock yourself in a room and never leave. Not move, not do anything. Everything is always more stupid and more incomprehensible than what one can deduce."

He got lost in his thoughts. When Croce came back, he said he'd go return to his burrow and keep working. The walk was over. Renzi watched Croce head off toward his block. He walked in a nervous zigzag, swaying slightly, as if he were about to lose his balance. He stopped before he went in, turned around, raised his hand, and waved weakly in the distance.

Was that goodbye? Renzi didn't like the idea, but he didn't have much left. They were pressuring him at the newspaper to get back to Buenos Aires, they barely published his articles anymore, they thought the case was closed. Junior told him to stop fooling around and to come back to work on the literary pages. Kidding, Junior had proposed that Renzi put together a special on gauchesque literature—since he was already out in the country.

When he got back to the hotel, Renzi found the Belladona sisters sitting at a table in the lounge. He went to the bar, ordered a beer, and watched the twins reflected in the mirror behind the bottles. Ada was speaking excitedly, Sofía was agreeing, there was much intensity between them, too much… *If it was a man*. Every time he got himself in deep, Renzi remembered something he'd read. The line came from a story by Hemingway, "The Sea Change," which Renzi had translated for his newspaper's Culture section. *If it was a man*. Literature doesn't change, you can always find what you are looking for there. Life, instead… But what was life? Two sisters in the bar of a provincial hotel. As if she were reading his thoughts, Sofía waved at him, smiling. Emilio raised his mug to toast in the air. Then Sofia sat up and called him over, a flare. Renzi left his glass on the bar and walked to their table.

"How're the girls doing?"

"Sit down, have a drink with us," Sofía said.

"No, I'm moving on."

"You're going back already?" Ada asked.

"I'm staying for the trial."

"We'll miss you," Sofía said.

"What's going to happen?" Emilio asked.

"Everything will work out. Everything always works out around here," Ada said.

There was a silence.

"I wish I was a fortune-teller," Emilio said. "So I could read your thoughts."

"We take turns with our thoughts," Ada said.

"Yes," Sofía said. "When one of us thinks, the other rests."

They kidded around for a while longer, told him some local jokes, fairly loopy,[40] until Renzi finally said goodnight and went up to his room.

He needed to work, organize his notes. Renzi was restless, scattered, he felt as if he'd never been with Sofía. *I was inside her*, he thought, a stupid thought. The thought of an idiot. "You screw a chick, she never forgives you," Junior would say, with his little

---

40   A man in the country, riding a spirited colt in the plains at dawn, a splotch on the bright line of the horizon. In the distance, a gaucho drinking *mate* under the eaves of his country house. When the rider passes in front of the house, the country man at the house says hello. "Nice little morning," the rider says. "I made it myself," the other answers, adjusting the shawl on his shoulders.

cynical and winning tone of voice. "*Unconsciously*, of course," he'd clarify, opening his eyes wide, knowingly. "Look, Eve had the first orgasm in female history, after that everything went to hell. And Adam had to go off to work." He'd had loads of women, Junior had, and to every one of them he'd explain his theory about the unconscious battle of the sexes.

After a while Emilio picked up the telephone and asked for his answering service in Buenos Aires. Nothing important. Amalia, the woman who cleaned his apartment, asked if she should keep going on Tuesdays and Thursdays even though he wasn't there. A woman who didn't leave her name had called and left a telephone number. Renzi did not bother to write it down. Who could it be? Maybe Nuty, the cashier from the Minimax supermarket around the corner from his house, with whom he'd gone out a couple of times. There were two messages from his brother Marcos, calling from Canada. He wanted to know, the woman from the answering service told Renzi, if he'd already emptied out the house in Mar del Plata and put it up for sale. He also wanted to know if it was true that Perón was coming back to Argentina.

"What did you say?" Renzi asked.

"Nothing." The woman seemed to smile in the silence. "I only take messages, Mister Emilio."

"Perfect," Renzi said. "If my brother calls again, tell him that I haven't checked my messages and that I'm not back in Buenos Aires yet."

The family house on España Street had been left vacant for a few months after his father's death. Renzi had traveled to Mar del Plata and gotten rid of the furniture and the clothes and the pictures on the walls. He'd boxed the books and put them in storage, he'd see what to do with them when the house was finally sold. There were also a lot of papers and photographs, and even a few letters Renzi had written his father when he was a student in La Plata. The only thing he took with him from the bookshelves was an old edition of *Bleak House* that his father had purchased in a used bookstore somewhere. Renzi had discovered—or he thought he'd discovered—a connection between one of the characters in the Dickens novel and Melville's "Bartleby." He thought he might be able to write an article about this and send it to Junior, along with the translation of the chapter from the Dickens novel, so his newspaper would leave him alone.[41]

Apparently his brother was going to cancel his trip. If he finally sold the house and they split the money, he'd get about thirty thousand dollars. With this money Renzi could quit the paper and live a while without working. Dedicate himself to finishing his novel. Isolated, without any distractions. Out in the country. The expiatory goat runs away to the deserted countryside. *Straight to where the sun hides / inland I must ride.* But living in the country was like living on the moon. The monotonous landscape, the chimango birds of prey circling above, the girls who amuse themselves.

---

41 "Chapter 10 of the novel "The Law-Writer," is centered around the copyist Nemo (No One). Melville (who wrote "Bartleby" in November of 1853) probably read that chapter of the Dickens novel in April of that year, when it was first published in *Harper's* magazine in New York. Dickens's *Bleak House* which narrates the story of an endless trial and describes the world of the courts and its judges, was much admired by Kafka" (Note by Renzi).

19

The trial was an event. It was actually a hearing, not a trial. Still, everyone in town took it as a decisive event and referred to it as *the lawsuit, the trial, the proceedings*—depending on the point of view of the speaker—to indicate its transcendent nature. Like every transcendent occurrence, it was related—or so everyone thought—to justice and truth, but what was really at play behind these abstractions was the life of a man, the future of the region, and a handful of very specific, practical questions. You couldn't say that there were two equal sides opposing each other, because the two opposing sides were not equal. And yet, one had the impression of attending an actual contest. On the streets of the town that day small groups of people commented time and again on the facts, as if all past history was to be decided in the lawsuit against Luca Belladona, or in the lawsuit that Luca Belladona had initiated against the municipality—depending on the point of view of the speaker. What was being litigated, apparently, was the $100,000 that Luca was seeking to reclaim. But plenty of other things were at stake, too, all of which became evident as soon as Cueto started to speak and the judge nodded along to every one of the Prosecutor's statements.

The judge, the Honorable Gainza, was a justice of the peace;

that is, a municipal functionary assigned to resolve local disputes. He sat on an elevated dais, at the front of the Misdemeanor Court of the Municipality, with a court clerk to his side. The prosecutor Cueto was at a table below, to the left. Sitting next to Cueto was Saldías, the new Chief of Police. At another table, to the right, was Luca Belladona, dressed in his Sunday best, with a gray shirt and a gray tie, very serious, with papers and folders in his hands, occasionally consulting with the ex-seminarian Schultz.

A lot of people were authorized to be present at the hearing. Madariaga was there, as well as Rosa Estévez, several estancia owners and auctioneers from the area, and even Cooke the Englishman, the owner of the horse at the center of the dispute. The Belladona sisters were there, but not their father. Everyone was smoking and talking at the same time, the windows in the room were open, and you could hear the rumble of the voices from those who hadn't been able to get in and were crowded, instead, in the hallways and the neighboring courtrooms. Inspector Croce wasn't there either, although he'd already signed himself out of the asylum and was living now above the Madariaga Store and Tavern in a small room that he was renting there. Croce thought that everything was already fixed, and he didn't want his presence there to legitimize his rival, Cueto, who was certain to win the hand with his shady dealings. There weren't very many women present; the five or six who were there stood out because of their self-assured attitude. One of them, a beautiful woman—Bimba, Lucio's wife—sat impassively, haughty, behind her dark sunglasses.

Renzi walked in late and had to nudge his way into the room. When he finally settled in at a wooden bench near Bravo, his eyes met Luca's. The Industrialist smiled at him calmly, as if he wanted to transmit his confidence to the few people there to support him. Renzi looked only at him the whole afternoon, because he thought that Luca needed to be supported by the presence of an outsider who truly believed in his words. In the course of the next two or three hours—Renzi didn't know exactly how long he spent in the courtroom, although there was a clock hanging on the wall that rang every half hour, and it rang several times—Luca looked at Renzi every time he was in a difficult position, or when he'd made a good point in his arguments. As if Renzi were the only one who understood him precisely because he wasn't from there.

The justice of the peace, of course, had already taken sides before the so-called reconciliation hearing started, as had most of the people there. Those who speak about reconciliation and dialogue are always the ones already holding the pan by the handle with the whole affair cooked up. That's the truth. Renzi realized right away that there was an air of anticipated victory, and that Luca—with his clear eyes and the slow, calculated movements of someone who feels violence all around him—was lost before he began. The judge pointed at and ceded the floor to him. Luca wavered for a moment before speaking, as if hesitating, as if he couldn't find the words to start. Finally he got up, stretched out his close-to-two-meter frame, and stood sideways to the court, looking directly at Cueto—because it was to Cueto to whom he was really speaking.

Luca looked like someone with a skin condition suddenly exposed to the sun. After so many months of living in the factory, the large courtroom, with all the people, gave him a kind of vertigo. Returning to town and appearing there, in front of everyone he hated and held responsible for his ruin, was the first affront he suffered that afternoon. He felt and looked like a fish out of water. Luca raised his hand to ask for silence, even though not even a fly was stirring. Cueto leaned toward Saldías, smiling and relaxed, and said something in a low voice, and the other smiled back. "Good, okay, friends," Luca said, as if beginning a sermon. "We have come to ask for what is ours." He didn't speak directly about the money under dispute, but rather about the certainty that the gathering that day was a necessary procedure—an uncomfortable procedure, if one were to judge by his mistrustful attitude—for the factory to remain in the hands of those who'd built it. The money—which Luca didn't talk about, and which belonged to his family, and which his father had decided to cede to him as an advance on his inheritance from his mother—was destined solely to pay off the mortgage that weighed upon his life like the sword of Damocles. They'd been threatened and attacked, they'd been surprised in their previous goodwill by the intruders who'd infiltrated and eventually taken over the company. But they'd resisted, which is why they were there that afternoon. He didn't talk about his rights, he didn't talk about what was at stake, he talked only about what he cared about: his insane project to continue by himself in the factory, building what he called his works, his inventions, and his illusion that they might leave him—"that they might leave us"—alone. He paused and there was a murmur, but it wasn't clear if it was a murmur of approval or condemnation. Luca remained standing for a moment in front of the room, looking back and forth from his sisters to Cueto and Renzi, the only ones who seemed to understand what was happening. Luca spoke without raising his voice, with confidence and self-assuredness, without ever realizing the trap he was falling into. It was a catastrophic error—he rushed toward his own end without a thought, without seeing anything, blinded by his pride and his credulity. You could tell he was only chasing a dream, that he was chasing one dream after another, never knowing where the adventure would end, always certain it was the only thing he could do: defend his dream, which everyone thought was impossible. He said something along these lines, Luca did, as a conclusion. The Honorable Gainza—a cunning old judge who spent his nights playing dice in the clandestine casino near the coast—smiled at Luca condescendingly, and gave the last word to the Prosecutor.

Luca sat down and remained motionless for the next phase of the hearing, almost as if he weren't there. He may even have closed his eyes—only the back of his head, upper back, and shoulders could be seen as he sat in the front row facing the judge now—and he was so still that, for a while at least, he seemed to be asleep.

There was silence, and then another murmur, and Cueto stood up, always smiling, with an expression of superiority and indifference on his face. He was tall, his skin looked splotchy, and he had a strange air about him, perhaps because his posture was at once arrogant and obsequious. Immediately he focused the attention of the matter on Durán's murder. In order for the money to be reclaimed, the other case, the criminal proceedings, had to be settled. It was known that the murderer was Yoshio Dazai, it had been a classic crime of passion. Yoshio hadn't confessed because when the crime is this obvious the murderer never confesses. They hadn't found the murder weapon because the knife used to kill Durán was run-of-the-mill and could be found in almost any kitchen in the area. All the witnesses confirmed that they'd seen Yoshio enter the room at the time of the crime. Of course Yoshio knew about the existence of the money and had taken the bag to the storage room in the basement hoping to go back for it when everything calmed down. Cueto stopped and looked around. He had managed to change the topic of the session and refocus everyone's attention by reminding them of the sordid story of the crime. The version of the events, as presented by Croce, was delirious and could be seen as evidence of the ex-Inspector's dementia. That a jockey would dress up as a Japanese night porter and kill an unknown man to buy a horse was ridiculous. Everyone understood that Croce's version was impossible. Even more ridiculous was the idea that a man would kill another man that he didn't know, and that he would take only the money he supposedly needed to buy a horse, and that he would take the trouble to leave the rest of the money in the hotel storage room in the basement, instead of just leaving it in the same room where he'd committed the crime.

"The letter and the suicide might be true," the prosecutor concluded. "But we've gotten used to reading letters of that kind thanks to the letters that Croce has been writing us in his night-time deliriums."

Cueto shifted the question at hand and articulated the actual dilemma with extreme judicial clarity. If Luca, in his role as plaintiff, would accept that Yoshio Dazai had killed Durán, the criminal proceedings could move forward, the murder case could be closed, and the money could be returned to its legitimate owner, Mister

Belladona. If Luca didn't sign on to this agreement and continued instead with his own suit, then the criminal case would remain open and the money would remain confiscated for years, since they would be unable to close the criminal case and the evidence couldn't be removed from the court's power while it remained open. It was perfect. Luca's claim sealed the murder case because it presupposed that Durán had come to Argentina to bring him the money.

It took Luca a minute to understand. When he did, he looked stunned. He lowered his head and sat like that for a moment while the silence spread through the courtroom like a shadow. He'd thought that everything was going to be simple, but he realized that he'd fallen into a trap. He seemed crushed. Whatever decision he made, he was crushed. If he wanted to get the money, he'd have to help send an innocent man to jail, but if he told the truth, he'd lose the factory. He turned around and looked at his sisters, as if they were the only ones who could help him. Then, as if lost, he looked at Renzi—but Renzi looked away, because he thought that he wouldn't have wanted to be in his place and that if he were in his place he wouldn't have accepted the deal, he wouldn't have agreed to lie and send an innocent man to jail for the rest of his life. But Renzi wasn't him. Never had he seen anyone look as pale, never had he seen anyone take as long to speak, to say just one word: Okay. Once again a murmur ran through the room, but this one was different, as of confirmation or revenge. Luca's left eye was twitching slightly and he fidgeted with his necktie as if it were the rope from which he was about to hang. But Yoshio was the one about to be condemned for a crime he hadn't committed.

There was a big commotion when the session ended, an explosion of happiness. Cueto's friends all got up to speak to each other. Ada joined the group, too, and Cueto took her by the arm and whispered something in her ear. The only one who approached Luca was Sofía, she stood in front of him and tried to cheer him up. The factory was saved. They hugged, she held him in her arms and spoke softly to him, as if she were trying to calm him down, and she went with him to the other room, where the judge was waiting for him to sign the papers.

Renzi stayed in his seat while everyone got up. Outside the courtroom, he saw Luca shuffling down the hallway, like a boxer who's accepted winning the title in a fixed match. Not the boxer who's forced to take a dive because he needs the money. Not—as usual—the humiliated, offended party who knows that he didn't really lose even though someone has beaten him. No. Luca was like a boxer who's retained his title as champion thanks to a racket—which only he and his rival know is a racket—and all he has now is the illusion that his dreams have finally come true, but at an unbearable cost. Luca moved as if he were extremely tired and could barely move. Sofía was the only one with him, walking next to him, without touching him. When they crossed the main hallway she said goodbye and left out a side door. Luca continued by himself to the door of the other room.

He'd been subjected to a trial like a tragic character without a choice. Anything he chose would have been his downfall, not for him but for his idea of justice. In the end, it was justice that had put him to the test, an abstract entity—with its rhetorical apparatuses and its imaginary constructions—which he'd had to confront that afternoon in April, until he capitulated. That is, until he accepted one of the two options he was offered. Luca Belladona, who'd always boasted of making clear decisions, unhindered by any doubts, supported by his self-assuredness and his fixed idea. He chose his work, we might say, over his life, and he paid a very high price, but his illusion remained intact to the end. He remained true to his precept, he'd been sunk, but he hadn't defected. He was so proud and stubborn that it took him a while to realize that he'd fallen into a trap with no way out. By the time he realized what was happening, it was too late.

The townspeople watched him walk down the hallway in silence. They'd known him forever and were now at peace, they seemed magnanimous, because by doing what he'd done—after years and years of his impossible battle, held up by his demoniacal pride—the town had succeeded in getting him to capitulate. Now it could be said that Luca was like everyone else, or that everyone else was like him: now that Luca had revealed a weakness that he'd never revealed before. Renzi hurried to try to talk to him, but was unable to catch up and could only follow behind as they walked down the stairs leading outside. Then an incredible thing happened. When he came out onto the sidewalk, Croce's mutt appeared, walking crookedly as always, but this time when he saw Luca walk out into the daylight, the dog rushed and started barking at him, baring his teeth as if to bite, with hatred, his yellow fur on end, his body tense. That barking was the only thing that Luca got that day.

20

The next day, when Renzi went back to the Madariaga Tavern, the atmosphere was somber. Croce was at his usual table by the window, wearing his dark suit and tie. That morning he'd gone to the prison in Dolores to visit Yoshio and give him the news, before the official word reached him, that his case had been closed with the consent of Luca Belladona. "Jail is a bad place to live," Croce said. "But it's the worst place in the world for a man like Yoshio to live."

Croce seemed dejected. Luca was going to pay off the mortgage and save the factory, but the cost was too high. Croce was sure it would end poorly. He had an extraordinary ability to grasp the sense of events and anticipate their consequences, but he could do nothing to prevent them. When he tried, the only thing waiting for him was madness. Reality was his field of play, he could often see a series of events before they occurred and anticipate their outcome, but the only thing he could do to prove his theories and demonstrate that he was right was to let the events happen of their own accord. He had no influence over them.

"That's why I'm no good as an inspector," he said after a while. "I take events that have already occurred and imagine their consequences, but I can't prevent them. What comes after a crime? More crime. Luca believes he's condemned both Yoshio and me.

If he hadn't accepted Cueto's offer, if he'd refused to help him close the case, I might have had a chance with Cueto." Croce paused and looked at the plains through the bars of the window against which he always sat. The same motionless landscape that was, for him, the image of his life. "I blew it," Croce added, "my version of the crime was no good for anyone."

"And in the end, what's the truth?"

Croce looked at Renzi with a resigned expression on his face and smiled with the same sparkle of tired irony that always burned in his eyes.

"You read too many detective novels, kid. If you only knew what things were really like. Order doesn't always get restored, the crime doesn't always get solved. There's never any logic to it. We struggle to establish the causes and deduce the effects, but we're never able to understand the entire network of the intrigue. We isolate facts, we stop in front of a few scenes, we question a handful of witnesses, but for the most part we move blindly in the dark. The closer you are to the target, the more you get tangled in a web without end. In detective novels the crimes are always solved, whether with elegance or with violence, so readers will be satisfied. Cueto has a tortured mind, he does strange things, he kills by proxy. He leaves loose strands behind on purpose. Why did he have them leave the bag with the money in the hotel's storage room? Was Old Man Belladona involved? There are more unknowns than confirmed certainties."

Croce sat still, staring out the window, lost in his thoughts.

"So you're leaving," he said after a while.

"I'm leaving."

"You're doing the right thing."

"Better not say goodbye," Renzi said.

"Who knows," Croce said, referring either to his conclusions about Tony's death, or Renzi's eventual return to the town which he seemed to be leaving forever.

Croce got up ceremoniously and gave him a hug. Then he thumped down again in his chair and leaned over his notes and diagrams, distracted, as if Renzi were already gone.

While Croce keeps going, Cueto will never have peace, Renzi thought as he walked out into the street. The story goes on, it can go on, there are several possible conjectures, the story remains open and is only interrupted. The investigation has no end, the investigation cannot end. Someone should invent a new detective genre, *paranoid fiction* it could be called. Everyone is a suspect, everyone feels pursued. Instead of being an isolated individual, the criminal is a group with absolute power. No one understands what's happening, the clues and testimonies contradict each other as if they changed with each interpretation, and all suspicions are kept open. The victim is the protagonist and center of the intrigue, instead of the detective hired to solve the case or the murderer hired to kill. Renzi thought along these lines as he walked—perhaps for the last time—down the dusty streets of the town.

He went back to the hotel and packed his bag. The days he'd spent in the countryside had taught him to be less naïve. It wasn't true that the city was the place for experiences. The plains had geological layers of extraordinary events that returned to the surface with the blowing of the southern winds. The evil light of the unburied shimmers in the air like a poisonous fog. Renzi lit a cigarette and smoked, gazing out the window over the main square. Then he looked around the room to make sure he wasn't forgetting anything, and went downstairs to settle his bill.

The train station was quiet, the train would arrive soon. Renzi sat on the bench, under the shade of the casuarina trees. All of a sudden he saw a car pull over out in the street and Sofía get out.

"I wish I could go with you to Buenos Aires."

"So come."

"I can't leave my sister," she said.

"You can't, or you don't want to?"

"I can't and I don't want to," she said, and stroked his face. "Come on, my little dove, don't start trying to give me advice."

She was never going to leave. Sofía was like all the people Renzi had met in town, they were always on the verge of leaving the countryside and running away to the city. They always said they were suffocating in the plains, but in the end they were never going to leave—and they knew it.

She was worried about Luca. She'd gone to visit him, he seemed relaxed, concentrating on his inventions and his projects, and yet he couldn't stop going back over and over to the deal he'd made with Cueto. "It was the only thing I could do," he told her, but he seemed withdrawn. He'd spent the whole night wandering around the factory with the strange feeling that now that he'd finally gotten what he'd always hoped for, his resolve had left him. "I can't sleep," he'd told her. "I'm tired all the time."

The train arrived. In the loud commotion of the passengers getting on the train, laughing and saying their farewells, the two of them kissed and Emilio placed a gold charm with the figure of a rose engraved on it in her hand. It was a gift. She held it up to her forehead, it was the only kind of rose that didn't wither...

When the train started, Sofía walked along the window, until she finally stopped, gorgeous in the middle of the platform, her red hair on her shoulders and a peaceful smile on her face, illuminated by the afternoon sun. Beautiful, young, unforgettable, and—in essence—another woman's woman.

As he traveled, Renzi looked out at the countryside, at the quiet of the plains, the last houses, the men on horseback riding alongside the train. A group of kids ran along the embankment, barefoot, flashing obscene gestures at the travelers. Renzi was tired, the monotonous jolting of the train made him sleepy. He remembered the beginning of a novel (it wasn't the beginning, but it could've been the beginning): "Who loved not his sister's body but some concept of Compson honor." And he started translating: *Quien no amaba el cuerpo de su hermana sino cierto concepto de honor...* But he stopped and rewrote the line. *Quien no amaba el cuerpo de su hermana sino cierta imagen de sí misma*: "Who loved not his sister's body but some concept of herself." He fell asleep and heard confusing words. He saw the figure of a large wooden bird in the country with a caterpillar on its beak. Was there such a thing as incest between sisters? He saw the shop window of a gunsmith. His mother wearing a parka on a freezing street in Ontario. And if it had been one of them? Sitting on his foldout bed in the asylum, Croce had asked him: "How tall are you?" And: "There's an obvious solution, and a false solution, and finally a third solution," Croce had said. Renzi woke up, startled. The pampas were still the same, endless and gray. He'd dreamt about

Croce and also—his mother? There was snow in the dream. As the afternoon grew darker, the reflection of Emilio's face on the train's window became more and more clear.

The town remained the same as always. In May, with the first low temperatures of fall, the streets seemed less hospitable, the dust swirled about on the corners, and the sky was bright, livid, as if it were made of glass. Nothing moved. The children weren't heard playing, the women didn't come out of their houses, the men smoked in the doorways, and the only sound that could be heard was the monotonous whirring of the station's water tank. The fields were dry, so they started burning off parts of the pastures, the workers advanced in a line burning the weeds and the cuttings, tall waves of fire and smoke rose above the empty plains. Everyone seemed to be waiting for some kind of sign, the confirmation of one of those dark predictions sometimes announced by the old folk healer who lived alone in a shack on a hill. The gardener walked by at dawn, his cart filled with horse manure from the nearby army encampment; the girls strolled aimlessly through the square, sick with boredom; the young men played pool in the Náutico bar, or set up drag races on the road to the lake. The news from the factory was contradictory. Many said that activity in those weeks seemed to have picked up again, and that the lights in the plant's garage were on all night long. Luca had started dictating a series of measures and regulations to Schultz for a report he intended to send to the World Bank and to the Argentine Industrial Union. He stayed up through the night walking the upper galleries of the factory, followed by his secretary Schultz.

"I have lived, attempted, and achieved *so much* that they had to carry out a certain violent chain of events to separate and distance me from my accomplishments. We were caught in a trap, through a series of tricks and ruses, not by doubt, but by certainty" (Dictated to Schultz).

"To attribute to the means of industrial production a pernicious action about *effects* is to recognize in them a *moral potential*. Do economic actions not create, in fact, a structure of feelings built on reactions and emotions? There is an economic sexuality that exceeds the conjugal norms needed for natural reproduction" (Dictated to Schultz).

"Men have always been used as mechanical instruments. In the old days, in the harvest season, farm workers used to sew steadily, using bale needles to close up the burlap sacks. They were incredibly fast at their sewing, they could produce more than thirty or thirty-five sacks per hectare. Once in a blue moon they'd have to scoop one of the laborers out of the platform. In the rush, he'd have sewn in the tip of his shirt and he'd be stuck to a sack. He'd be rolling on the ground like a fallen brother" (Dictated to Schultz).

"I've been thinking about the local weaving. String, knot, string, cross and knot, red, green, string and knot, string and knot. My grandmother Clara learned to knit the blankets they weave in the pampas, her fingers deformed from arthritis, they were like hooks or vine shoots—but with her fingernails painted! Very elegant. We recall Martin Fierro's sentence: *every gaucho you see / a tapestry of misfortunes.* The mechanical spinning and weaving of fate! The local weaving penetrates to the marrow. Somewhere someone weaves, and we live woven, flowered in the weave, plotted in the plot. If I could go back even for an instant to the workshop with all the tapestries. The vision lasts only a second, then I fall into the brutal dream of reality. I have so many terrifying things to tell" (Dictated to Schultz).

"I've confirmed several times that my intelligence is like a diamond that can pierce pure glass. Economic, geographic, climactic, historical, social, and family determinations can, in very extraordinary occasions, be concentrated and embodied in a single individual. Such is my case" (Dictated to Schultz).

Schultz would get lost at times, he couldn't follow Luca's pace, he wrote what he thought he heard.[42] Luca marched in long strides through the facilities, talking nonstop, he didn't want to be alone with his thoughts. He asked Schultz to write all his ideas down as he walked nervously from one end to the other, across the garage of the plant, by the large machines. Sometimes Rocha would follow him instead, he'd sub in for Schultz while the ex-seminary student slept on a cot, they took turns taking dictation.

"Soon I will not have anything else to say about the past, I will be able to talk about what we will do in the future. I will climb to the top and stop living in these plains, we too will reach the highest peaks. I will live in the future tense. What is to come, what is not yet—is that enough to live on?" Luca said as he walked along the balcony above the inner courtyard.

Even though he hadn't slept in several nights, he still recorded his dreams.

---

42   "The flash of lightning that illuminated my life with a neat zigzag has been eclipsed" (Dictated to Schultz).

Two lost cyclists from the Doble Bragado Race turn off the road and continue on, just the two of them, far from everything, in the middle of the deserted pampas, pedaling evenly toward the south on their light Legnano and Bianchi bicycles, leaning over their handlebars against the wind.

Some time later Renzi received a letter from Rosa Echeverry with sad news. She found herself with the "painful obligation" of having to inform him that Luca "had suffered an accident." He'd been found dead on the floor of the factory's garage. It seemed like such a well-planned suicide that everyone could believe—if they so chose—that he'd died by falling from the height of his viewing machine, where he was taking one of his usual measurements. This is how it was explained in the letter from Rosa, for whom Luca's last gesture was yet additional proof of his goodness and his extreme politeness.

Luca had an extraordinary sense of himself and his own integrity. Life had tested him. In the end, when he finally got what he wanted, he'd *failed*. Perhaps the failure—the crack—was already there and it finally gave in because he couldn't live with the memory of his own weakness. Yoshio's shadow, the fragile Nikkei in jail, would return to him like a ghost whenever he tried to sleep. One fleeting flash in the night is enough to break a man, as if he were made of glass.

Once the priest accepted the version of the death as an accident—because suicides, like hobos and prostitutes, were buried outside the church graveyard—Luca was buried in the cemetery. The entire town attended the ceremony.

It was raining slightly that afternoon, one of those light, freezing drizzles that go on for days and days. The cortege went down the main street, up the so-called northern slope, and as far as the large gate of the old cemetery, with the black-covered horses of the funereal carriage trotting along rhythmically and a long line of cars following behind at walking pace.

The Belladona family vault was a sober structure imitating the Italian mausoleum in Turin that contained the remains of the officers who'd fought with Colonel Belladona in the Great War. Luca had made the worked bronze door, the light webbing above the small windows, and the hinges of the vault in the family workshop when his grandfather had died. The door opened with a soft sound; it was made of a transparent, eternal material. The tombstones for Bruno Belladona, Lucio, and now Luca seemed to condense the history of the family. They'd rest together. Only the males died. Old Man Belladona stepped forward, lofty, his face wet with the rain, and stood in front of the coffin. He'd buried his father, his oldest son, and now he was burying his second son. His two daughters took their place next to him; dressed in mourning like widows, standing arm in arm. His wife, who'd only left her "lair" three times—one for each of the three deaths in the family—wore dark sunglasses and gloves, and her shoes were dirty with the mud from the cemetery grounds. Cueto observed the scene from the back, standing under a tree, in a long, white raincoat.

The ex-seminary student approached the sisters and asked permission to say a few words. Wearing all black, pale and fragile, he seemed the most appropriate person there to bid farewell to the remains of the man who'd been his mentor, and for whom he'd been a confidant.

"Death is a terrifying experience," the ex-seminary student said. "It threatens, with its corrosive power, our possibility of living a humane life. There are two kinds of experiences that can protect those—those able to turn to them—from the terror of the danger of death. One is the certainty of truth, the continuous awakening toward the understanding of the 'ineluctable need for truth,' without which a good life is not possible. The other is the resolute and profound illusion that life has meaning and that the meaning of life is found in performing good deeds."

He opened his Bible and announced that he would now read from the Gospel of John, 18:37.

"And Jesus said: *For this I have come into the world, to bear witness to the truth. Every one who is of the truth hears my voice.* To which Pontius Pilate answered: *What is truth? Of what truth do you speak?* After he said this, he turned to the judges and the priests and said: *I find no crime in this man.*" Schultz looked up from the book. "Luca lived in the truth and in the search for the truth, he was not a religious man but he was a man who knew how to live religiously. The question of our time has its origins in Pilate's answer. This question implicitly supports the sad relativism of a culture that ignores the presence of the truth. Luca lived a good life, we should say farewell to him knowing that he was enlightened by his illusions of reaching meaning through his works. He rose to the height of those illusions and gave his life to them. We should all be grateful for his persistence in the realization of his dreams and for his disdain of the false lights of the world. His work was done with the stuff that dreams are made of."

Croce attended the ceremony but stayed in his car, without

getting out, and although no one saw him, everyone knew he was there. Smoking, nervous, his hair graying, the traces of his "suspected dementia" burned in his clear eyes. Everyone eventually left the cemetery, and in the end Croce was the last one there, the murmur of the drizzle on his car's roof and the rain falling monotonously on the road and the tombstones. When night fell on the plains and the darkness too became like the drizzle, a beam of light flashed in front of him. The circular brightness of the light pulsed back and forth, like a white ghost amid the shadows. Then, all of a sudden, it went out, and there was just the darkness.

EPILOGUE

Many times, in different places, through the years, Emilio Renzi remembered Luca Belladona. He always remembered him as someone who'd had the courage to live up to the heights of his own illusions. Months could go by without Renzi thinking about him, and then some fortuitous event would bring him back to mind, and he'd resume the story where he'd last left it—with new clarifications and details for his friends in a café in the city, or having a few drinks at his place at night with a woman sometimes—and the images of Luca would return vividly, his frank, reddened face, his clear eyes. He remembered the empty factory, the building in the middle of the plains, Luca wandering among his instruments and his machines. Always optimistic, always finding a way to find hope, unable to imagine that reality would deal him a fatal blow, like so many others. A fall brought about by a small change in his behavior, as if he were being punished for making a mistake, not for a character flaw but for a lack of foresight, for a failing he could not forget and would return like a remorse.

That night Renzi was talking with a group of friends after dinner in an open balcony facing the river, in a weekend house in the Tigre Delta, and he felt as if that night—always in spite of himself, mocking such a natural state—he'd gone back, and that the delta was an as-of-yet unknown quadrant of reality, like that town in the country had been for him, where he'd spent a few weeks in a kind of archaic interruption of his life as a city man, unable to understand such a return to nature—even if he never stopped imagining a drastic leaving that would take him to an isolated, quiet place where he could dedicate himself to what Emilio, like Luca, also imagined was his destiny, or his vocation.

"Luca couldn't imagine that there might be a defect in his character, because he'd reached the conviction that his way of being was something separate from his decisions, that it was a kind of instinct that guided him through every conflict and every difficulty. But he'd been defeated—or at least he'd been forced to make an unforgiveable decision, he must have thought that he'd deserted—and he couldn't forgive himself. Even though any other decision would have been just as impossible."

The light from a kerosene lantern and the smell from the coils that kept the mosquitoes at bay reminded Renzi of the nights of his childhood. His friends listened to him in silence, drinking white wine and smoking, sitting before the river. The steady glow of the cigarettes in the darkness, the flickering light of the occasional boats passing by, the croaking of the frogs, the rustling wind in the trees, the clear summer night—were like the landscape of a dream.

"He was so proud and stubborn that it took him a while to realize that he'd fallen into a trap with no way out. By the time he realized what was happening, it was too late. I think about that when I remember the last time I saw him, a few days before leaving town."

He'd called a taxi and asked the driver to wait by the side of the road while he walked up to the factory. There was light in the windows. Renzi knocked a few times on the iron gate. It was getting dark and a freezing drizzle was falling.

"After a while Luca open the front door a crack. When he saw me, he stumbled backwards, waving his hand. *No, no*, he seemed to be saying as he retreated. *No. Impossible.*"

Luca closed the door, followed by a sound of rattling chains. Renzi stood there for a while before the tall front of the factory. As he made his way back to the street, he thought he saw Luca behind the lighted windows of the upper level, pacing, gesturing, speaking to himself.

"And that was all," Renzi said.

Thank you all
for your support.
We do this for you,
and could not do
it without you.

DEEP
VELLUM

DEAR READERS,

Deep Vellum Publishing is a 501c3 nonprofit literary arts organization founded in 2013 with the threefold mission to publish international literature in English translation; to foster the art and craft of translation; and to build a more vibrant book culture in Dallas and beyond. We seek out literary works of lasting cultural value that both build bridges with foreign cultures and expand our understanding of what literature is and what meaningful impact literature can have in our lives.

Operating as a nonprofit means that we rely on the generosity of tax-deductible donations from individual donors, cultural organizations, government institutions, and foundations to provide a of our operational budget in addition to book sales. Deep Vellum offers multiple donor levels, including the LIGA DE ORO and the LIGA DEL SIGLO. The generosity of donors at every level allows us to pursue an ambitious growth strategy to connect readers with the best works of literature and increase our understanding of the world. Donors at various levels receive customized benefits for their donations, including books and Deep Vellum merchandise, invitations to special events, and named recognition in each book and on our website.

We also rely on subscriptions from readers like you to provide an invaluable ongoing investment in Deep Vellum that demonstrates a commitment to our editorial vision and mission. Subscribers are the bedrock of our support as we grow the readership for these amazing works of literature from every corner of the world. The more subscribers we have, the more we can demonstrate to potential donors and bookstores alike the diverse support we receive and how we use it to grow our mission in ever-new, ever-innovative ways.

From our offices and event space in the historic cultural district of Deep Ellum in central Dallas, we organize and host literary programming such as author readings, translator workshops, creative writing classes, spoken word performances, and interdisciplinary arts events for writers, translators, and artists from across the world. Our goal is to enrich and connect the world through the power of the written and spoken word, and we have been recognized for our efforts by being named one of the "Five Small Presses Changing the Face of the Industry" by Flavorwire and honored as Dallas's Best Publisher by *D Magazine*.

If you would like to get involved with Deep Vellum as a donor, subscriber, or volunteer, please contact us at deepvellum.org. We would love to hear from you.

Thank you all. Enjoy reading.

Will Evans
Founder & Publisher
Deep Vellum Publishing

LIGA DE ORO ($5,000+)

Anonymous (2)

LIGA DEL SIGLO ($1,000+)

Allred Capital Management
Ben Fountain
Judy Pollock
Life in Deep Ellum
Loretta Siciliano
Lori Feathers
Mary Ann Thompson-Frenk
   & Joshua Frenk
Matthew Rittmayer
Meriwether Evans
Pixel and Texel
Nick Storch
Stephen Bullock

DONORS

Adam Rekerdres	Cheryl Thompson	Mary Cline
Alan Shockley	Christie Tull	Maynard Thomson
Amrit Dhir	Daniel J. Hale	Michael Reklis
Anonymous	Ed Nawotka	Mike Kaminsky
Andrew Yorke	Grace Kenney	Mokhtar Ramadan
Bob Appel	Greg McConeghy	Nikki Gibson
Bob & Katherine Penn	Jeff Waxman	Richard Meyer
Brandon Childress	JJ Italiano	Steve Bullock
Brandon Kennedy	Kay Cattarulla	Suejean Kim
Caroline Casey	Kelly Falconer	Susan Carp
Charles Dee Mitchell	Linda Nell Evans	Theater Jones
Charley Mitcherson	Lissa Dunlay	Tim Perttula

SUBSCRIBERS

Adam Hetherington

Adam Rekerdres

Alan Shockley

Alexa Roman

Amber J. Appel

Amrit Dhir

Andrew Lemon

Anonymous

Antonia Lloyd-Jones

Ariel Saldivar

Balthazar Simões

Barbara Graettinger

Ben Fountain

Ben Nichols

Betsy Morrison

Bill Fisher

Bjorn Beer

Bob & Mona Ball

Bob Appel

Bob Penn

Bradford Pearson

Brandon Kennedy

Brina Palencia

Cayelan & Quinn Thomas

Charles Dee Mitchell

Chase LaFerney

Cheryl Thompson

Chris Sweet

Christie Tull

David Lowery

David Shook

David Wang

David Weinberger

Dennis Humphries

Dr. Colleen Grissom

Ed Nawotka

Ed Tallent

Elisabeth Cook

Fiona Schlachter

Frank Merlino

George Henson

Gino Palencia

Grace Kenney

Greg McConeghy

Guilty Dave Bristow

Heath Dollar

Horatiu Matei

Jacob Siefring

Jacob Silverman

James Crates

Jane Watson

Jeanne Milazzo

Jeff Whittington

Jeremy Hughes

Joe Milazzo

Joel Garza

John Harvell

John Schmerein

Joshua Edwin

Julia Pashin

Julie Janicke Muhsmann

Justin Childress

Kaleigh Emerson

Katherine McGuire

Kenneth McClain

Kimberly Alexander

Lauren Shekari

Lena Saltos

Linda Nell Evans

Lisa Pon Lissa Dunlay

Lissa Dunlay

Liz Ramsburg

Lori Feathers

Lytton Smith

Mac Tull

Mallory Davis

Marcia Lynx Qualey

Margaret Terwey

Mark Larson

Martha Gifford

Mary Ann Thompson-Frenk
   & Joshua Frenk

Meaghan Corwin

Michael Holtmann

Mike Kaminsky

Naomi Firestone-Teeter

Neal Chuang

Nicholas Kennedy

Nick Oxford

Nikki Gibson

Owen Rowe

Patrick Brown

Peter McCambridge

Sam Ankenbauer

Scot Roberts

Sean & Karen Fitzgerald

Shelby Vincent

Steven Norton

Susan Ernst

Taylor Zakarin

Tess Lewis

Theater Jones

Tim Kindseth

Todd Mostrog

Tom Bowden

Tony Fleo

Will Morrison

Will Pepple

Will Vanderhyden